SCHEMES

Also by Kiki Swinson

The Playing Dirty Series: *Playing Dirty* and
Notorious
The Candy Shop
A Sticky Situation
The Wifey Series: *Wifey, I'm Still Wifey, Life After Wifey,*
Still Wifey Material
Wife Extraordinaire Series: *Wife Extraordinaire* and *Wife*
Extraordinaire Returns
Cheaper to Keep Her Series: Books 1-5
The Score Series: *The Score* and *The Mark*
Dead on Arrival
The Black Market Series: *The Black Market, The Safe*
House, Property of the State

ANTHOLOGIES
Sleeping with the Enemy (with Wahida Clark)
Heist and *Heist 2* (with De'nesha Diamond)
Lifestyles of the Rich and Shameless (with Noire)
A Gangster and a Gentleman (with
De'nesha Diamond)
Most Wanted (with Nikki Turner)
Still Candy Shopping (with Amaleka McCall)
Fistful of Benjamins (with De'nesha Diamond)
Schemes and *Dirty Tricks* (with Saundra)
Bad Behavior (with Noire)

Also by Saundra

Her Sweetest Revenge Series, Books 1-3
If It Ain't About the Money Series: *If It Ain't About the*
Money, Hustle Hard
A Hustler's Queen

ANTHOLOGIES
Schemes and *Dirty Tricks* (with Kiki Swinson)

Published by Kensington Publishing Corp.

SCHEMES

Kiki Swinson
Saundra

KENSINGTON PUBLISHING CORP.
www.kensingtonbooks.com

DAFINA BOOKS are published by

Kensington Publishing Corp.
119 West 40th Street
New York, NY 10018

All Kensington Titles, Imprints, and Distributed Lines are available at special quantity discounts for bulk purchases for sales promotions, premiums, fund-raising, and educational or institutional use. Special book excerpts or customized printings can also be created to fit specific needs. For details, write or phone the office of the Kensington special sales manager: Kensington Publishing Corp., 119 West 40th Street, New York, NY 10018, attn: Special Sales Department, Phone: 1-800-221-2647.

Dafina and the Dafina logo Reg. U.S. Pat. & TM Off.

ISBN-13: 978-1-61773-367-3
ISBN-10: 1-61773-367-9
First Kensington Trade Paperback Edition: October 2016
First Kensington Mass Market Edition: December 2019

ISBN-13: 978-1-61773-366-6 (ebook)
ISBN-10: 1-61773-366-0 (ebook)

10 9 8 7 6 5 4 3 2 1

Printed in the United States of America

DEVIL IN SHEEP'S CLOTHING

Kiki Swinson

PROLOGUE

NEVER BITE THE HAND THAT FEEDS YOU

"Karlie, please make them stop." My sister begged me through sobs. But I couldn't do anything. I was tied up too. All I could do was beg these goons for their mercy.

"No! Please!" I begged, gagging from the mixture of snot and blood running over my lips and into my mouth. The salt from my tears stung the open wounds on my bottom lip. But that was the least of my pain. Another slap across the face almost snapped my neck from my shoulders. The hit landed with so much force, blood and spit shot from between my lips and splattered on my assailant's crisp white shirt. I wasn't going to escape this assault. That much was clear.

"Just let her go. It's my fault," I groaned through my swollen lips. "Please. She didn't do anything wrong. It was all me. I swear," I rasped, barely able to get enough air into my lungs to get the words out.

"Oh yeah? It was your fault? Well, look at what you've done," he growled evilly. "Just look!" He grabbed my face and forced me to watch.

"Agggh!"

Miley let out a pain-filled scream. I could hear another crackling round of electric shocks rocking through her body. It sounded like the sizzle, crackle, and pop of the mosquito light in my uncle's backyard, cooking the little nuisance bugs when we were kids. I couldn't even stand to look over at my baby sister's naked body dangling like a captured animal. They had Miley's arms extended over her head and her wrists bound to a thick, silver pipe that ran across the warehouse ceiling. Her face was covered in a mix of tears, snot, and blood. Her hair was soaked with sweat and matted to her head. I could see tracks of burn marks running up and down her stomach and extending down her thighs. I knew then that even if by some miracle we made it out of this shit, Miley would never be the same again. I sobbed at the sight and at the thought. It was my greed that had landed us here. It was my need to prove a point to the world. A world that didn't give two fucks about me or what I had anyway. More skin-searing sizzles interrupted my thoughts. More screams from my sister sent my emotions over the top.

"Miley!" I screeched until my throat burned. I strained against the restraints that held me to the cold metal chair. "Miley! I'm sorry! I'm so sorry!"

"Agh!" She let out another scream. This time, urine spilled from between her legs and splashed all over the floor. I was so close I could feel the warm fluid hitting my feet. The smell of my sister's piss, mixed with my own blood, threatened to make me throw up.

"I . . . I . . . I'm sorry," I rasped. "I wish I could just take it all back," I murmured, barely able to formulate the words. The loud laughter that followed told me all I needed to know. There was nothing else I could say or do to make up for what had already happened. Shit had officially gone down the tubes. I had only been trying to find a way for us to survive, but it had turned out to be our destruction. I had singlehandedly killed us.

"Oww!" I yelped, as my downturned head was yanked up by my hair. Pain shot through my scalp as the large gorilla-like hand clenched my long hair.

"Open your fucking eyes," the deep, scratchy voice demanded. I could feel his hot breath on my face. The stench of old cigarettes and alcohol shot up my nose and to the back of my throat. I forced my battered eyelids open and squinted. The blurry image of his face came into focus, but quickly went fuzzy again.

"You're going to watch your little bitch sister die now," he growled in my face. "All you had to do was be loyal. Be smart. But a bitch like you ain't neither, and now you gotta pay."

I felt my heart sink. I was powerless. My legs trembled fiercely and sweat danced down my spine. I couldn't stop obsessing over the what-ifs. What if I had just accepted my position in life? What if I had refused the plan, never gotten involved? What if I had just stopped?

My actions had put us in this predicament, and now nothing could save us.

"Miley. Baby girl, I'm sorry." I cried so hard my entire body rocked. I heard my sister scream one more time. It was a deep, guttural scream that I would imagine coming from an animal at slaughter. She gurgled a few times. And then there was silence. The silence seemed louder to me than her screams. I just knew right then and there my baby sister was gone.

"Didn't any fucking body ever teach you not to bite the hand that feeds you?" he said. Then he let out the most evil, maniacal laugh that I've ever heard come from a human being. He let my hair go with so much force the chair I was in toppled over and my body crashed to the floor. My jaw cracked against the concrete and shattered under the skin. The mixture of grief for my sister and the pain of the fall sent me into a deep darkness and reeling back in time.

What did you do, Karlie? What did you do? I asked myself.

CHAPTER 1

FED UP

Two months earlier

"Another damn cut-off notice," I huffed as I dumped yet another bill onto the growing mountain of bills that sat atop my rickety kitchen table. "This shit don't make no sense. I work every damn day and can't get ahead for shit. All of the money that slips through my hands every day, and for what? I ain't seeing none of that shit." I let out a long breath and shook my head. "I'm fed up. Real damn fed up. Being broke is for the birds."

Of course, my prima donna little sister, Miley, was popping her gum while scrolling through her iPhone, like she was going to magically find some hidden money to help us out of our situation. She was the only person I knew who was broke but acted like she was rich. The latest iPhone, expensive bags and shoes . . . you name it, my sister had it. She spent every dime she made on material things.

"Do you hear me? I need more money from you, Miley," I said, bending my head into her face so she could understand what I was saying. "Together we shouldn't be struggling this bad. I know you like to floss for the streets, but we don't have it like that," I said bitterly.

"What happened to your hustler robbing boyfriend?" Miley said, looking up from her phone for a second, her face folded into an expectant frown.

I cocked my head to the side like I hadn't heard her correctly. "What?"

How dare this spoiled-ass girl!

"Sidney. Where is that nigga?" she said, smacking her full, lip-gloss-painted shiny lips. "I thought he said he was gon' hold you down. Yeah, right. That nigga out here sticking up hand-to-hand corner boys. You probably make more working at EZ Cash than he makes robbing them lil broke niggas," Miley scoffed.

"I know you gotta be kidding me right now," I retorted.

My nostrils flared at the audacity of her stupid-ass comments. She was always trying to put my boyfriend, Sidney, down, and it irked my nerves more than the mounting bills.

"Shut the hell up, Miley. I don't wait for a man to take care of me. Unlike somebody I know," I snapped back, raising an eyebrow at her to let her ass know that her situation was no better. She was way out of line. "You talking about me, but last I check that nigga you running with ain't laying no bread on these bills either. Your ass is just as broke as me. We broke together, chick. If I don't have lights, gas, and water up in this bitch . . . you don't have lights, gas, and water either," I reminded her. "You want to be around here looking like a million bucks but ain't got no cable, lights, and gas. You a fucking hood rat."

"What-ev-er," Miley mumbled. She knew I was telling the truth.

"Say what you want. We both working at that damn slave ship EZ Cash, and neither one of us ain't got shit to show for it but bills. You lucky I hooked you up with the job at the other location, or your ass wouldn't even have no damn iPhone to scroll through or no damn weave to flick over your shoulders. Not that you ain't running around here with Taz's wannabe so-called big-time weed-dealer ass too. Broke is broke. If we both got niggas we fuckin' with and we both broke, then neither one of us ain't no better than the other. Period," I lectured. "Bottom line is I need more money from you. Either that or you better come up with a get-rich-quick scheme fast."

It was bad enough we lived in the Carriage House apartments. Some of the worst apartments in Virginia Beach. I had hopes and dreams of someday getting the hell out of the slum-ass place. It was one of the worst neighborhoods in the area too. I don't think my sister got it. She had her head in the material clouds all of the time.

Miley sucked her teeth and stormed out of the kitchen. I flopped down in one of the raggedy kitchen chairs. I covered my face with my hands and inhaled deeply. Thinking. I always felt bad when my sister and I argued.

Miley never liked to hear the truth, but as her older sister, it was my job to make sure she did. I mean, let's face it, Miley and I were in the same boat so there was no sense in us pointing fingers. My mother left us both for dead when she died of a heroin overdose. I was fourteen and Miley was ten when we found our mother, slumped over, face gray, lips blue, with the needle still jammed in her arm. I had been the one who wiped Miley's tears away and rocked her to sleep at night after that tragedy. I had to grow up fast after that. I had always played mother to my sister, even before our mother died, but after her death I became a fourteen-year-old adult. I had tears in my eyes now just thinking back to that time.

Miley and I knocked around to a few of our relatives after our mother died, but that shit didn't last. My mother's sister—yes, I refer to her as my mother's sister and not my aunt—tried to sell us to her men friends for money. Verona straight tried to turn us into little prostitutes. One night, some big, fat white dude came to the house and requested a night with Miley. This nasty motherfucker said he wanted the youngest one in the house. That was the last straw for me. I had to whoop Verona's ass, threaten that white man with a butcher's knife, and take Miley and run like hell.

My mother's brother, Darwin, another trifling ass family member, was collecting our Social Security check but leaving us starving with no clothes or shoes. Living with him was no better than being on the damn street. We never had food or clothes. This dude would be fly while Miley and I walked around with clothes so raggedy we looked like two homeless people.

Our last resort was my mother's aunt, our great aunt. My grandmother's sister, Bernice. As old as that bitch was, she had to be the worst of them all. She would make Miley and me get up at the crack of dawn to clean her house every day. When I say clean, I don't mean straighten up or make up beds. I mean dust, mop, scrub, clean windows, and shit like that . . . every single day. Who needs their house cleaned every single damn day? Then that evil bitch Bernice would give us one meal of plain, watered-down grits but not until after all of the cleaning was done to her standards. After she used her white-gloved hand to inspect for dust and dirt, she'd feed us the slop and then make us leave the house. She would tell us we could not return until 9 PM at night when it was time for us to go to bed. Dinner . . . yeah right, that was a joke. We never got dinner unless Bernice was having company from her church. We would literally be roaming the streets all day long because going to school wasn't even an option with the dirty, threadbare clothes she had us in. The fucking worst. I got so fed up, I grabbed Miley one day and dragged both of us downtown to Social Services. I signed myself and my sister into the system without even thinking twice. It was either that or we'd be homeless on the streets.

People complain about foster care, but trust me, it was a hell of a lot better than dealing with my own low-down, dirty family. I only had one condition when we entered the system—I was not going to be separated from my sister. Ever. Period. No matter what. I don't care how old I got and how many homes wanted Miley and not me; I would have the foster care workers turn them down. Finally, we were placed with a really sweet Spanish woman named Magda. She loved us until the day she closed her eyes. We loved her too.

Miley was the only family I had in the entire world. We fought like archenemies sometimes, but I loved her little conceited ass no matter what. Nothing was ever going to change that. Not even now with her riding on my last good nerve.

"Are you going to Beans's party?" Miley asked, slipping back into the kitchen and breaking up my little blast-from-the-past daydream. I looked up at her, my face folded into a scowl.

She can't be serious right now!

"Bitch, didn't I just say we got a damn cut-off notice and you asking me about some damn party!" I shot back. This was what I meant about her. She didn't believe shit stunk unless she fell face first into the shit. She was so used to me always thinking of a master plan to bail us out. Not this time. "You really have your priorities fucked up, Miley," I grumbled, shaking my head in disgust.

"Well, I heard from one of Taz's boys that Sidney and his crew supposed to be rolling deep to the party. Which means bitches will be circling like buzzards on dead meat. So . . . humph, if I was you, I would be pulling my shit together to be there. Fuck them bills. Ain't like we haven't lived without lights n' shit before. You better make sure ya nigga ain't out there throwing his paper at the next thot. Especially if you could use that paper to pay some of your bills." The tension in my face quickly eased into worry. Miley knew exactly what buttons to push to get my attention.

"Yeah, that's what I thought," Miley mocked once she saw my facial expression. "I guess you ain't thinking about them bills now, right?" She sashayed out of the kitchen with that hateful-ass teasing giggle she always did. Her words about Sidney being surrounded by chicks in the club was playing in my ears and nagging me. I knew how these hungry hoes in Virginia Beach operated. For every one man there were about fifty chicks so keeping your man faithful was a daily chore.

I got up from the chair and fixed myself a drink. Even that didn't ease my mind. I growled and let out a long sigh. "Fucking fed up," I grumbled under my breath. I took another swig of my drink. Still, I felt no relief. It was so damn frustrating that I worked around so much money on a daily basis, yet I was struggling like a damn welfare recipient. I slammed my empty glass down on the chipped Formica counter top.

"Fuck it."

Miley was right. If I didn't go to the party God only knew what and who Sidney would be doing without me there watching his ass.

Sidney and I had been together two years and we'd had our fair share of side chick incidents. Sidney was six feet, two inches of caramel gorgeousness. Women all over Virginia Beach knew about his fine ass and wanted him just the same. When we met, Sidney had the East Side drug game on lock. He was the boss of the streets. That was until he got knocked after one of his runners got bagged and snitched. After Sidney came home from his time in the feds, there was no way he could touch a drug, so he resorted to robbing hustlers. It was risky, but at least he wasn't on the Narcotics Unit's radar anymore. Sidney may not have as much money as he used to back then, but his dick game was still the best so I was always on the lookout for chicks trying to get at him.

"So what's the damn verdict?" Miley came back into the kitchen. She was like a damn annoying fly buzzing in my ear. Unrelenting and annoying. I rolled my eyes.

"Hook my hair up for me." I caved. Miley busted out laughing.

"I knew your ass wasn't going to let that nigga be up in there without you."

"Oh shut up. You better worry about coming up with your half of these damn bills. And . . . I'm wearing my Gucci stilettos, *not* you," I stressed. That shut Miley up real quick.

CHAPTER 2

THIS CAN'T BE LIFE

"Mmm-hmmm. See what I mean. Boom! Just like I suspected," Miley yelled in my ear over the music. "That nigga is busted!"

She didn't have to say anything else, nor did she have to point out the obvious. We both noticed Sidney at the same time. He was so engrossed in a conversation with a female that included a lot of laughing and smiling, that he never looked up or noticed me. Of course the bitch that was in his face also smiling and blushing like whatever they were sharing was making her pussy wet. I bet she thought she had snagged her a trick for the night for free drinks and VIP treatment. As I scanned the little huddle of people around him, my insides began to boil. There were lots of bitches hanging all around Sidney and his entourage. I felt heat rising from my feet and climbing my body as I watched

Sidney cheesing like some little thirsty young boy about to get his first piece. I squinted my eyes into slits. I felt my hands curling into fists on their own. My heart pumped furiously too.

"Oh, this nigga said he ain't have no money, but he look like he got a lot of bottles on his table though," I grumbled under my breath. "Want to be smiling at a bitch?" I gritted. Before I could even get my full thoughts together, I was on the move. My sister was right on my heels. She always had my back in situations like this. Miley would fight an old lady too. She didn't give a damn.

As I navigated through the sea of bodies in the club, a few dudes tried to get my attention. Some grabbed my hands and some touched my arms trying to holler at me, but I was so focused on Sidney, I just yanked my arm and hand away from them and stormed in the direction of Sidney's table. The attention I was getting from dudes let me know I wasn't a slouch in the looks department. I knew I had it going on. I was twenty-nine years old, stood five feet five inches tall with light brown-sugar-colored skin and I had curves for days. I'm talking about thirty-six-D-cup breasts, twenty-eight-inch waist and forty-inch hips. That was an hourglass shape with a little more on the bottom than the top. Sidney would always joke that he was going to send me to the strip club with my booty because I could be making a lot of money with my perfect shape and gorgeous face.

For the party, I chose to wear an all-black BCBG spandex cat-suit and my purple Gucci stilettos. Miley straightened my hair so it hung straight down my back and stopped right before my butt.

It was all mine too. The makeup that I applied was natural because my clear, baby-soft skin didn't need much makeup at all. Miley was also looking like a joint. My sister was a few shades lighter than me, more on the fair side. She was taller by a few inches but just as gorgeous in the face. Miley wore a Chinese bang long weave, but she didn't have to because she had long hair of her own. She wasn't as curvy as I was, but she had enough tits and ass to keep the men swooning over her. She was also swatting dudes away as we moved through the sea of bodies.

By the time Miley and I made it to Sidney's table, a fine sheen of sweat beaded my upper lip and fire flashed in my eyes. I had approached, and this nigga was still so enthralled with this chick he didn't even notice me.

"This what you do when my back is turned!" I yelled over the music, immediately getting in Sidney's face. He jumped and sat up straight. His eyes went wide like he'd seen a ghost. I wanted to slap him in the face just seeing the way his eyes bulged out and his mouth dropped open. That smile he was wearing a few minutes earlier had quickly faded off of his face.

"Oh you didn't think I was coming up in here, right!" I screamed, pointing in his face accusingly. Sidney stood up and pushed away from the table. The chick he was all comfortable with a few minutes earlier had her head cocked like she was about to say something. Sidney didn't even bother saying anything else to her. He knew better.

"Oh, she got something to say?" I gritted, turning my sights on the bimbo.

"She better not," Miley interjected threateningly.

"C'mon man. This ain't even necessary," Sidney said, immediately grabbing me in a bear hug. He knew me very well. So he probably knew that the next thing coming was a punch in that bitch's face. He also knew if I jumped, Miley was going to jump as well.

"No! Get the fuck off me! Who is that bitch? You seemed real fucking chummy with her ass!" I barked, pointing my finger directly at the ho. She was just one of the many who seemed to be enjoying all the expensive liquor Sidney and his boys had laid out on their table like they were celebrity ballers or some shit.

"Chill, Karlie. It ain't even like that. These bitches ain't with me," Sidney placated me, speaking in my ear as he held on to me and walked me backwards toward the club's exit. "You my bae. You ain't got shit to worry about. Shhh. C'mon. You wifey, you ain't got to act like that over no next bitch."

"That's not what it looked like to me," I said, my voice beginning to crack. I had been through this enough times with him.

"You know you my only one. Stop the madness," he said. I felt myself softening.

"Why you always have to try me? I hate this," I whined, on the verge of tears. Sidney was the only dude to ever have me wrapped around his finger like this.

"Yo, that shit meant nothing," he said, grabbing me even closer to him. I melted against his strong, muscular body and let him lead me right out of the club. Miley stayed inside. She was going to find her man.

"C'mon, we going home," Sidney said once we were outside. He was licking my neck and breathing hard in my ear, which always made me weak in the knees.

"I . . . I . . . can't just leave Miley," I huffed. I could already feel my thong getting wet with my own juices. "Plus, I just got here. I didn't pay money to get inside just to turn around and leave."

"Miley is a big girl. Her man up in there. I need you right now," Sidney breathed into my ear. "I need to show you who got me. It definitely ain't none of those chicks up in the club."

My insides were melting like butter left in the sun. Sidney was saying and doing all of the right things. I wasn't thinking straight at all. It was true. Miley was a big girl. She had probably found Taz and his crew. Knowing my sister, she had her a drink and was blunt by now.

"C'mon. I need you," Sidney whispered hotly in my ear. I couldn't even control my own thoughts with Sidney sucking on my ear like he was.

Sidney opened the back door of his Suburban and pushed me inside. Before I could protest, he climbed up into the truck, slammed the door, and planted his mouth over mine. I let out a low moan. It was half protest, half acquiescence. I tried in vain to push him off. I also tried to stay mad at him. All to no avail.

Sidney touched me gently on my breasts—my "trigger buttons" was what I called them. My chest rose and fell with every hot minute that my man kissed me deeply. Our tongues danced seductively to the beat of our hearts. My hips were writhing involuntarily. I could feel my clitoris beating as it swelled. I wanted to feel Sidney inside of me so badly. Miley's face flashed in my mind for a quick second. I couldn't just leave her at the club. We had come together.

"We can't. I . . . I . . . have to . . . um . . . Miley," I panted, barely able to make complete sentences.

"Shhh."

Sidney moved from my mouth and trailed his long anaconda tongue down to my titties. I became so weak. My body tingled all over. I was at the point of no return now. I didn't just want Sidney. I needed him.

I gulped in a lungful of air. It was all I could do to keep from hyperventilating. I tried to pull Sidney's head up, but he had taken in a mouthful of my left nipple. He sucked hard and let his tongue roam over the sensitive ridges of my areola. I arched my back in response. My inner thighs quivered. I was dying for the dick by the time Sidney finished his tongue massage. We were both frantically working to get me out of my clothes. My hands trembled with anticipation.

"Sit up and ride it," Sidney grunted. He quickly slid the rest of my jumpsuit off of my body as I rose up. Although the tints on his windows were police grade, I didn't care if anyone watched us. I was sure with all of the moving the truck was rocking from the outside. The electric pulses of lust coursing through my body sent all of my inhibitions out of the window.

"Damn. Your ass is fine as fuck," he murmured,

his hot breath on my face. I was feeling a mixture of fear, excitement, and lust. It was enough to make my eyes roll up into my head like I had just taken a long pull on the fattest Purple Haze–filled blunt.

"I want to feel you so bad," I groaned. I fumbled around, trying to find a comfortable position. I embedded my knees into the soft leather seats and grabbed Sidney around the neck for leverage.

I straddled him and eased myself down onto his long, thick dick. As soon as the meaty girth of his love muscle filled me up, I let out a satisfied squeal. I lifted myself up and lowered myself down slowly at first. With each repetition, I picked up speed until I was riding his dick like a jockey bouncing on a race-horse. Sidney clutched onto my plump, round ass cheeks and squeezed. That caused the sensations I was feeling in my pussy to intensify.

"Shit!" he said gruffly. He clutched onto my ass tighter like he never wanted to let me go. I lifted all the way up, and this time I swirled my hips as I sat down on his dick. The feeling that rippled through my loins told me this was it.

"Yes! *Agh!*" I yelled out as I bounced up and down and swirled and bounced some more. Every time I went down on it, I made sure I swirled my hips, twerked my hips and rocked a little bit. I wanted to make sure it was the best sensation for Sidney but also to make sure his body made contact with my clitoris. This was how a woman needed to be fucked. At that moment I didn't care what chick Sidney had in his face earlier. I just knew he was mine.

"I love you, girl," Sidney groaned.

"I love you too, baby," I panted. "Oh shit, Sid! Oh shit!" I bucked even harder on the dick. "Aggh!" I belted out as my pussy convulsed with an orgasm. I felt my love juices leaking from my hot wet center. It didn't take Sidney too long to follow. He filled me up. A warm sensation heated my insides.

My body went limp against his. I closed my eyes and inhaled the scent of his cologne mixed with his sweat. I just loved his ass. If only he had more money, he would be perfect. That was always the problem. Both of us being broke. The struggle was so real. There had been many dudes in Virginia Beach with money that had tried to holler, but their dicks were whack or they were corny. Sidney had the right swag, the right dick, but not enough money. It was so messed up. I guess there were no perfect men out there, but money would've definitely made Sidney perfect.

After a few minutes of silence, Sidney slapped my ass and laughed.

"Damn, girl. You gangster. You just gon' fuck ya nigga right here in my truck parked in the club parking lot. Fuck anybody who wanna look, huh?" he joked.

I chuckled coyly. "I told you I was a ride-or-die bitch. Literally," I joked back. We both busted out laughing. That didn't last long though. I wasn't ready to let Sidney off the hook that fast. While he was digging me out, I had temporarily forgotten about the chick that I had found him flossing in the club with, but it didn't take long for it to all come flooding back to my mind.

"So, where you get money for all them bottles

you was popping with those basic bitches in the club?" I asked with a sour attitude. I had immediately broken up the light mood we were having. I didn't care. I loved his dick, yes, but I was not stupid.

"C'mon, Karlie. You really going back to that bullshit?" Sidney sighed and rolled his eyes. I climbed off of him, onto the seat. I bent over and snatched up my jumpsuit and began getting dressed.

"Hell yeah, Sidney. I'm around here with cut-off notices from the electric company, gas company, and my car needs a transmission, but you out here flossing with other chicks, popping bottles like you Drake or some shit. I mean, you would fucking think I was a single bitch with no man as broke as I am," I whined, moving my head like it was on a swivel as I got shrugged into my jumpsuit with so much attitude I hit my head on the ceiling of the truck.

"You act like I don't do shit for you though. When I have it . . . you have it," Sidney came back as he folded his limp dick back into his boxers. "If I ain't good enough, I don't know what to tell you."

"I'm just saying, Sidney. You must have it to waste," I snapped, putting my clothes on with attitude. "That same money you flossing with could be used for bills. Or you could be trying to find a legit way to get some money."

"Nah, I don't have it to waste. That wasn't even me buying them fucking bottles. . . . It was Cess. You think I like having other niggas front me in the club? Huh, Karlie? I ain't got it. If I wasn't on parole, I would hit these streets hard, but it ain't like that for me no more. A nigga can't get bricks from overseas and flip them. I'm on the radar. You know that. I can't even understand why you tripping like this. It's not easy for me to hear about you struggling, but it's either that or you will be visiting a nigga in the feds. That's what you want? Huh?" Sidney barked, his tone serious. I lowered my eyes and shook my head. I knew he was right. The last thing I wanted was to see him get locked up again. At least now, even if he couldn't give me the world, he could still rock my world in bed. If he was locked up I would lose on all ends.

"You're right. I'm sorry. I'm just so frustrated being broke. This can't be life," I lamented. There were a few minutes of uncomfortable awkward silence that settled around us inside of the truck. It seemed to make the air inside heavy. Intolerable even. We both shifted uncomfortably in our seats.

"Shit, you the one working with all the money every day. You better get on your Jada Pinkett, Queen Latifah, *Set It Off* shit," Sidney said, breaking the silence. I snorted and shook my head. He laughed. I realized he was trying to cut through the tension with that joke. I shook my head and smirked.

"Yeah, right. Those motherfucking owners would know it was me right off the back. Wig on, mask on, and those fuckers would still know it was me. Especially because I basically run those damn spots," I said, followed by an uneasy fake laugh.

"It probably don't be a lot of money up in that shit anyway," Sidney said, his words trailing off as if he didn't even believe that himself.

"What? Please. You're wrong. I'm always scared

of getting robbed. That shit may look like a hood hole-in-the-wall, but trust me; we keep over a hundred thousand in each store on a daily basis for the loans. It's crazy having my hands around that much money knowing how broke I am. Trust me, sometimes the temptation is real. But they do a daily count so it's not like I can steal. If money ever went missing, it would definitely have to be through a strong-arm robbery," I said. I shook my head for emphasis.

There was more silence. It was like Sidney and I were both just thinking real hard about how even half of that money could do us damned good.

"They would know it was you if you tried it, but if it was a random strong-arm robbery, would they know then?" Sidney asked. "Like if a few niggas ran up in that joint, guns waving and snatched the loot." He wasn't looking at me. He was staring off in a zone, like his mind seemed to be racing.

I had to move a little on the seat so I could look at him. "What you mean?" I asked, turning my head so that I was looking him in his eyes.

"You know . . . if somebody else did it, but that person knew the ins and outs so that it would go down fast. Like it was random, but really not," he replied, throwing a knowing glance in my direction. I crinkled my eyebrows and looked at him to see if he was serious. He couldn't be seriously asking me what I thought he was asking me.

"It would definitely have to be a random robbery for them not to suspect an inside job," I replied seriously. "I mean only a few people know how much money is kept inside." Sidney shook his head real slow like he was in deep thought.

"Random robbery," he repeated with an eerie tone to his voice. "Ain't no robbery really ever a random robbery. Even in *Set It Off* them chicks had the inside woman," he said, a sinister smile curling on his lips. I turned my face away from his and stared out of the truck's windshield. In my peripheral vision, I could see that Sidney was also staring straight ahead. I didn't say another word that night, and neither did Sidney. I had always heard that what was understood did not have to be said. That was how shit was.

CHAPTER 3

THE BEST LAID PLANS

"*Aghhh!*" Amy Gaines, the youngest loan clerk at EZ Cash, let out an ear-shattering scream that threatened to burst my eardrums. I was standing right next to her, but my back was turned toward the store's door. Amy was the first one to notice them. Her screams startled me. I whirled around on the balls of my feet just in time to come face-to-face with the barrel of a shiny, silver, long-nose Desert Eagle.

"Don't move, bitch!"

My heart sank and my stomach curled into a tight knot. I gasped and clutched my chest. Amy would not stop screaming.

"Shut the fuck up!" the masked man snarled at her. She quickly clamped both of her hands over her mouth to stifle her screams. I swallowed a hard lump that had formed in my throat.

"Y'all bitches better get down right now before I put one of these slugs in your fucking heads!" the masked, gun-waving assailant barked. He was so tall I had to crane my neck to look up at him. I didn't have any trouble seeing his gun though. It was leveled in my face.

I was the manager at the EZ Cash so I felt like I was responsible for everyone's safety.

"Just do what he says," I instructed. Immediately, the two loan clerks I was in charge of got down on the floor like they had been told. Both started begging and pleading for their lives. It made me cringe to see them so scared. For some reason, I wanted to yell and tell them to shut the hell up, but the words just wouldn't come. I guess everyone handled fear differently. Since I was a kid, even when I was scared, I'd always pretended to be tough.

"Bitch, did you hear me! This ain't the movies. I will lay all y'all asses down with no problem!"

Those words snapped me back into reality. My hands were shaking. I swallowed hard as my eyes darted around wildly. There were two gunmen in my immediate sight. All sorts of things ran through my head, but my thoughts were quickly interrupted when I noticed the third gunman barreling toward us, his gun waving out in front of him like he was nervous.

"Please don't kill me," Amy begged, tears streaming her face. Amy was a young black girl from North Carolina who attended Norfolk State University. She was a junior in school and had taken the job to help her with her books and her small bills.

"Yes, please let us live. I have kids. You can have it all. My kids ain't got nobody else. I can't die," Trina Long, the other clerk, rambled pitifully. I could hear the fear rattling through her words.

Trina was a twenty-four-year-old single parent of two kids. She always expressed how much she needed this job to pay her rent and make up for the no-good baby daddies she had chosen to procreate with.

That was it. Amy had a future ahead of her. Trina had kids to take care of. I was the manager. I was their boss. I was responsible for them. I had to step up. It was my duty. With sweat beads dancing down the sides of my face, I moved forward apprehensively. I was trying to find the softest voice to speak in.

"Listen, leave them out of this. Please don't hurt them. I . . . I am the supervisor here, and no one is going to call the police if you just take what you want and leave us be," I said, raising my hands in surrender to let the masked gunmen know I wasn't going to resist. "There is a safe. I'm the only one who can get you inside," I offered, nodding my head toward the back of the store. Maybe too easily when I thought of it, but I offered nonetheless.

"I want every fuckin' thing you got in here! Every dollar, bitch!" the second assailant growled through the black material of his mask. A strange feeling flitted through my chest. I swore I saw the devil dancing in his eyes. A shot of heat engulfed my body, and for the first time since they had burst through the doors, I felt a dizzying mixture of anger and fear grip me tight around the throat.

"Look, all we got right here is fifteen hundred dollars. It's in my top right drawer. That's all we keep in the immediate vicinity. The safe is in the back. So, just take it all and leave," I said, my tone a little testy. It was a bold move and I instantly regretted it.

"Oh my God, Karlie, please don't make them angry," Amy whispered from the floor, her fingers laced behind her head like a hostage in some movie. "Take them to the safe. Give them everything," she whimpered.

"Oh yeah?" The biggest of the robbers took three steps toward me and pointed his pistol toward my head. "Bitch, you don't run shit in here right now! I do. Now, get the fuck over here before I kill you in this motherfucker!" he boomed. His words reverberated through my chest like the booming bass of a party speaker. I swayed on my feet a little. I hadn't been expecting that.

"I'm only trying to . . ." I began but before I knew it, the monstrous, gorilla-sized assailant lunged forward, snatched me from behind the counter, and shoved his gun into the small of my back.

"Shut the fuck up and show me where the safe is!" he barked, pushing me forward. I stumbled toward the back office with my hands over my head. My insides were churning so fast I just knew I'd throw up.

This nigga doing too much! All of this ain't even called for. You just wait!

Once we were in the back office, I quickly went to the safe, which was wedged between two tall, old-school grey filing cabinets. I got to my knees.

My hands were shaking so badly that I didn't get the combination on the first try.

"Don't fuck around! Open that safe or else," the gunman ordered, swiping his gun across the back of my neck. I let out an exasperated breath as I fumbled with the ancient combination dial again. This was one of the times I resented how cheap my bosses were. What thriving business didn't have an electronic keypad safe these days? What thriving business kept its old-school safe just sitting on the dusty, torn-up tile floor too? I went to work on the combination lock again with my hands trembling. Left. Right. Left.

Click.

Finally.

I breathed out a long, unsteady breath of relief. It has taken me six fuck-ups to finally get it right.

"Move," the gunman demanded, pushing me aside so hard I scraped my knee on the raggedy, ripped-up linoleum tile on the floor. He was definitely working my last nerve. Gun or no gun, I wanted to spit in his damn face.

"Jack-fucking-pot! Yo, bring that duffel bag," he called out to the others.

The other two assailants herded Amy and Trina into the back office, where I was just easing myself up off the floor. Amy was shaking like a leaf in a wild storm. Trina moved clumsily, her nerves clearly muddling her movements.

"Sit the fuck down," the tallest and meanest of the gunmen commanded. Both girls flopped to the floor without hesitation. Me, on the other hand, I had had enough. I just wanted this shit to be over. My knee was itching with pain. I had a headache. And, I was thinking, *Just take the damn money and get the hell out already!*

"Okay, I gave y'all everything we have in the store. Just please go," I said sassily.

"What, bitch?" the mean one snarled. "You don't tell us what to do, we tell you," he growled, getting close to my face. He was so close I could smell his cologne. It was a scent I had smelled before.

He can't be fucking serious. I'm trying to keep it together. I'm about to lose it up in here. My mind raced and my jaw rocked feverishly. Trying to pretend to be scared was wearing me down.

"I'm just trying to . . ." I started. I never got a chance to finish. Before I could react, I felt metal connect with the bone of my skull. My teeth clicked, and my eyes snapped shut on their own.

Crack. Crunch.

The gunman had swung the butt of the pistol at me and cracked it over my head. Flashes of light sparked behind my eyes like someone had set off a round of fireworks in my brain. I smelled the blood before I tasted the metallic, tinny flavor on my tongue. The scent and the taste only lasted a few seconds. My ears went deaf. I remember emitting a mousy squeak right before the impact from his strength and the blow of the gun knocked me out like a light. After I hit the floor, everything in my world went black.

"Miss Houston. Miss Houston. Can you hear me? Let me know if you can hear me." The sound of the strange voice filtered into my ears. It sounded muffled, like it was coming through some kind of cone or funnel.

I groaned and tried my best to open my eyes. "Let me know if you can hear me," the strange voice came again.

I wanted to tell the voice that I could definitely hear it, but I couldn't move or speak. I tried in vain to force my eyelids up, but the daggers of pain that shot through my skull each time I tried were like little elves were using my head as a dartboard. I quickly snapped my eyes shut again. It hurt too much to open them. My temples throbbed, seemingly with every beat of my heart. My ears were ringing now too.

"Ms. Houston? Let us know if you can hear us," a different voice shouted this time. I wanted them to stop speaking. The voices were fading now, but I could sense that there were people circling around me on all sides. Their presence made goose bumps rise on my skin.

A crowd? Strange voices? What the hell is going on?

Then I heard the crackle of a police radio and a dispatcher's voice. "Robbery and crime unit needed at Newtown Road and Baker." *The cops!*

Someone had called the police to the store. The thought sent a cold chill over my entire body. My head hurt even more now. My first thoughts went to Amy and Trina. I wondered if they were okay. If I was in this condition, what about them?

"Mmm," I moaned. It was all I could muster.

"She's conscious. Let's get her in the ambulance and take her to the ER. Maybe a precautionary MRI is best," I heard a man's voice say levelly.

"You may want to run a line," a woman replied, her voice slightly more frantic.

"Ms. Karlie! Oh my God! I'm so glad you're alive!" I heard Amy cry out. I couldn't miss the squeal of her annoying high-pitched voice anywhere. That prompted me to fight to open my eyes again. Pain or no pain, I needed to know what was going on. Had Amy and Trina already spoken to the cops? Had the robbers gotten away? All kinds of thoughts ran through my head, and my entire skull was pounding even more fiercely now.

"I'm so glad to see that you're okay," Amy went on, rushing to my side as the EMTs pulled the stretcher upright onto its retractable legs.

"Wh . . . what . . . happened?" I croaked through dry, cracked lips. I was going to pretend I didn't remember for as long as that would work. Why be bothered with answering questions?

"It was so terrible. They just came in with guns waving, and the next thing I knew we were all being . . ." Amy rambled, her arms flailing like an animated character's. Amy's story was suddenly interrupted by loud voices. She stopped in midsentence and turned.

There was a small commotion to my left. I had a hard time turning my head toward the confusion, but Amy's eyes darting in the direction of it was enough to speed my heart rate up.

"Excuse me. Ms. Houston," a tall, bald, kind-of-fine black guy finally wedged himself between Amy and me, interrupting our little reunion. Amy eyed him suspiciously. My face crumpled in agitation as soon as I realized where he was coming from.

"I'm Detective Castle. I need to speak to you about what happened here this evening," he said, flashing his shiny, gold badge in my face. My heart throttled up in my chest even more. Suddenly I couldn't catch my breath. I waved my hands wildly and started coughing uncontrollably.

"Hyperventilating. Pulse skyrocketing over one hundred. Let's get her to the ER now," a female EMT shouted, brushing past and shooting Detective Castle a dirty look. The detective stumbled back a few steps as the other EMTs rushed to my side. I couldn't take my eyes off of him. Not only was he gorgeous, but something about the determination in his eyes made my entire body tremble with live-wire nervousness.

"Catch her at the hospital. When she's in better condition, Detective," the female EMT grumbled. With that, they hoisted me into the back of the waiting ambulance and slammed the double doors right in Detective Castle's face. I closed my eyes tight. This was far from over. I could just feel it. Even the best laid plans could go awry. If only I'd known then just how much that would ring true.

CHAPTER 4

SEE NO EVIL, HEAR NO EVIL

"Oh my God, Karlie!" Miley rushed into my hospital room with tears streaming down her face. "When I heard that you were hit in your head with a gun, I was so scared. Are you okay? Look at your head."

"Shhh. I'm fine. In a lot of pain . . . but fine," I comforted, reaching a weak, shaky hand out to my sister. That's when I took a good look at her face too. She had a vicious green, blue, and purple ring around her left eye. My eyebrows rose to the middle of my forehead.

"Oh my God! What the hell happened to you?" I asked incredulously.

"They hit up my store too. One of them punched

me right in the face," she relayed, roving her head around to make sure we were alone. "So fucking unnecessary," she whispered harshly.

I closed my eyes. My jaw rocked feverishly.

"Fucking idiots," I mumbled.

"It was over the top. Too fucking much," Miley said, disgusted. "I mean, make it look . . ."

"Shh. Not here," I warned. I knew my sister, and she was about to go off. Good thing I shushed her because as soon as I did, my room door swung open. The polite nurse stuck her head in first. She had a kind, caring face. Kind of like the motherly face I had missed all of my life.

"Ms. Houston. You have a visitor," the nurse said, her tone kind of suspicious. "It's a detective. Are you feeling up to it? I can always tell him to come back tomorrow." She winked. I inhaled deeply and exhaled.

"No, it's fine. I might as well get this over with," I replied. Miley immediately raised her eyebrows at me.

"Why don't you wait, Karlie? They know what happened. I mean shit, look at you. You are in no condition to be trying to remember anything," Miley said, a tinge of nervousness lacing her words. I knew my sister all of her life, so I definitely knew she was uncomfortable at that moment.

"If I keep putting it off, he will just keep coming on more aggressively. Let him in. I don't have anything to hide," I told the nurse and my sister at the same time. I could hear Miley blow out a defeated breath.

Detective Castle came through the door with the kind of sexy authority that reminded me of Denzel Washington in the movie *Training Day*. His coffee-bean skin was clean, smooth, and well taken care of. His pants were so neat and creased so sharp he could've cut something with them. Everything he wore was starched and pristine. I could tell the detective had swagger. He looked more like a *GQ* model than a cop. I could just imagine how he looked in regular street clothes.

Snap out of it, Karlie! He's not your friend. He's definitely not fuckable.

"Ms. Houston." Detective Castle nodded at Miley. "Ms. Houston," he repeated, this time turning his head toward me. Miley responded with a grunt. I didn't respond at all.

"I'm sorry to keep bothering you, but the best information in cases like these is obtained within the first couple of hours after the crime," he explained, cautiously regarding a brooding Miley. It was curious to me that he didn't have a partner with him. Didn't they usually come out in pairs and play good cop/bad cop?

"It's all good. I can only tell you what I remember," I rasped, my throat suddenly gravelly and dry.

"That's a start," he said, digging into the inside pocket of his obligatory sand-colored trench coat and pulling out a miniature composition notebook. "Tell me how your day started . . . I mean, before the robbery."

"It was a regular day. I came in at my usual time of nine A.M., I opened the store, counted the cash up, and set everything up to start business for the day."

"And then what?" Detective Castle asked, looking up from his little annoying notebook.

"And then what, what?" I repeated rhetorically and sarcastically. Detective Castle shot me a knowing look. I inhaled and exhaled. "Like I said, I came in, took care of a few customers."

"Anything strange or different about any of the customers?" he interrupted. I rolled my eyes.

"No. The usual broke-ass people borrowing against their paychecks so that they will be in the same broke predicament next paycheck. But you wouldn't understand that, I'm sure," I answered with much attitude, eyeing him up and down. I just got a stomach-sickening feeling about him for some reason.

"Listen, Ms. Houston. I'm on your side. I want to find out who did this and who assaulted you," he replied, his voice pacifying. I had to catch myself. He was right. He was on my side.

Yeah, right. Me, trust the cops. Never.

"Well, I was in the store with my back turned. I had just finished doing the count when I heard my employee scream. Next thing, I saw a masked man with a gun pointed in my face. Everything else happened fast after that," I said evasively, closing my eyes as if the memory itself was causing me great pain. Miley shifted in her seat garnering a glance from the detective.

"Details. I need to know details. What you saw. What you heard," he replied, agitation underlying his words now. I guess his good-cop act was wearing thin along with his patience. The heart monitor to my left began beeping a little faster. My temples began throbbing again.

"It . . . it . . . all happened very fast. One of the men was yelling, my employees were crying, and I was trying to stay calm. I told them to just take what they wanted and leave us alone. I guess that pissed one of them off. I saw the gun. I saw more masked men. I got hit. No. I got knocked out," I countered with urgency. "It is one of those 'see no evil, hear no evil' situations for me, Detective. I didn't want to see or hear the evil that stormed into my store. I saw my life . . . all of our lives, flash right before my eyes. I'm sorry. I just want to put this all behind me. All I know is I'm glad we all made it out of there alive," I told him, closing my eyes again. I wanted that to signal that this was the last of this conversation. He sighed.

"Ms. Houston, I understand this is traumatic. But, the fact that the stores you and your sister work at both got hit at the same time, same time of day, same number of assailants in each store, same way . . . is gnawing at me," he said, shoving his notebook back in his pocket as if to say he was going off the record. That seemed to anger Miley even more.

"Listen. She told you what she knows and so did I. What you gonna do . . . arrest us because we both work at EZ Cash?" Miley snarled. Before the detective could get another word in . . . "If not, then we don't have anything else to say about this. As you can see, my sister is a little under the weather right now. That would be your clue to leave this alone," Miley snapped, almost coming toe-to-toe with Detective Castle. Her attitude was making me nervous, and the heart monitor was certainly telling the story. It was ringing off so loudly that the nurse came rushing into the room.

"Is everything okay, Ms. Houston?" the nurse asked warily. Her eyes darted between all of us.

"I'm just exhausted," I whispered, turning my face away from where Miley and Detective Castle stood facing off.

"Enough said. I'm going to have to ask all visitors to leave. With these types of head injuries, a patient can take a turn for the worse really quickly," the nurse announced, pulling the door open and holding it open expectantly.

"I'll be speaking with you, Karlie. Sooner rather than later," Detective Castle said, keeping his disapproving eye on Miley although he was speaking to me. Miley sucked her teeth as he strode for the door. He turned and smirked at us both before he ducked out of the door.

Miley simply shot me a look. *I got this*, she mouthed to me. I shook my head slightly, letting her know I didn't agree with the way she had carried on. My little sister was notorious for telegraphing her guilt in hot situations. She had been doing it since we were kids. I could hear Magda's voice in my head. "A guilty dog always barks." I just don't know why Miley didn't get that concept.

CHAPTER 5

HONOR AMONG THIEVES

"You stupid muthafucka!" I hollered as soon as I stormed into the hollowed-out warehouse. My voice reverberated loudly off of the cement walls, grabbing everyone's rapt attention. All eyes were on me, and I didn't give a damn. I was still steaming mad at how everything had been carried out.

"I said to make it look real . . . not fucking gun-butt me so hard that you put me in the goddamn hospital! This scar is going to be on my head for life! Ten damn stitches ain't no fake-ass hit. You did that shit on purpose, right? You never fucking liked me!" I got right up in Walt's face. He had definitely taken our little act too far. There was something about the way he had spoken to me during the robbery that had some truth to it. I'd known for a long time that Walt didn't care for me. I had had some beef with one of his baby mothers back in the day, and I don't think he got over it. I didn't care if he was Sidney's cousin. He had taken it too far. Walt stood there smirking at me. That made me even angrier.

"What if you had done some real damage? You stupid bastard! Are you going to pay for me to see a fucking plastic surgeon to cover up this scar? Hell no! You broke-ass nigga!" I went on. I had been waiting for the moment I could get at his ass.

"Yo, nigga, get ya bitch," Walt said calmly.

"A bitch? Who the fuck you calling a bitch . . . bitch!" I screamed.

"Calm down, Karlie. Calm the hell down," Sidney chastised, pulling me back out of his cousin Walt's face. Walt laughed out loud this time like I wasn't even standing there and like I was a joke. That just infuriated me even more.

"Oh it's funny to you, asshole?" I yelled, reaching out and taking a swipe at him with my left hand. Sidney pulled me away just in the nick of time. My bravado garnered a few snickers from the other dudes standing around. Either that or they were laughing at me like I was a big joke.

Truth be told, Walt could've knocked my ass out again with his bare hands if he really wanted to. And I think if I wasn't Sidney's girl, he probably would have with the way I was embarrassing him. Walt was a big guy who stood about six foot, five inches and weighed about three hundred pounds. He had been the ringleader at the robbery at my store. He was also the one who'd sent me to the hospital and opened up a nasty gash on my beautiful face. He'd definitely taken our little ruse too damn far. When we had all sat around and planned the robberies, I had told the guys that a light assault on me and Miley would make it look real and throw the cops off from thinking we had anything to do with it. Walt had done his fair share of time in the feds. He had a reputation for being violent with women and men. Sidney told me that more than one of Walt's babies' mothers had filed domestic violence charges on him.

"Look, you said make that shit look real so that's what I did," Walt finally said brusquely. "How was I supposed to know you was gonna fall like a little frail-ass bird? I ain't even hit your ass that hard. So count yourself as lucky."

"*Look* real," Miley chimed in before I could say anything else. "That's the operative word . . . *look* real. Like make pretend, you asshole. You didn't have to bust my sister's head to the white meat to make them girls in that store believe it was a random robbery. And your boy could've definitely used much less force to punch me in the face too. Look at this shit. I'll be wearing shades for a month. You niggas went way too far with it," she lectured, turning her covered eyes toward Troy, the dude who had punched her.

"Fuck all this complaining. What's done is done. Let's get down to the business at hand," Sidney's homeboy Craig interrupted. That was just like him—always no nonsense and about straight business. Craig was a marijuana head and a stick-up kid from the downtown section of Norfolk. He was that real down-ass nigga who would rob anybody he felt was a big enough score. Craig was the guy who young street dealers hated—or feared, I should say. After them little boys bust their asses all day selling crack rock, here comes Craig like a thief in the night, taking all of their profit and whatever drugs they have left too. I was still surprised that no one had taken Craig's life yet behind his low-down dirty ways. Something about Craig had always scared me. There was a ruthlessness in his eyes that said he'd kill his own mother over a few hundred dollars. I shuddered just thinking about it. I had told Sidney when we were planning the robberies that I didn't know if Craig could be trusted. I'd always felt like he'd kill all of us and take everyone's share of the money if he could. He had a real nasty vibe, and my stomach didn't take to him. Sidney had assured me that, although Craig was a grimy street dude, he was loyal to people who were loyal to him. I went along with it, thinking . . . if Sidney trusted him . . . I trusted him. I still didn't like the feeling I got when I was around him though.

"I agree. Shit is done already," Sidney said. "We can't change what happened. But we can count up this guap right now. Seems like we came up off this lick. This shit right here feels nice and heavy." Sidney hefted one of the familiar black duffel bags up onto the table. Troy, their other boy, did the same with the duffel bag that was holding the proceeds from Miley's store.

Sidney unzipped his bag first. He opened the top wide so that the green stacks inside could be seen. A collective round of gasps filtered through the warehouse. It was as if niggas had never seen that much cash in their lives. They probably hadn't. Shit, the only reason I had was because I worked at the EZ Cash. I smiled. The money made me feel euphoric, like I had just taken a long pull off a blunt.

"Yo! We came the fuck off!" Walt cheered, walking into Craig to exchange a pound and chest bump. "There gotta be over a hun'ed stacks in this m'fucka."

"You think it's that much paper there?" Sidney asked. "Nah. We probably ain't that lucky. But, it might be damn close to that."

"Yes, there is over a hundred thousand dollars because I know what was in the store when I opened the safe," I said with attitude, cutting my eyes at Walt. Walt sighed. He turned to Sidney and flashed a telling glance.

"Kill the attitude now, Karlie. Let's get this done," Sidney instructed with authority in his voice. "Let bygones be bygones. We came off. Period. Ain't nothing to be acting negative about now."

I lowered my eyes and bit down on my bottom lip. I exhaled. I had to agree with Sidney. There was no need to act miserable with all of that money sitting there in front of us. I was a few days away from getting rid of my financial problems. We had pulled off what seemed like the perfect heist. All of the loose ends had been tied up at the stores. I was confident that I'd eventually get rid of that lurking-ass detective. Life was about to be good. Or so I thought.

Sidney nodded at me and then to the first duffel bag. I directed a small smile at my man. I walked over and peeked inside the bag, and my smile grew wider. It felt damn good that I was the first one to dig in to the duffel bag, to touch the familiar, neatly bound stacks of cash. They were taped in bundles of five thousand dollars each. That was how we kept them at the store.

"Five, ten . . ." I started counting as I lifted each stack one at a time and put it on the table. After a few minutes, I glanced up from the bag to notice all six of the guys practically salivating over the money. Miley was rubbing her hands together like a mad scientist too. I realized at that moment that money could turn anybody into a beast. I shook my head slightly. All I could do now was pray that the aftermath went as smooth as the actual robbery.

"Soon as I get my shit, I'm about to get the hottest fits," a dude named Mega announced cheerfully. He was a little young nigga who worked with Craig. Mega was six feet, six inches tall and as skinny as a rail. He had blown a basketball scholarship to college because he just couldn't let the streets go. Mega still lived at home with his mother, and he wasn't doing anything with his life. He was obviously very immature.

"Shit, not me. I'm going straight to my weed dude. A nigga gon' be high for life," Ant, Sidney's nephew, followed up with a big stupid smile on his face. Ant was a little spoiled brat. All he did was take handouts from Sidney and smoke weed all day and all night. Ant had gotten shot when he was fourteen years old. Sidney always blamed himself because he felt that whoever had shot Ant was trying to send a message to him. Sidney was fiercely protective of his nephew, sometimes to a fault. Listening to Ant and Mega talk about their plans for the money sped my heart rate up. Immediately, heat flashed through my chest and turned my face red. I pursed my lips and turned toward the two immature boys like I was their mother.

"Shut up! Shut the fuck up with all that hood nigga talk!" I chastised, my pointer finger jutting out at them accusingly. "If you dummies go out there spending all crazy right away, y'all don't think people gon' take notice and start talking?" I asked and told at the same time. Everybody suddenly got quiet. "And then y'all not even talking about doing something with the money that will benefit you in the long run? Clothes and weed? Where the fuck is that going to get y'all? Ridiculous. It's stupid shit like that keeping our people down now. I told Sidney to pick people that were mature enough to handle this shit. You two dummies obviously weren't the right ones," I ranted, shaking my head in disgust.

Both Mega and Ant hung their heads. The other dude that Sidney had put down on the heist, Troy, started mumbling under his breath. He knew better than to say anything about whatever dumb plans he had for his share of the money. I kind of liked Troy. He was one of Sidney's finer friends with his gorgeous hazel eyes and his LL Cool J physique. Troy had just had a baby, but he was constantly trying to holler at my sister. I liked Troy so I didn't expect him to say anything ignorant about his money. I could only believe that he would take care of his new family with the money. It was all too much to think about. Worrying about these dudes spending crazy or running their mouths had been so far from my mind when I'd planned the robbery. I suddenly had an ill feeling in the pit of my stomach about all of this. I just knew that somebody out of this crew was going to be running their mouth in the streets. It was too late to go back on that now.

"Karlie is right. We gotta lay low until they forget all about this shit. Now, let's get to the business of it all. We got the surveillance tapes. Right?" Sidney asked, looking around at everyone's faces. A collective murmur in the affirmative rose and fell around the room. I saw a look of relief come over Sidney's face.

"A'ight. We shot out the eye in the sky that was on those corners. Right?" Sidney confirmed. This time, heads went up and down. More relieved body language from Sidney.

"So, we got few eyewitnesses, but Amy and Trina and that fat girl that was in Miley's store are all too scared to say shit to the cops. They work for Karlie and they are pretty much convinced that she and Miley were victims just like they were. We should be golden. *IF* . . . I repeat, *IF* . . . y'all dumb niggas keep y'all mouths shut and be easy," Sidney lectured on.

I twisted my lips and shook my head in agreement. I moved my eyes from Ant to Mega and then over Troy, Craig, and Walt. Walt was still glaring at me like he wanted to kill me. And, Craig still had that grimy look in his eyes like he was going to rob us all at any minute. Another wave of uneasiness came over me. I shifted my weight from one foot to the other and averted my eyes back to the bags with the money. Maybe if I focused on everything I could accomplish with the money, I wouldn't feel so bad. Nah. That didn't work either.

Stop being paranoid, Karlie. Shake it off. Everything is all good, I told myself. That sixth-sense feeling wasn't letting up though. From the beginning, something about this heist made me leery.

"We not splitting this money up right now either. I'm about to put it up some place safe, and when the DTs stop circling and shit stops being hot, everybody will get their fair share," Sidney continued. My heart fluttered a little bit watching him take the lead. I loved a strong man. I despised weak-ass men.

A collective rumble of displeasure rose and fell over the group. Everybody wanted their share right away. It was what we had promised them. Their displeasure at not getting the money right away was understandable, but Sidney and I both knew that some of these dudes would get us caught.

"Y'all not even gon' slide niggas a grip to get by for a few days? I mean like something for all our hard work," Mega asked, his hands shoved down into the pockets of his jeans. I shot him a look. My hands curled into fists at my side and my eyes hooded over. *This little nigga has to be kidding me. Ungrateful bastard!*

"Word. That's crazy. I got a baby to feed. I took a chance doing this lick," Troy followed up, shaking his head in disgust.

With my breathing heavy and my nostrils flaring, I literally had to bite my tongue to keep from saying anything in response. Instead, I let out a long sigh to show my irritation. Miley sucked her teeth. Everybody was throwing dirty glares at one another. The tension in the room was palpable, to say the least. I was still watching Craig though. I just felt like he would pull out on us at any minute and take flight with all of the money. Through all of the arguing, Craig seemed unfazed by it all. Like he knew something none of us knew. I shook my head from left to right trying to shake away those thoughts. I was bugging out. Craig was still Sidney's boy.

"Nah. We all get our money at the same time. When shit dies down," Sidney stood firm. "Let's give it about five days to a week. That is not that long. By then, the cops will decide that the robbers got away. They will clear Karlie and Miley of any suspicions and we can all live happily ever after with our guap. Then you dudes can buy whatever the hell y'all want."

I could tell those dudes were not happy. I watched as their faces folded into frowns and they whispered their displeasure amongst one another. At the time, I didn't care. All I was concerned with was all of the things that money could do for me. Knock out some bills. Maybe a new apartment for Miley and me. Maybe even separate apartments this time. A trip or two . . . the Caribbean always seemed like someplace I wanted to go, but could never afford. My hands started shaking just thinking about the possibilities.

I zipped up the first bag and started counting the money in the second bag. I wanted everybody to know how much was there and how much each person was going to get. I was hoping and praying that would at least garner some honor amongst thieves and be motivation for everybody to keep their mouths shut once they left. A girl could hope. Right?

CHAPTER 6

MURPHY'S LAW

"Where's the money? Where's the fucking money! I want it now!"

"I . . . I . . . don't have it. Please just don't hurt me. Please!"

"Bullshit! Where's the money?"

"Ahhh! Please don't hit me again. I'm begging you!"

"Naw. I'm not going to hit you, bitch. I'm just going to blow your fucking brains out!"

"Noooo!"

"Ahh!" I jumped out of my sleep with my arms flailing so wildly I hit myself in the head. My chest heaved up and down like I had been running an Olympic race. Sweat had my hair plastered to my forehead, and I had goose bumps all over my skin. I moved my head around frantically, making sure I had really been dreaming.

"Shit. That was so real," I said with a long sigh, closing my eyes and exhaling in relief. I touched my cheeks roughly to make sure I was awake and there wasn't a gun in my face like in the dream. "You are paranoid, Karlie," I whispered to myself, letting my tense muscles ease and relax again. "These dreams are going to send you to the crazy house." I swiped my hands over my face.

I had been having the same recurring nightmare that a man was threatening me about the money since the robbery. I could hear his voice, but I could never see his face . . . just the glare from the shiny silver gun he pointed in my face. It was always so real. My head was pounding from jumping out of my sleep like that.

Just as I went to lie back down . . .

BANG! BANG! BANG!

I almost jumped out of my skin. This time, I knew I wasn't dreaming. I also knew I wasn't deaf.

"Oh my God. What the hell was that?" I grabbed my chest. It took me a few minutes to realize the loud noise was actually coming from the front of my apartment. It was coming from the door. Someone was banging on my door like a maniac. Either that or banging like the damn police.

"What the hell?" I grumbled in response to more loud knocks rattling my door. Still a little dazed for a few minutes, I finally gathered my thoughts enough to attempt to get out of the bed. Sleep still clouded my mind, but it wasn't long before the incessant banging made those sleep clouds dissipate. I looked at my bedroom window and the sun was barely up so I knew it was very early. I picked up my cell phone and checked the time. My face immediately folded into a scowl.

"Who the hell is banging on my door at six o'clock in the morning on a Saturday?" I grumbled some more. I threw my legs over the side of my bed, grabbed my favorite orange and black tiger-striped terrycloth robe, and shrugged into it. I also grabbed the baseball bat I kept at the side of my bed for protection. A girl couldn't be too careful. Especially in the neighborhood I lived in. Especially when you got down on a heist with grimy dudes you might not be able to trust.

The knocks resounded through my apartment again as I padded down the hallway leading to the door.

"Wait a damn minute," I complained, my own stale morning breath stinging my nose. Now I was really annoyed. I gripped my bat tighter as I approached the apartment door.

"Who is it?" I yelled at the door, inching my ear closer. At first there was no answer. Then another round of knocks scared me and caused me to jump back, slightly off balance.

"Who is it?" I screamed again. This time with an attitude.

"It's Sid. Open the door, Karlie!"

My shoulders slumped with relief hearing that it was Sidney. But I was immediately alarmed.

Sidney? He has keys so why the hell would he be banging like that at this time of morning.

I set my bat down and went about unlocking the four padlocks on the door.

"Why the hell you ain't use your . . ." I started

as I swung my door open with much attitude. I couldn't even finish my sentence before Sidney came barreling into my apartment like a six-foot tornado. He literally pushed past me with so much force that he almost knocked me over.

"Damn, Sidney. What the hell?" I whined.

"Close the door," he demanded with urgency. I stared at him incredulously for a few seconds. "Hurry up and close the fucking door, Karlie!"

"Okay, okay," I snapped back. "What the hell is wrong with you?" I asked as I closed the door behind him.

"Lock it. All of the locks," Sidney said cryptically. With his hand on his waistband, he rushed over to my windows, peeked through the blinds, and then started closing all of my blinds and pulling all of the curtains together. I watched him, confused.

"Okay, Sidney, you're starting to scare me now, damn it. What the hell is up?" I said, one hand on my hip. "You come here this early in the morning all frantic. Didn't use your key to get in. Now you acting like somebody watching us or after you? Tell me what is going on. Did you get into a fight or beef with somebody? Where is the key I gave you to my apartment?"

"Shh." Sidney motioned for me to lower my voice. I snapped my lips shut, but the look on my face probably said it all. Sidney knew he had better start talking and fast, or he was going to hear my mouth going off.

"I think I dropped it on the way here."

"Well, tell me what's going on."

"Yo, Karlie. We need to move the money. We have to find another hiding place right away," Sidney whispered, his words coming out almost breathlessly as he finished shutting us out from the outside world. He moved from my windows and immediately started pacing around my little glass coffee table in circles. He was biting his bottom lip fiercely. Something I knew him to do only when he was extremely angry or extremely nervous.

"What? Move the money? What are you talking about, Sidney?" I asked skeptically. "You are truly bugging out right now, Sidney, and I just need to know . . ." I started with my hands up in front of me.

"Troy is dead," Sidney blurted. Just like that. Sidney dropped a bomb on me. No warning. No kind of clue about what was coming. Just . . . *bam!* At that point, whatever I had been saying when Sidney interrupted me with that news just completely went out of my head. My words clipped short like a needle being snatched from a record. My mind immediately became muddled . . . almost blank.

"What?" I asked as if I hadn't heard him the first time. I truly could not process what he had just said. "What did you say?" My voice came out like a hoarse whisper. Suddenly my mouth was cotton-ball dry. I could feel my left temple throbbing.

"That nigga is dead, Karlie," Sidney said. "Troy is fucking dead!" he continued more frantically now. Sidney used his hands to grab each side of his head.

"Yo. I can't even fucking think straight right

now, Karlie. This nigga was murdered. Shot in his head in cold blood. I'm fucked up right now," Sidney went on.

I started pacing the floor right along with Sidney. My heart was pounding, while veins in my neck pulsed fiercely against my skin.

Troy was shot and killed? I repeated in my head. Then I abruptly stopped moving. I had a thought. Sidney had first said we had to move the money. Then he'd said Troy was dead.

"But what does Troy's murder have to do with us . . . the money . . . moving it?" I asked. "How do you know he wasn't murdered over some beef? Or some drug shit?"

Sidney shook his head like I had just asked him the dumbest question in history. He obviously knew something that I didn't know.

"I'll tell you what it has to do with us. When they found him, there was a note that said something like . . . 'we know about the money, he won't be the last if we don't get all of it,' " Sidney relayed. My heart sank. I guess that had answered my question. It was obviously all about the money.

My legs suddenly got so weak I couldn't stand. I flopped down on my little threadbare couch . . . exasperated. I lowered my face into the palms of my hands and exhaled a windstorm of breath. Sidney kept pacing; the rustle of his jeans was the only sound I could hear. The silence that fell over the room was deafening. Our minds raced in a million different directions. This was supposed to be a foolproof heist. Easy in, easy out. There should have been no complications . . . unless someone on the inside of the crew was running their mouth.

Troy had to have been bragging about the money for anyone else to know about it. Either that, or somebody else already knew and wanted what we had. If I was a smoker, I would've smoked an entire pack of cigarettes in that few minutes we sat there in silence.

After a few minutes, I lifted my head. I turned my eyes toward Sidney and stared right into his eyes. I could not only see the fear dancing in his eyes, I could feel it gripping me around my neck now.

"Somebody knows," I said hoarsely. "Somebody knows what we did and they want in. This is not over."

"Yeah, it's obvious. I bet it's because those little niggas been running their mouths. I told all of them to keep their damn mouths shut," Sidney replied. "I think this is some street dude trying to scare us. Whoever it is better hope I don't find his ass before those homicide detectives find him. I bet the whole hood looking for the come-up off this shit now. I can just imagine what these little niggas think we got now. You know everybody trying to come up. Like I said . . . we have to move that money."

"No. You're wrong. There is more to this, Sidney. Trying to scare us would be beating Troy up to send a message. Trying to scare us would be holding Troy hostage and demanding a ransom to get the money. Trying to scare us would be leaving a note to tell us where to drop the money and if we didn't more of us would die. This is more than someone trying to scare us. This is someone trying to get that fucking money for a reason. Somebody who has more than just a hood come-up in mind," I told Sidney seriously. I shuddered as chills came over my entire body like I had been splashed with ice water. I was so scared, my teeth started chattering. Sidney stopped moving for a few seconds and turned to me like he'd just had a revelation.

"You're right. There is more to this shit. But why kill the nigga and leave no way for us to give them the money? Even if it was somebody who wanted the money for a reason. Even if it was somebody who felt they had a right to the money . . . if we can't get it to them, then what's the point?" Sidney asked, rubbing his chin and squinting his eyes like he was contemplating his own questions. "No ransom demand. No request to meet to turn the money over. Makes no sense. You don't just murder a nigga off of GP with no end game in mind. Unless . . ." Sidney paused. I was hanging on his every word. "Unless you feel like niggas violated you in some kind of way by having that money."

I was quiet. I had to think about that. It was true. Which meant whomever killed Troy wasn't satisfied with just him and didn't want the money just yet . . . if they wanted it at all. This seemed more like revenge to me. Like they had a point to prove.

"Who found him?" I asked Sidney in a barely audible tone. I could feel tears welling in the backs of my eyes. I didn't know Troy as well as Sidney did, but that didn't mean I would want to see him die. I knew he had just had a baby too. I had gone to the baby shower with Sidney. Just the thought of that little baby with no father, possibly because of me, made my skin crawl. It was my fault.

"His moms found him. Right in the doorway of his crib. It was like he was trying to get home and somebody just ran up on him . . . and BLAM . . . right in his head. Stuck the note to his open wound like the cowards they are," Sidney answered. I shook my head and closed my eyes.

"She called me. She gave me the note. She picked it up before the cops got on the scene. She didn't want them pigs to find that note. You know how that shit is. She's a church lady and didn't want it to get out that Troy might have been into some ill shit. She wants him to be buried like a saint. Don't they all."

"Thank God for her pride," I exhaled my words. "So we are the only ones who know about the note?"

"Yeah."

"Don't tell anyone," I warned. "All that's going to do is spook all of them. We need to keep this quiet until we can split up the money."

"C'mon. I'm not stupid, Karlie. Shit getting serious right now. I know if those other dudes hear about the note, they're going to request their money off the rip," Sidney said, annoyed.

"Getting serious. It's been serious. I thought this would be the perfect heist. Easy breezy. One, two, three. But, no. From the beginning of this shit we have been battling Murphy's Law—what can go wrong, will go wrong. I got a feeling more things are going to go wrong too. I got a real sick gut feeling that this is just the beginning."

With that, Sidney flopped down next to me and wrapped one of his strong arms around me. I have to admit. It was the first time I didn't feel protected by my man. In fact, with the whole heist idea being his in the first place, I felt like he had got me into some shit I was never going to be able to get out of alive.

CHAPTER 7

POINTING FINGERS

Sidney removed the black, wrought-iron grate that covered a deep cavern in the cement floor of the warehouse. Craig, Walt, Mega, Ant, Miley, and me all watched, holding our breath. Everybody was probably saying the same silent prayer—*Dear God, let the money still be here.*

"It's still here," Sidney announced with a relieved sigh as he reached down and tugged on the strap of the first bag. "Open it and count it," he told me as he held the bag out toward me.

I quickly took the bag from him. Miley snatched up the second bag. We both opened the bags and confirmed that the stacks of cash were still in place. I didn't have to count the money in my bag. I had become a pro at eyeing money and estimating the amount.

"Yo, I'm saying. Let's just split this shit up and go our separate ways," Craig spoke up. "There's already one nigga dead. What we going to wait for us all to be dead before we get our cut?"

"Word. Might as well enjoy our shit just in case Troy getting hit means that somebody out there is after this loot," Walt said, followed by a chuckle. "I'm just saying. That nigga Troy ain't have no enemies, so if he got murked, I'm thinking it gotta have something to do with this paper. That shit is common sense. He had to be running his trap about it."

"Nah. I think we all getting paranoid. Just give it a few more days. That detective is still creeping up on Karlie and Miley, lurking and looking for information. We don't even know if what happened to Troy was about this money or not," Sidney answered.

"Yeah. Three more days should do the trick," I followed up.

"If y'all ain't think Troy getting murked has anything to do with the money then why we here talking about moving the shit from this spot?" Mega asked, his words dripping with suspicion. He had a point. I had to think quickly on my feet.

"We just want to make sure that the money is safe. We didn't have to call all of you here. We could've just moved the money without saying shit and none of y'all would've known about it. If we were grimy, that's what we would've done. Or better yet, we would've taken it all and bounced without giving y'all shit. So let's just stick to the plan. We will split up the money in a few days. I can't take the risk of the cops finding out about me and

Miley. I'm sure y'all can understand that. If we get knocked . . . y'all all get knocked too," I reminded them all.

"You saying all of that, but how we know somebody you know ain't murking niggas so you get away with all the money in the end anyway," Walt said accusingly. He stepped closer to me with his eyes squinted into dashes and his nostrils flaring like a bull's. I guess he still hadn't gotten over me cursing him out after the robbery. I stood my ground. I didn't even flinch under his glare.

"Oh please, nigga. How we know your grimy ass ain't the one doing the shit. Last I checked, you was the grimiest nigga in this bunch. You probably shot the nigga," I snapped, rolling my neck and my eyes. Walt started toward me with his fists balled.

"Chill, man. Just chill." Sidney stepped in Walt's path just before he could hit me. I was scared as shit, but I had to play it off.

"Yeah, grimy nigga. I must be right—that's why you so mad," I mocked as I hid behind Sidney. I was playing tough. If Walt or any of the other dudes saw one bit of fear out of me or Miley, I'm sure they would take advantage of us.

"Nah. Any bitch that robs her own workplace is the grimiest in this bunch," Ant interjected. "All y'all niggas sound stupid. Arguing about when to split up money and who shot who. All of this is childish. Give me my paper and let me skate away from all this bullshit."

"Fuck you! Don't speak to my sister like that, you bitch-ass nigga," Miley stepped to Ant. "You wasn't saying she was grimy when she was putting you down on that lick, you thirsty, bum ass."

"Fuck out of here, bitch!" Ant spat, shoving Miley out of his face so hard she almost fell.

"Oh hell no!" I yelled, charging toward Ant. "Don't put your hands on my sister! I will kill your ass!" Just before I got to him, Sidney grabbed me around the waist and pulled me back.

"Let me go! I'm sick of all of these dudes! Let me go!" I gritted out, kicking my legs wildly trying to get at Ant.

"I will fuck y'all bitches up," Ant barked, his fists curled at his side. "Let her go. Let me show her what a real man does to chicks who run their mouths like these two."

"Both of these chicks probably setting niggas up," Walt said, moving his hand like he was going for something in his waistband. The entire room erupted with accusations and insults. Everybody was pointing fingers at each other. Miley and I were ready to fight. It wasn't hard to see that we were all coming apart mentally.

"Shut the fuck up!" Sidney finally screamed so loud he startled everyone into silence. All of our faces were in different stages of shock and surprise. "All this finger-pointing bullshit stops right now! I'm sick of all of it!" Sidney announced, moving his eyes from person to person as he walked past each of us like the principal in the movie *Lean on Me*. "None of us are responsible for what happened to Troy. All we know is right now shit is too hot with the cops to split this money up. In a few days, when this cop stops snooping around the stores and stops lurking around my girl, we will all get what's owed to us. Until then, everybody shut the fuck up. Stop running your mouths in the street and lay fucking low. Period. I don't want to hear another word about this."

"Yeah. A'ight. Y'all niggas got three days tops. If I don't get my money, it's going to be a problem," Craig threatened.

"Whatever," I mumbled under my breath. I was sick of all of them and their threats. I turned my attention back to the bags of money.

"Now . . . here's my idea for where to move the money to," I said, pulling out three sheets of paper from my bag. That had everyone's attention again. And that's when I laid everything out.

CHAPTER 8

BODY COUNT

Two days had passed since we'd moved the money. We had another day or so before it would be time for us to split up the money, which would mean, hopefully, this whole ordeal would be over. I looked through the front glass window of the EZ Cash and saw Sidney's truck parked outside. I smiled.

Sidney had been keeping me close since Troy's murder. He had been like a fixture at my house, even spending the night, which, he usually didn't do. He was taking me to work and picking me up too. I couldn't front. I was enjoying his attention. It was definitely something I was hoping to get used to once the dust settled.

I turned away from the front desk and started my process of shutting things down for the evening. I was emptying the drawers when I heard the front door chimes ring signaling that someone was coming in.

"I'm coming now. . . ." I started without turning around. I figured it was Sidney coming to tell me to hurry up.

"No need to rush. I've got time."

I whirled around on the balls of my feet, my face crumpled in confusion at the sound of the familiar deep baritone. It definitely wasn't the voice of my man. All of the wind left my lungs when I saw Detective Castle standing there with a smirk on his face. My heart sped up in my chest. I quickly hid my trembling hands behind my back. I had to play it off. I definitely couldn't let him see me sweat.

"You must like me," I said sarcastically, rolling my eyes in disgust. "Either that or you just have no criminals to catch."

Detective Castle laughed. "Trust me, Ms. Houston, it's neither," he said, pulling a yellow folder from under his arm at the same time. "I wish this was a pleasure trip, but unfortunately it's not. Definitely not," he continued as he placed the folder down on the counter in front of him. He opened it and took something out.

"Ms. Houston, do you recognize these two men?" Detective Castle said, sliding a shiny eight-by-ten glossy photo toward me. I sucked in my breath and then I let out a gasp. My left hand instinctively flew up to my open mouth. The first thing I saw was all of the blood. I could barely make out the faces, but I recognized the dreads and the gold chains right away. My stomach did flips. I clutched the side of the counter.

"Whoa. Whoa," Detective Castle yelled, racing around the counter, grabbing me right before I hit the floor. "You all right?"

"I . . . I . . . get . . . get . . . weak at the sight of . . . of . . . blood," I replied weakly, barely able to get the words out.

"How about you sit down, Ms. Houston," he said, helping me to my chair. I swallowed hard and closed my eyes. My head was spinning.

"I understand your difficulty, Ms. Houston. But, I need to know your association with these victims," he said.

"I . . . I . . . don't," I started, lowering my forehead into my hand. I couldn't even be sure if it was who I thought it was.

"Before you lie," he said, throwing his hand up to halt my words. "I just want you to know that I'm asking you the questions, but there are some things I already know. Now these men are dead and I need to know your relationship with them."

I was shaking my head no. Tears immediately sprang to my eyes. It had finally set in my mind that it was Ant's dreads that I recognized and Mega's gold chains that I had seen just the other night. My heart was pounding. I was responsible for three people's deaths now. Troy, Ant, and Mega were all dead.

"Um . . ." I mumbled.

"Speak up, Ms. Houston," Detective Castle urged. "Do you recognize this SUV?" I opened my mouth to speak, but no words came out. I wanted to just tell him everything so that maybe the murders would stop. I couldn't afford for the body count to keep rising. I opened my mouth again, but just as I started to speak, Detective Castle turned his attention toward the chimes ringing on the front door and so did I.

"Yo, Karlie. What's going on?" Sidney rushed into the store in a huff. He paused as soon as he saw the detective. My eyes popped open. I immediately averted my eyes from Sidney to Detective Castle and back again. The minutes that they stood there facing off felt like hours to me.

"Mr. Coles." Detective Castle smirked. He acted like he was Sidney's long lost friend or something.

"Fuck is you?" Sidney gritted, although he knew exactly who Detective Castle was.

"I think you know who I am. I surely know who you are. I was just telling your girlfriend that this"— he slid the gruesome picture across the counter toward Sidney—"probably has something to do with your other friend's death. Which brings the body count of people associated with you and Ms. Houston to three . . . in just three days. And maybe, just maybe, they all might've been bragging around the streets about coming into a lot of cash recently. And . . . there just happened to be a lot of money missing from this establishment where *your* girlfriend works. You think this is all just a strange *Twilight Zone* type of coincidence?"

"Listen, Inspector Gadget, if all you got is speculation and allegations then I ain't got shit to say. When you got an arrest warrant and I got a

lawyer, I will speak to you. Until then, you can get
the fuck out before I file a citizen's complaint for
harassment," Sidney said with so much powerful
bravado I felt my heart and my pussy thump. Detective Castle looked defeated, like Sidney had just
taken a piss on his leg. That quickly changed to
anger.

"Have it your way, Mr. Coles," Detective Castle
grumbled, his jaw rocking. "I'm sure your sister is
not going to be a happy camper when she finds
out that you put your only nephew in danger," Detective Castle said cruelly.

"Fuck you, pig!" Sidney spat. I could tell that
the detective's words had hit him below the belt.

"You might just be the one to get fucked in the
end." The detective turned his attention back toward me. "You should think long and hard about
what's going on around you, Ms. Houston. Sometimes the company you keep can cost you everything you have . . . including your life," the detective
said with an eerie finality that sent chills down my
spine. After he said everything he needed to say, he
slid the photos back into the folder and left.

Miley was biting her nails down to the quick. I
was moving around with nervous energy, straight-
ening things in the house that didn't need fixing
or cleaning. I had already rearranged my *Essence*
and *Ebony* magazines on the coffee table about
fifty times. I had taken all of my dishes out of the
cabinets and stacked them back in twice. I didn't

have any more liquor in my cabinets or else I would've probably been pissy drunk by now.

"It gotta be the money," Miley said, gnawing on her thumbnail now. I let out a long sigh. I really didn't want to go over this again. We had talked about it over and over again. We had speculated fifty times. We had blamed a hundred people around Virginia Beach. It was all for nothing. We still had no damn clue if Troy's murder was related to Ant and Mega's murders.

"All three of the dudes that robbed my store are dead. Like, in some kind of order. All shot in the head or face. Mad cold-blooded." Miley went on like Sidney and I didn't already know the facts. "Y'all still don't think it's some kind of message?"

"Somebody *is* sending us a message," I agreed, annoyed. "But who? I mean, who would go as far as just killing dudes to send a message? Shit, just rob us and get it over with. There is more to this. You would think we stole money from some drug cartel or kingpin or some shit," I said. For that moment, I stopped flitting around like a busy bee. Everyone got quiet and so did I. My own words had hit me like an open-handed slap to the face. I suddenly remembered when I first started working at the EZ Cash, my old manager, Earl, had said to me jokingly, "You don't know this shit owned by the Black Mafia? Don't play with their money, girl. If one dime ever came up missing, they would be on some shit." I had laughed at Earl because the man who showed up as owner of the EZ Cash was an older white man named Mr. Sherra, who, everyone in Virginia Beach knew, owned several franchises. Mr. Sherra certainly wasn't a member of the Black Mafia. In fact, he was a feeble-looking old man who was as sweet as candy. Earl had disappeared one day. He'd left work the night before and never showed up again. After about two weeks, I'd grown suspicious and wondered what had happened. When I'd asked Mr. Sherra about Earl, he had laughed and then said Earl had just up and quit. I never thought anything of it at the time, but maybe Earl was right. Maybe there was some truth to the Black Mafia myth. Maybe we had stolen from some dangerous people and now it was payback time. There were so many possibilities, it was starting to make my head hurt.

"I'll be back. Y'all make sure y'all keep this door locked up. Don't open it for nobody," Sidney said, breaking the silence as he stood up and started toward the door.

"Oh hell no!" I raced around and got in front of him. "You're not going out alone. You think our safety is all that matters? Your friends are popping up dead everywhere. Hell no. You are not leaving without me," I proclaimed, blocking the door with my body. Sidney started shaking his head. I was dead serious. I was not letting him out of that door.

"Listen, love. I'm good. I got my best friend right here with me," he said, lifting his shirt a little so I could see the handle of his gun. "I have to go make sure my sister and my moms is okay. I just lost my nephew. I can't sit here all day and just not be with my family. I promise I'll be right back when I'm finished checking on them. You know a nigga like me. Ain't nobody running up on this." Sidney was playing tough, but I could tell he was a little nervous about leaving too.

Tears instantly sprang to my eyes. With everything that was going on, I couldn't even imagine having Detective Castle show up at my house with a picture of Sidney dead.

"Please, Sidney. Just stay. Tomorrow we can split up the money and run."

"We should do it today." He spat.

"But you know we gotta be careful. That detective could be lurking and watching our every move." I reminded him. "It's just one more day. We just have to survive one more day. Don't go out there. We can see your family and give them Ant's money. I know how you feel, but if you get killed, what would I do? If anything happened to you, I'd die," I cried. My entire body quaked with sobs. Sidney pulled me into his chest. "Shh. I love you," he whispered. He stroked my hair while he kissed the top of my head. That just made me sob even more.

"C'mon, baby. I'm good. I just need to make this quick run. I wouldn't be able to live with myself if I didn't check in on them. It's bad enough I feel guilty for what happened to my nephew. I can't just leave my sister to grieve alone. I'll be back before you know it. You think I'm going to let anything happen to me and risk something happening to you? Nah . . . I would never. I told you I won't ever let shit happen to you and I meant it," Sidney said. His words were no consolation. I also didn't have the strength to fight him. When Sidney was determined, he was determined. He moved me away from his chest, bent down, and kissed me. He used his thumb to swipe the tears from my cheeks.

"Shh. I love you, Karlie," he comforted. I closed my eyes and shook my head from side to side. If something did happen to him, at least I knew that he loved me. He probably had no idea how much I loved him.

"C'mon. Just lock up. I'll be back in no time," he said, kissing me on my forehead one last time. I opened my eyes and watched in terror as Sidney unlocked the door and pulled it open. I stood behind him waiting to lock it once he left, but he stopped right before he got all the way out of the doorway. I realized that something had made him pause like that.

"What? What is it?" I asked, trying to peek around him. Sidney didn't say anything. He bent down and picked up a box that had been left at my door.

"What is that?" Miley asked, crossing the living room to see what was going on. "Who is the package for? Is it addressed to one of us?" she pressed.

Sidney carried the box back into my apartment. "Lock the door back," he demanded.

"Are you going to open that? What if it's a bomb?" Miley asked, her eyes wide. "Karlie, are you going to let him open that? What do you think it is? I don't know. . . ." Miley rambled. She was making me nervous with her frantic questions.

"Be quiet!" I snapped. "Just be quiet." I threw

my hands up in front of me. My nerves were frazzled enough. I didn't need her carrying on.

Sidney was playing it cool. He didn't say a word. He calmly walked to the kitchen counter, set the box on the counter near the sink, retrieved a knife, and cut the tape away from the cardboard. I rushed over, and so did Miley. My heart was galloping in my chest. Miley was bouncing on her legs like she had to pee. The entire apartment was eerily quiet. I couldn't even hear any of us breathing, which told me we were all holding our breath.

"What is it?" Miley asked again, being very annoying. I shot her an evil look. We both turned our attention back to the strange package. All I could see was wadded-up newspaper at first. Sidney slowly removed the top layer of newspaper.

"Oh, shit! Aggh! Goddamn!" Sidney shrieked, backing away from the box and its contents so fast he almost fell. He had his forearm covering his mouth and nose.

"Agggh!" Miley screamed. "Oh my God! Get it out of here!" She had seen what was inside too.

My mouth hung open. I wanted to scream, but no sound would come. I knew that I was in shock because even the pungent smell of death didn't faze me. I could not take my eyes off of Walt's dead eyes staring up at me. His mouth hung open like a scary Halloween mask. Dried blood covered his entire face and head. The loose tendons and jagged flesh around his neck told me that he'd suffered when he was killed. Someone had sent us Walt's decapitated head in a box like it was a gift. My legs finally gave out, and I collapsed to my knees. Miley leaned over and threw up. Sidney growled and swiped everything off my kitchen counter onto the floor. Then he punched a hole into one of my cabinets.

"Motherfuckers! I will kill all of you motherfuckers!" he hollered. I had never seen him cry until now. Walt had just been added to the body count. All we could think about was who would be next, because someone was going to meet their maker.

CHAPTER 9

ON THE RUN

Instead of waiting until the next day, we grabbed the box with Walt's head in it and left the apartment. After we dumped the box in a nearby river, we went into plan mode.

"We have three stops to make before we can bounce. All we have to do is make it to each place and keep our eyes and ears open for anything and anyone suspicious . . . including that stalking-ass cop that keeps popping up everywhere," Sidney instructed as we all sped out of my apartment building. "So, just like we discussed, I'll go into the first stop just to make sure nobody is following us and nothing goes down," he continued.

I could see that Miley's hands were trembling. I reached down and grabbed one of them and gave it a reassuring squeeze.

"We got this. We are going to get the money

and get out before anything else happens," I whispered to her. She inhaled deeply and exhaled.

"I hope you're right. This is just too much," she said, her bottom lip trembling.

"Have I ever let anything happen to you since Mommy died?" I asked, giving her a weak smile. Miley shook her head no and gave me a small, halfhearted smile back. "Well, I'm damn sure not going to now. I always have your back. . . . Remember that." It sure sounded good coming out of my mouth, but I was having a hard time even convincing myself.

"I have faith in you," Miley said.

"Good. You should. I have a pretty good track record," I replied with a dry chuckle.

Secretly, I was saying a silent prayer that I didn't let her down this time. Things were crazy. I was just hoping that I could keep both of us alive.

We finally made it to Sidney's truck and we all loaded in. Once inside, Sidney picked up his cell phone to call Craig.

"I have to let Craig know what's up. He needs to lay low for his own safety," Sidney was saying as he dialed Craig's number.

Craig was one of the last men standing. Sidney hadn't heard from him since we'd found out about Walt, but Sidney still wanted to give Craig his cut of the money. That's just the kind of dude Sidney was. We were about to be on the run, but his integrity wouldn't let him leave his boy out on his cut. I had to admire that about my man.

"Damn. Where is this nigga?" Sidney mumbled,

clearly flustered. "It's not like him to ignore my fucking calls like this. Man, I hope this dude is good. I can't take no more dead bodies. I don't like not hearing from him."

I felt a chill run down my back like I had just stepped barefoot onto a block of ice. I bit down on my bottom lip just thinking about it. What if Craig wasn't answering because he was already dead? I knew if I was thinking it, Miley and Sidney were too. I wrung my hands together in my lap as I watched Sidney frantically try Craig's number over and over again. Each time he got Craig's voice mail, my hopes that Craig was still alive lessened more and more. A feeling of dread washed over me. I leaned my head back on the headrest and closed my eyes. This time, I was praying in earnest. *God, please let him be alive. Please spare our lives. Please forgive me.*

"Fuck!" Sidney belted out, slamming his fists on the steering wheel. "This shit right here got me fucked up in the head right now. I wish I knew who was fucking with my crew. On everything I love, they would be sorry. When I find the person doing this, they are dead. I swear on everything I love, they are dead," Sidney growled with his nostrils flaring.

"I know, bae," I comforted, rubbing Sidney's shoulder. "It's no use in getting upset. It's totally out of your control right now. At this moment, we have to focus on us. We have to get out of this block, get the money, and get the hell out of dodge," I told him. I was trying to keep my composure when I really wanted to tell Sidney, *Fuck that nigga Craig! Let's get the hell out of here before who-*

ever is after us for this money finds us! I never liked or trusted Craig anyways.

After a few seconds of thinking about what I said, Sidney finally gave up trying to get Craig on the phone.

Sidney checked his mirrors for any signs of any suspicious cars. When he was comfortable with our surroundings, he drove out of my neighborhood. I kept watching the rearview mirror to make sure we weren't being followed. Miley had her head on a swivel as well.

We pulled up to the first stash spot—an Anytime Fitness on Wesleyan Drive. I dug in my purse and pulled out the locker key.

"This one you have to get. Remember Walt put this one in the men's locker room and I can't go in there," I said, handing Sidney the key. He looked at me expectantly. My mind was so muddled I just stared back at him.

"What? What's the matter?" I asked.

"The locker number, Karlie," he replied.

"Oh, goodness. My mind is so gone. Walt had said it was number four-thirty. That's what I have written down," I answered, still trying to shake the cobwebs from my brain.

"A'ight. When I get out, Karlie, you get in the driver's seat, just in case anything goes down and y'all have to pull out of here," Sidney instructed, obviously thinking way ahead of me and Miley.

"Oh, hell no! I'm the better driver," Miley protested from the backseat. "I'll get in the driver's seat. No way I'm trusting *Driving Miss Daisy* over here to save my life if things get hot. You know damn well my sister cannot drive fast. We will be dead depending on old sugar foot here to get us out of danger."

"Fine. You drive, Mario Andretti," I snapped at her. "That's why your ass always got tickets from the Virginia state troopers. But, whatever. You're the expert driver, I forgot." Miley could be real annoying sometimes. Everything wasn't a competition. She was lucky that I loved her behind unconditionally.

"I don't care who drives. Somebody get your ass in the seat just in case. When I come out, if everything is good, I'll hop in the back and we can pull over somewhere and change back after we are free and clear from this area," Sidney interjected. "And stop all of this stupid arguing. We have to stick together more than ever now." My face flushed red, and so did Miley's. We both knew that Sidney was right.

Miley and Sidney both exited the truck. She slid into the driver's seat just like he had instructed. Sidney whipped his head around, hyperaware of his surroundings, as he headed into the gym. I did the same from inside the truck. I looked up the block through the windshield. Then I turned around and looked down the block through the back windows. I even checked the side mirrors and rearview mirror inside the truck. The block seemed normal to me. Just the usual hustle and bustle of the midday crowd. There were no strange cars around that I could see. My heart sank once Sidney disappeared into the gym though. Just because outside looked good, that didn't mean there wasn't someone inside waiting to pounce. It had been my idea to rent lockers at three different gyms as stash spots for the money. I remembered this old-school hustler named Benny who used to hang around my mother telling her to stash some of his money at a YMCA locker once. Even as young as I was then, I'd thought that idea was genius. Who would think to check those lockers for anything other than sweaty gym clothes or changes of clothes? I knew we could take a gym bag full of money inside without people getting suspicious. Once we put our own locks on the lockers, nobody would mess with it. If the gym attendants saw a locked locker, they would just assume someone working out had locked up their stuff. I already knew how lax those gym attendants were anyway. It's not like they'd perform nighttime checks to see if any of the lockers remained locked. It was a genius idea in my mind. I guess everyone else in the crew thought so too because they had all agreed to the idea.

As we sat and waited for Sidney, Miley started swinging her legs in and out nervously. It was driving me crazy.

"Would you keep still?" I grumbled.

"What?" she snapped. "What does my legs moving have to do with you?" She sucked her teeth.

"It's annoying and it's just making my nerves even worse. So stop," I retorted, rolled my eyes. There was so much tension between us. I knew it was both of our nerves being on edge that had us at one another's throats. Miley stopped shaking her legs for a little while. I said a silent thank-you for the peace.

I looked at my watch and back at the gym door. I let out a long breath. It seemed like an eternity since Sidney had gone inside.

"What time did he get out of the truck?" I asked Miley.

She shrugged and turned her face away from me.

"Oh, now you're not speaking to me?"

"I said I don't know."

"You didn't say anything," I snapped. "Just forget it." I looked at my watch again. Now my legs were swinging in and out with uneasiness. Of course Miley shot me a look and then looked down at my legs.

"What?" I growled at her. We were both on edge.

"There he is!" Miley said excitedly. "Finally. Now we can get the hell out of town."

I whipped my head to the left and smiled. My heart melted when I saw Sidney's gorgeous caramel face and sexy physique rushing from the gym doors. Miley threw the SUV into drive. We were ready to go. My stomach did a few anxious flips. I felt like a giddy child who'd just received a new toy.

"Yes. Finally." I sighed. I was smiling because Sidney was almost to the truck, which meant freedom for all of us. Before he got to the door, a loud noise caused me to twist my head to the right. It was the squeal of vehicle tires that had snatched my attention away from Sidney. My mouth dropped open when I saw a black van speeding toward us.

"Oh my God," I gasped, the words barely audible when I noticed that the van had abruptly stopped directly in front of us.

"Aghh!" Miley screamed when she noticed it.

"Oh shit!" I yelled. The van had blocked us. Before we could even react, two men jumped from the van, guns drawn and rushed Sidney. Sidney had stopped walking when the screeching tires startled him. He had been so caught off guard that he didn't have time to react fast enough to get to his gun before the masked men threw a black bag over his head and dragged him towards the open back door of the van.

"Sidney!" I squealed so loud the back of my throat itched. "No! Sidney!" I jumped in my seat. I could feel blood rush to my face as I continued to scream. My screams didn't throw my sister off her game at all.

Instinctively Miley threw the SUV into reverse and sped backwards away from the van. I could see them throw Sidney inside and the men jump in after.

"No! Wait! We can't leave him!" I screamed, reaching over and hitting Miley on the arm. "Stop the fucking car! We can't leave him!" With my eyes bulging almost out of my head, I watched as Sidney's truck sped backwards, farther away from the van.

"Miley! Don't leave him! No! We can't fucking leave him!"

Miley ignored me and continued to skillfully drive the vehicle in reverse.

"Goddamn it! They're coming!" Miley shouted. She stepped on the gas even harder. "They have him already. Do you want to die right now? There is nothing we can do to save him, Karlie! He is gone!"

"Aghh!" I screamed. Both out of the fear of being

chased and out of the agony of leaving Sidney behind. I knew Miley was right, but the aching in my heart at that moment would not allow me to let it go.

"No! We have to save him! He is my man!"

"Oh my God!" Miley screamed when she saw the black van gaining on us. "Nah! Fuck this! I got this. They will not get us!" she gritted out, moving the steering wheel like a movie stunt driver. My body swayed left to right and then back again. I had already hit my head twice with the way Miley was swinging that SUV.

When we got to the corner, Miley quickly put the car into drive, wheeled it around and, with tires screeching, sped down the street opposite the gym.

"Fuck! I can't believe this shit!" Miley yelled as she looked up into the rearview mirror. "They are right behind us! I can't shake these bastards. We are fucked!"

"Miley! We have to go back for Sidney!" I cried out. "We have to stop and go back for him." I don't think the danger we were in was registering in my mind. My thoughts were too clouded by the fact that I had lost Sidney . . . forever. Tears were running down my face in streams. "We can't just leave him like that! They are going to do him worse than they did Walt." I cried some more.

"Karlie! Snap the fuck out of it! There are five men in that van chasing us right now. You think the two of us can save Sidney if we stop? Hell no! We are on the run from God knows who and you're talking about stopping! Be quiet!" Miley screamed at me as she floored the gas pedal and wheeled the

SUV better than a NASCAR driver. I put both of my hands up to the sides of my head and began rocking in the seat. I knew Sidney was a dead man. I looked up into the mirror as Miley eased onto Highway 264.

"Fuck it. If we get pulled over for speeding at least the cops will save our lives," she said in a frantic voice. Every move Miley made in Sidney's truck, the van followed.

"We can't even go get the rest of the money. To me, it's like whoever is after us knows exactly where to look for us. How would they know to come to that gym? How did they know it would be our first stop? So now we are fucking broke and homeless and in danger," Miley spat as she maneuvered Sidney's truck in and out of traffic. My heart was racing and my stomach was in knots. Miley whipped the SUV down the highway, switching lanes like a pro.

"All right, Karlie. I'm about to fuck their heads up," Miley told me. She looked up into the mirror, and the only thing separating us from the van was one minivan filled with a mother and her kids.

"Hold on tight. This is about to be some stunt movie shit," Miley warned me. She was focused and in a zone. I had never seen my sister this focused. It felt kind of nice depending on her for a change instead of it being the other way around.

"Here we go!" she yelled out. Before I could grab on to the door handle, Miley turned the steering wheel to the left with so much force my body was pushed to the right.

"Oww!" I hollered as my head banged into the passenger-side window. Miley whipped the truck again, and this time I was able to hold on in time. I heard tires from other cars squealing behind us. There were also car horns blaring all around us. We were in a high-speed chase like something out of a movie. Miley started for the next highway exit and so did the van chasing us.

"If you get off the exit, they'll catch us at the light!" I screamed at her.

"Shut up, Karlie! Let me do this! I got this!" Miley screamed back.

"Oh my God! They are following us off, Miley! We can't take the streets or they'll catch us!" I hollered.

"Would you shut the fuck up!" she spat. At the last minute, my baby sister wheeled the SUV to the right, drove over the shoulder and grass off the side of the exit, sped down the shoulder of the road for a few seconds, zipped back onto the highway, and flew past the exit instead. The van had already sped into the exit ramp and couldn't back up in time without hitting the cars behind it. Miley had forced them to get off the highway, but she had gotten back on. That move was pure genius.

"Ahhhh! Hahahah! I got them! I fucking got them! I outsmarted their asses!" Miley screamed in victory. She slammed her right hand on the steering wheel as she sped down the highway and farther away from the danger.

"You did that!" I cheered. "You handled that like a pro."

"Hell yeah! Woohoo! Don't play with this bitch when it comes to driving. I am that bitch!" Miley celebrated. We were finally able to drive at just above the speed limit. Things slowed down. As we rode down the highway, my heart grew heavy all over again. I fell silent and hung my head.

I couldn't take part in the celebration anymore. I was glad we were safe now, but I couldn't stop thinking about my man. I covered my face with my hands and began sobbing. I couldn't believe I had let Sidney get snatched and done nothing about it. Sidney was probably already dead. The thought sent another round of wracking sobs through my body.

"All of this is my fault," I cried. "This is my karma for being greedy. I just let it happen. Just like that."

"Karlie, you can't beat yourself up. We were all down with that robbery. We all have to take responsibility for the shit that's happening to us. Sidney knew the danger after everybody started popping up dead. It is not all your fault, so stop blaming yourself. There was nothing either one of us could've done for him against those goons with guns. Even Sidney didn't expect that. He couldn't even get to his gun in time. It all happened so fast. It's not your fault so stop saying that," Miley lectured.

"What now? What will we do now?" I cried out. "Our entire life is fucked. All of this over some goddamn money. Money is the root of all evil, I swear. Why couldn't we just accept that we were meant to be broke? This is what the universe had planned for us."

"Would you stop it? Damn. Nobody wanted to be broke so we came up with a plan. Okay . . . it didn't go according to our plan, but that doesn't mean we had to accept being broke," Miley replied.

"But what will we do now? That's the question.

You think we can go back to the apartment? Hell no. You think either one of us can go back to work? Hell no to that too. I have about two hundred dollars to my name right now. How far will that get us, Miley?"

She was quiet for a few minutes.

"I don't know the answer to any of those questions yet. But whatever we decide, it needs to involve trying to get to the rest of that money. If we can get to the last two stash spots some kind of way, we will be good. I know we don't have anything right now . . . not even a damn place to stay, but just like when we were kids, Karlie, we have each other," Miley said on the verge of tears. She was right. The seriousness of her words exploded in my ears like small bombs, and it made me feel even worse. Since our mother died and left us to fend for ourselves, I was usually the one who had all of the answers for the both of us. At that moment, with the odds stacked against us, I was drawing a blank. We were on the run with no place to run to. But, like my sister had said, we still had each other. For now.

While I tried to figure out my next move, I took out my cell phone and made a call to the only person I knew that could help me right now.

CHAPTER 10

LAST RESORT

Miley and I had made it out of the Virginia Beach area unharmed. I had my arms folded across my chest, hugging myself in an attempt to calm my nerves as I paced in the parking lot of a Marriott Fairfield Inn off Mercury Boulevard in Hampton. I could not get Sidney off of my mind. I could not stop thinking about our situation. I was all cried out.

When I saw the minivan pull to a stop, my heart jerked in my chest. I breathed out a heavy sigh of relief when I saw her face.

Yes. She came through like she said she would.

"Oh my goodness. Ms. Karlie, are you okay?" Trina asked, rushing toward me with concern etched on her face. "Sorry it took me so long. You know how it is. I got here as soon as I could. I was so thrown off by your call. It's not like you not to be at work, so everyone was worried sick about you. I had to drop the kids at daycare or else I would've been here faster. I have so many questions. . . . What is . . ." Trina rambled. I put my hand up to stop her from rambling on. I knew her, so I knew that could go on forever.

"Yeah. I'm good. Nothing to worry about," I assured her, lying through my teeth. "It's just one of those situations."

"You sure you're okay?" Trina asked, eyeing me suspiciously. I am sure I probably looked like a damn mess.

"Yeah, girl. There's nothing to worry about. I'm cool. Just needed a little time away for myself. Kind of want to go off the grid for a little bit and didn't want anyone to know. Thanks for coming right away. Sorry for making you come so far out. I guess it wouldn't be getting away if I had stayed in Virginia Beach, right?" I replied, letting out a phony giggle and giving Trina a quick hug. "You didn't tell anyone I called you, right? Or where you were going?" I clarified. I had told her not to say anything to anyone, but I had to make sure.

"No. No. I didn't tell anyone anything. Not even that pain-in-the-ass baby daddy of mine. I did exactly what you asked. I called in to the job and said I had an emergency with one of the kids and I rushed right down here. Of course, Amy was asking a bunch of questions about what happened and when I would be in. You know how nosey she can be. Plus, she always thinks somebody is trying to make her do all of the work. I was one minute from telling her to mind her damn business, but I was nice about it. I just told her I simply had an emergency and I'd see her later. I think that got her off my back for now," Trina said reassuringly. The tension in my body eased a little bit hearing that. I smiled.

"Good. Yeah, you can certainly handle Amy. She's so corny. One day, I hope she gets a little bit of swag about herself. Or maybe a man that will give her a little swag," I said, chuckling nervously. I kept looking around and over Trina's shoulder suspiciously. Checking my surroundings had become like second nature now. It must've made me look crazy and paranoid. I could tell it was making Trina a little nervous.

"So like you said on the phone . . . you just want me to get you a hotel room in my name?" Trina asked for clarification, her eyebrows furrowed. I realized after she repeated back to me that it seemed like a ridiculous request for a manager to be asking an employee—especially because I had chosen a hotel so far away from our city. I was desperate. I had no choice. Trina was my last resort. When I was trying to come up with a plan, Trina was the only person I came up with that I could trust to do this kind of a favor. I had pegged her as more trustworthy than Amy. I just hoped that I was right.

"Yeah, that's it. Like I said, I just need some time off the grid. Away from everyone and everything. Since the robbery, I've been overwhelmed. I can't really eat. My man is stressing me out." I lied. "I can't sleep. I can't get my mind to calm down. Honestly, I feel like I'm losing my mind. I need this time or else I might lose it," I said. It was halfway true. Since the robbery I had been a wreck emotionally. My appetite was nonexistent, and sleep was like an elusive, rare diamond.

Trina was hanging on my every word like she was trying really hard to believe my story. I could tell by the skeptical creases in her forehead and the glint in her eyes that she didn't believe me for one second. I quickly and silently decided that she didn't have to believe me, so long as she did the favor for me. I knew that chances were I'd never see Trina again after that day.

"You sure you're okay? You say it's just a break you need, but to me you look like you've been crying," Trina pressed, tilting her head to one side inquisitively. "I'm not trying to get all up in your business. I just want to make sure that you're really okay, because you don't look okay." There she went again, rambling on and on.

I wanted to tell her to mind her damn business and just do what I say, but I bit my tongue. I needed her right now. I couldn't mess that up with my attitude. She was my only hope of getting a safe place for Miley and me to lay low until we could come up with another plan. I figured that, out of Trina and Amy, Trina would be less scary and less likely to run her mouth about my request for help.

"Yeah, I'm cool. I just need some place to stay for a few nights. I've got a few things to sort out. Just get the room in your name for two nights. That way, anyone looking for me won't be able to find me. I'll figure out the rest as I go. Here is the cash," I said, handing her a fistful of wadded-up bills. Trina looked down at the cash and back up at me.

"Tell them you don't want to give your credit

card. They will try to force you to leave a credit card for incidentals, but just tell them you'll pay in all cash. Don't let them bully you because they will try," I instructed. "There are no rules statewide that say you have to leave a credit card at a hotel."

Trina shook her head in agreement. She snatched the cash from me and smiled. I watched her as she rushed around to the front of the hotel. I didn't get a bad feeling about her. I was confident I had made the right choice in getting her to help me. The first damn thing I had done right in days.

When Trina was gone from my sight, I furtively signaled to Miley to lay low until I had the key. I had to keep up the ruse that I was alone and in need of time alone. Trina hadn't noticed my sister sitting across the parking lot in Sidney's SUV, and that was how I wanted it.

It took Trina longer than usual to get the room, which made me slightly uneasy. I had probably checked my watch fifty times in the twenty minutes she'd been inside. I exhaled when I finally saw her round the corner from the front of the hotel back into the parking lot. She was smiling like she had just won the lottery or something. My shoulders slumped with relief, and I was smiling right back at her.

Thank God for small favors.

"All done. Did everything you said. Just like you said, that bitch inside tried to force me to give her a credit card. She even called a manager, but I recited the law you told me about. Bam. There was nothing they could say. She had an attitude, but I bet you she checked me in and gave me the damn keys. Here you go, Ms. Karlie," Trina relayed, handing me the key.

"You said keys. Did you get more than one?" I asked. I had caught it.

"Um . . . no. You know what I meant. I only got one key since it's just you. You don't need more than one, do you?"

"No. No. One is enough," I quickly corrected myself. I didn't want her to get suspicious.

"Oh my God, girl, you're a lifesaver." I smiled, taking the key from her. "I will make sure I pay you back for this huge favor. As soon as I take this little break and get my mind together, I will take you out to dinner and give you a few days off . . . paid," I lied. Trina twisted her lips like she kind of figured I was lying, but she played it off anyway.

"Please, Ms. Karlie. It's nothing. I don't need anything in exchange. I'm glad to help. Anything else I can do to help you, just holler at me," she replied. I reached out and gave her a hug. *Wait, did she just say she'll help me with anything?* I thought to myself. *Because while I'm thinking about it, she may be the perfect person to get the other two duffel bags of money. And then Miley and I would be good.*

"Thank you," I said honestly, still contemplating asking her to get the duffel bags for me. Then I changed my mind. Trina seemed like the type that would look inside the bags once she retrieved them from the lockers. And then one or two things would happen. She'd get scared and put the money back or she'd take it and slip out the side door without being detected.

"Look, I know we've had our ups and downs as manager and employee, but I didn't hold a grudge at all. I'm not that type. When people are mean to me, I try to turn the other cheek. So, count this as my way of turning the other cheek," Trina said. It seemed like she had been waiting to remind me about our past disagreements.

My eyebrows flew up into arches. I was taken clearly aback by Trina's little speech. I felt guilty now. She was right. There were times as her manager that I'd come down on her hard for being late, leaving early, using the phone too much and making mistakes on loan processing. I didn't think she had taken any of it personally, but obviously she had. Trina wasn't an ideal employee at all. She was always using the kids as an excuse when I knew damn well she was late or missing days because of her most recent no-good baby daddy. Still, I didn't expect her to mention it at a time like this. I let out a nervous laugh.

"It was always all about the job, Trina. I just wanted you to be the best you could be. It was nothing personal," I assured her. "Thank you so much again for coming through for me." I wanted to get away from her now. There was uncomfortable energy between us.

"No problem. I forgive you. I think," she said followed by a fake laugh. "We all need a helping hand every now and then. I really didn't mind. In fact, it was my pleasure . . . really," Trina continued. "Let me get out of here and get back to the plantation. I won't tell anyone I saw you." She got close and gave me a quick hug.

"Thanks again," I said as she turned and started for her minivan.

"I'll see you soon. Try to get some rest. Seems

like you will need it," Trina called out over her shoulder. There was something about her parting smile that seemed sinister to me. But then again, there was something about everyone that seemed sinister to me at that moment. I didn't fully trust a soul.

I went into the hotel lobby so that Trina would see me go inside. Once she pulled out of the parking lot, I slipped out of the back door. I rushed over to Sidney's SUV and opened the door.

"C'mon. I got the key," I said to Miley excitedly. My excitement quickly faded when I noticed that she was on her phone. Right away, a hot, stomach-sick feeling came over me. I knew my sister and her mouth.

Who the hell could she possibly trust enough to be talking to right now?

"What the hell are you doing on the phone?" I whispered harshly. She put her hand up to tell me to wait. I twisted my face into a scowl.

"Don't shush me or tell me to wait. Who the hell are you talking to?" I growled. "Get the hell off the phone!"

Miley rolled her eyes. She wasn't supposed to be letting anyone know where we were, which meant there should've been no damn reason for her to be on the phone. We didn't know who to trust at this point so phone calls should've been out. Miley mouthed the name *Taz* to me. That was even worse. Taz was a street dude to his core so it wasn't beyond the realm of possibility that he could be one of the people after us for the money. I'm sure by now Miley had told him she was about to come into some good money.

Frustrated, I waved my hand in front of Miley's face. "I'm going inside. You want to stay out here like a sitting duck you can. But don't fucking tell that simple nigga where we are."

She sucked her teeth and told her boyfriend she would call him right back.

"What the fuck is your problem?" she grumbled. "I know what I'm supposed to do and not supposed to do, Karlie."

"Miley . . . do you understand that we can't trust anyone right now? You run your mouth and go tell Taz where we are . . . what if he tells one of his boys and it gets out? We have no idea who is after this money. It could be him you know. You think because he's your so-called man that it is not him? Think again. Niggas in the street will set their own mothers up for that amount of money, much less some chick. I'm sure you've run your mouth and told him about the money so don't act like I'm overreacting. Stay off the phones for now," I lectured. Why was this so hard for her to understand? Everyone around us was dead or missing. She had seen what had happened to Sidney right in front of our eyes. I was disgusted with her. I couldn't hide it either.

"Don't front like if the shoe wasn't on the other foot you wouldn't be calling Sidney to let him know you were okay. I hate when you act like what's good for you is not good for me," she replied with an attitude. She was acting really childish in my opinion, but it was not the right time to be arguing. We needed to stick together. I had to take a deep breath and count to ten in my head. *She's right. I can see her point. Does she see my point? Probably not.*

Just fix it, Karlie. I gave myself a quick pep talk. It wasn't about who was right or wrong. It was about making peace so that we wouldn't be under any more unnecessary stress.

"Look. I'm sorry for snapping on you, but this is a stressful time for both of us. I just want us to get out of this alive, Miley. I'm not telling you that Taz is a bad guy, but we just don't know who to trust right now. Once the dust is settled, you can reconnect with Taz. Shit, you can take your money and run off into the sunset with him, but for now no phone calls. And most importantly, no fighting and beef between us. Deal?" I said.

Miley pouted and rolled her eyes. "Deal," she replied reluctantly.

"Good. Now, let's go up to the room and get some rest. We have to sort out our next move," I said softly.

"I'm sorry too," Miley said, cracking that cute smile that had always melted my heart since she was a baby. We both knew that meant no more discussing it. When she got out of the truck, I grabbed her for a hug. At first she was reluctant. She was still playing mad. It was another game we played from childhood until now. After a few seconds she gave in and hugged me back. We giggled.

"We are going to get through this . . . together," I said, my tone lighter than it had been in days. Miley cracked a small smile and shook her head in agreement.

"Like always . . . together," she said. What was understood didn't need to be said. My sister and I knew that all we had was each other.

I was so grateful for a clean, safe place to stay that as soon as I opened the hotel room door, relief washed over me. I rushed through the door and quickly went about closing up the blinds. I wasn't taking any chances. It seemed like whoever was after our whole crew had no problem finding us somehow. Miley was obviously exhausted. After driving like she had, I could understand it. She rushed over to one of the beds, threw herself stomach-first in the center and sprawled out with her arms and legs splayed wide.

"Oh my God. I didn't even realize how tired I was. I guess adrenaline will do that to you," she said, clutching one of the pillows tight. "This bed feels like heaven. Like the best bed I've ever been in."

I laughed, but I wanted to feel it too. I walked over to the other bed and flopped down on my back. I slipped my shoes off and pushed myself back against the soft, fluffy pillows.

"Ahh. Yes. My entire body is aching. This definitely feels like heaven," I said. "My bed at home is better, but this will do for now. At least we are not stuck in that damn truck driving around aimlessly or worse . . . sleeping in it."

"Yeah, Trina really came through," Miley said.

"Shit, yeah. She was definitely a lifesaver," I said, my words starting to slur. I closed my eyes . . . exhausted. Miley was saying something to me, but after a few minutes, I couldn't hear her. Sleep overcame me so fast I didn't even know what hit me . . . until something actually hit me.

*   *   *

The force of the blow to my chest instantly took my breath. I made a loud sucking noise as I tried to keep the air in my lungs. My eyes and mouth popped open in shock in response to the pain crashing into my chest. I felt like a ton of bricks had been dropped on me from the ceiling.

"Mmm," I moaned when the sleep finally cleared my brain and I realized that my mouth and nose were covered. "Mmmmm," I feverishly protested, trying to move my head from side to side in an attempt to loosen the grip that was holding me captive. I could smell and taste the leather from the glove that was suffocating me. Suddenly it registered in my brain that I was being attacked. My body came alive like I'd been hit with a live wire of electricity. I started kicking my legs wildly, but another blow to my midsection abruptly stopped that. I felt vomit leap up from my stomach into my throat. I was choking. I was dying. The next vicious punch to my gut gave me pause. It landed with so much force that it made a small bit of urine escape my bladder.

"Stop fucking fighting or I'll blow your sister's fucking brains out right in front of you," the assailant hissed. I went stock-still at the mention of Miley. My heart was squeezing so hard it hurt. Tears leaked out of the corners of my eyes. This was it. They had found us.

But how?

How did they get into the room? They hadn't kicked in the door. There was no warning before they were standing over me and Miley while we slept. They must've had a key.

Suddenly I felt my body moving. Instinctively, I extended my arms, trying to find something to hold on to. My efforts were futile. The next thing I felt was my legs hitting the floor with a thud. My heels crashing to the floor sent small shockwaves of pain up my legs, causing my thighs to tremble. The carpet burned the heels of my feet as I was dragged. I tried to twist my head in protest, but that caused pain too. It wasn't until I finally was positioned in such a way that I could see my sister with a black cloth bag over her head that I started to fight with everything I had in me. It was like I suddenly had the strength of ten men. I reared my arm back and drove my elbow into my attacker's midsection.

"Fuck!" he wheezed and bent over slightly. That still didn't make him let go of his vise grip on my face. "You little bitch!" he growled, clamping down on me with even more force.

"Mmm!" I groaned under his black-gloved hand, twisting my body. I raised my hands and began punching and clawing at his hands, but the gloves kept me from being able to dig my nails into his skin.

"Mmm! Mmm!" I went wild, bucking my body with the ferocity of a caged animal trying to get away. My constant movement made it increasingly difficult for him to keep such a tight grasp on me.

"Keep still, bitch, or I swear I'll spill your fucking brains right now," he hissed viciously. I was no match for his power, but I kept fighting. If I was going to die, what did I have to lose anyway? I tried to drop my body weight down in order to loosen his grip on me. I'd seen that on a self-defense class on television. That little stunt just made the angry assailant tighten his grip on my face even harder. My neck felt like it would snap from my shoulders at any second. The pain rocking through my entire neck, back, and spine made my legs go limp. I was exhausted. I finally gave up my efforts to get away. I realized that with one false move he could snap my neck and end my life instantly.

"That's right. You better obey or else you're a dead bitch," he snarled in my ear. "But not before I make you watch me murder your sister."

I gulped and swallowed the large lump that had formed in my throat. I didn't care if they killed me, but I had to do whatever it took to save Miley. Even if I didn't make it out alive, I was praying she somehow could.

"Yeah. Atta girl. You learn quick," he said as I kept still. There was something eerily familiar about the assailant's voice. So familiar that the sound of it made my body go cold like someone had pumped ice water into my veins. My mind was so jumbled with thoughts of death that I couldn't immediately place the voice, but I knew I had heard it before. There was a commotion to the right of where I was being held. I stretched my eyes to see what was happening.

"Mmm!" I started protesting again as I watched one guy throw my sister over his shoulder like a big sack of potatoes. Miley's head dangled precariously over his back. She looked like a lifeless ragdoll.

"Mmm. Mmm!" I groaned, writhing in protest once again as the guy hauled Miley's limp body through the door. That was it. Not my sister! They couldn't separate me from my sister! I wouldn't keep still. I kicked my legs and twisted my body like a fish out of water. I didn't care anymore if they killed me. I needed to know where they were taking my sister. I was sobbing; tears ran down my eyes and over his glove. I kept writhing my body, trying to flail and kick. I couldn't understand why Miley wasn't screaming, kicking or fighting. It dawned on me that she must've been drugged. That would be the only thing to keep a spitfire like Miley quiet in a time like this. I didn't have to question that for long. Right after they disappeared through the room door with Miley, another dude rushed toward me. He came and stood in front of me, and I watched in horror as he sprayed something on a cloth and got closer to me. The one holding my face removed his hand.

"*Agh!* Help! Help me!" I screamed out in the second between one attacker moving his hand and the other one forcing the cloth over my nose and mouth. I had my wide mouth open so whatever was on the cloth went straight to the back of my throat and up my nose. I felt a burning sensation dull my senses. I began coughing and wheezing. I couldn't catch my breath. My eyes, nose, and throat started to burn like I'd swallowed a fire-lit sword. I knew I was moving my arms, but keeping control of my body was becoming increasingly difficult. My ears started ringing. I wanted to lift my hands to cover them, but I couldn't get my body parts to cooperate with my brain. Suddenly, the room began to spin. I could hear voices, but they sounded like they were coming through a tunnel. I could sense movement around me. I was fighting to keep my eyes open, but I was losing the battle. Darkness began closing in on me. I felt my chest heaving up and down as my breathing became labored. I opened my mouth and managed a scream. My screams were short-lived and so was my consciousness.

CHAPTER 11

DEVIL IN SHEEP'S CLOTHING

"Ah!" I gasped and gulped in a lungful of air so fast it made me cough and gag. *"Uhhh,"* I panted, my head whirling around in circles as I tried to catch my breath. My entire body trembled and shuddered so hard, all of my muscles ached. Finally my eyes fluttered open, my wet eyelashes partially obscuring my vision. I could see the shadowy figure standing in front of me holding the source of my torment. I was freezing from the bucket of ice-cold water that had been thrown on me. I finally got my eyes opened wide enough to see clearly, but that didn't last long before a blindfold was forced over them.

"Please," I whispered through trembling lips. "My sister?"

"That woke you right up, huh?" said a man with a deep voice and some sort of accent. I could tell he was walking back and forth in front of me because I could hear the sound of his shoes clicking against the floor. I attempted to move my body, but all I managed to do was feel the restraints cutting into the delicate skin of my arms and ankles. The cold steel of the chair I was tied to stung my ass and thighs too.

"Wh . . . what do you want?" I gasped. My head was pounding so hard even those few words hurt coming out.

The man stopped walking, his footsteps silenced. I could tell he was directly in front of me. I could smell the strong scent of his cologne.

"What do I want?" he repeated. "Do you motherfuckers hear this? She's asking me, what do I want?" he mocked. Then he let out a maniacal laugh that had such a depraved ring to it that it made my stomach churn. I gagged again as fear gripped me tight around my throat. Suddenly I was fighting off the vomit that threatened to come up my throat.

"You have the fucking nerve to ask me what do I want, you little bitch," the man spat venomously. "This bitch got some nerve. . . . Wouldn't you say? Show her what I want," he demanded loudly. The thunder of more than one pair of feet came in my direction. Whoever this man was, he was definitely the one in charge.

"*Agh!*" I hollered in agony as a punch landed on the left side of my face. I felt like my cheekbone had shattered under my skin. Another forceful blow landed on the bridge of my nose, sending stabs of pain ricocheting through my entire face. I felt blood filling up under my eyes, which told me right away that my nose had just been broken. I coughed, wheezed, gagged, and screamed as punches rained down on my face, head, back, and stomach. With the next round of blows, I felt one of my teeth crack and jump loose from the gums. I could feel blood spilling out of my nose like a faucet.

"Stop. Please," I begged. The pain was unbearable. "Wh . . . wha . . . what do you . . . you want?" I gasped. I didn't understand why he didn't just kill me and get it over with.

"Okay," the man said. With that one word, his goons immediately backed off.

"Now. What I want is for you to tell me where my money is," he said. "I already know you were the mastermind behind the robbery so don't try to deny it. I just want to know where my money is." I swallowed hard. I had no idea who this man was. It definitely wasn't Mr. Sherra, the owner of the EZ Cash.

"I . . . I . . . don't know what you're . . ." I started. Before I could finish, another slap landed on the right side of my face with so much force, it rocked the chair I was in.

"Don't fucking lie! If you lie . . ." he growled. He moved to my right side and got close to my head. Then he snatched off my blindfold. "She will suffer longer." The man snatched my head back so that I was forced to look in front of me.

"Miley! No! Miley!" I screeched. "Let her go! Please!" Screaming hurt so badly but I didn't care. I wanted to save my sister. I began bucking my body against the restraints so hard the thick nautical rope cut into my skin. I didn't care about that either. Seeing my sister in the condition she was in was breaking my heart.

"Now . . . I guess you know that I am not playing," the man hissed. They put the blindfold back on me. Not being able to see Miley was killing me.

"No! Please! I need to see her! Please!" I pleaded, the veins in my neck and arms cording against my skin. The man emitted that sinister, scary-movie, maniacal laugh again. This time, the sound of his laughter made goose bumps stand up on my skin. Only a vicious killer could look at a woman, bleeding and in pain, and laugh so raucously you would've thought he was watching a comedy show.

"Why did you do it? What made you think you could get away with it?" the man asked, his mood quickly changing back to serious. "Weren't we good to you? You were the highest-paid bitch in all of the stores. But you couldn't be satisfied, huh? Just like an ungrateful, ghetto piece of trash. Always wanting something for nothing," he spat vituperatively.

I shook my head up and down. "I . . . I'm . . . sorry," I rasped. Tears danced down my cheeks. The man was right. I was ungrateful. My greed had already cost so many people their lives.

"You're sorry? That's it? You're sorry?" he snarled. "This bitch has got to be kidding me. Humph, she's sorry, everyone," he announced loudly.

"Ow!" I howled as another bevy of punches and

slaps came down on me like a hailstorm. I could barely keep my head up. I felt my ribs buckle more than once under the force of several punches. I couldn't breathe now. It felt like a seven-hundred-pound man was sitting on my chest. I knew that one of my lungs had probably been punctured by one of my fractured ribs. I was going to die. I accepted it, but I didn't accept that Miley was going to die.

"Show her what we do to people who steal from us and then lie and say they're sorry," the man instructed his goons. Again, they snatched the blindfold off of my eyes. I squinted in an attempt to get my eyes to focus, but the light in front of me was so bright I couldn't see anyone's faces. My head lolled. It was a chore trying to keep it up. Finally, after a few seconds, Miley came into focus in front of me. I could see that she was badly injured, but it was hard to see anything else. Then I heard the crackling of what sounded like an electric current. A man walked over and put something up against my sister's naked body. The next thing I knew, her body was bucking and jerking and she was screaming.

"Oh God! *Agh!*" I shrieked. I snapped my eyes shut. I couldn't stand to watch Miley in so much pain. They hit her with the little machine again.

"No! Please!" I begged, gagging from the mixture of snot and blood running over my lips and into my mouth. The salt from my tears stung the open wounds on my bottom lip. But, that was the least of my pain. Another slap across the face almost snapped my neck from my shoulders. The hit landed with so much force, blood and spit shot from between my lips and splattered on my assailant's crisp white shirt. I wasn't going to escape this assault. That much was clear.

"Just let her go. It's my fault," I groaned through my swollen lips. "Please. She didn't do anything wrong. It was all me. I swear," I rasped, barely able to get enough air into my lungs to get the words out.

"Oh yeah? It was your fault? Well, look at what you've done," he growled evilly. "Just look!" He grabbed my face and forced me to watch again.

"Agggh!"

Miley let out another pain-filled scream. I could hear another crackling round of electric shocks rocking through her body. It sounded like the sizzle, crackle, and pop of the mosquito light in my uncle's backyard cooking the little nuisance bugs when we were kids. I couldn't even stand to look over at my baby sister's naked body, dangling like a captured animal. They had Miley's arms extended over her head and her wrists bound to a thick silver pipe that ran across the warehouse ceiling. Her face was covered in a mix of tears, snot, and blood. Her hair was soaked with sweat and matted to her head. I could see tracks of electricity burn marks running up and down her stomach and extending down her thighs. I knew then that even if by some miracle we made it out of this shit, Miley would never be the same again. I sobbed at the sight and at the thought. It was my greed that had landed us here. It was my need to prove a point to the world. A world that didn't give two fucks about me or what I had anyway. More skin-searing sizzles interrupted my thoughts. More screams from my sister sent my emotions over the top.

"Miley!" I screeched until my throat burned. I strained against the restraints that held me to the cold metal chair. "Miley! I'm sorry! I'm so sorry!"

"Agh!" She let out another scream. This time, urine spilled from between her legs and splashed all over the floor. I was so close I could feel the warm fluid hitting my feet. The smell of my sister's piss, mixed with my own blood, threatened to make me throw up.

"I . . . I . . . I'm sorry," I rasped. "I wish I could just take it all back," I murmured, barely able to formulate the words. The loud laughter that followed told me all I needed to know. There was nothing else I could say or do to make up for what had already happened. Shit had officially gone down the tubes. I had only been trying to find a way for us to survive, but it turned out to be our destruction. I had singlehandedly killed us.

"Ow!" I yelped, as my downturned head was yanked up by my hair. Pain shot through my scalp as the large gorilla hand clamped down on my long hair.

"Open your fucking eyes," the deep, scratchy voice demanded. I could feel his hot breath on my face. The stench of old cigarettes and alcohol shot up my nose and to the back of my throat. I forced my battered eyelids open and squinted. The blurry image of his face came into focus but quickly went fuzzy again. I was finally made to meet the person responsible for all of this pain.

"You're going to watch your little bitch sister die now," he growled in my face. "All you had to do was be loyal. Be smart. But a bitch like you ain't neither, and now you gotta pay."

I felt my heart sink, but I realized I was powerless. My legs trembled fiercely. Sweat danced down my spine until it tickled my ass crack. I couldn't stop obsessing over the what-ifs. What if I had just accepted my position in life? What if I had refused the plan? What if I had just stopped?

My actions had put us in this predicament and now nothing could save us.

"Miley. Baby girl, I'm sorry," I cried so hard my entire body rocked. I heard my sister scream one more time. It was a deep, guttural scream that I would imagine coming from an animal at slaughter. She gurgled a few times. And then, there was silence. The silence seemed louder to me than her screams. I just knew right then and there my baby sister was gone.

"Didn't any-fucking-body ever teach you not to bite the hand that feeds you?" he said. Then he let out the most evil, maniacal laugh that I've ever heard come from a human being. He let my hair go with so much force the chair I was in toppled over violently and my body crashed to the floor. My jaw cracked against the concrete and shattered under the skin. The mixture of grief for my sister and the pain of the fall sent me into a deep darkness, reeling back in time.

What did you do, Karlie? What did you do? I asked myself. *How could you let this happen?*

"Who are you?" I managed through my swollen lips.

"Who am I? You have the fucking nerve to ask me now?" he gritted, crushing my throat with his huge hand. My esophagus felt like it was going to crumble in his clutch.

"I'm the real owner of all of the EZ Cash stores in Virginia Beach, you thieving little bitch. I'm also the kingpin of the city. I own this fucking city. I am the motherfucker that fed all those bastards that helped you rob me," he growled as he squeezed until I could no longer breathe. Then, just like that, he let go. I began coughing violently as my body instinctively gasped for air.

"I am the boss. . . . That's who I am. *El Jefe . . .* don't you ever forget it," he said. Then he used his pointy-toed shoe to kick me in the ribs. I coughed up a mouthful of blood. I could feel myself fading. Either death or shock was setting in quickly. Then I heard it—a name I was familiar with.

"Trina, baby, get over here so she can see you," the man who'd identified himself as El Jefe called out. My heart immediately sank into the pit of my stomach. Even with all the pain wracking my body, nothing hurt like my heart. I could hear the click of her high heels getting closer to me. Then I felt the pain of another kick in my stomach. That one came from her. Trina . . . the one person I'd thought I could trust had betrayed me. I knew I was as good as dead now. There was no turning back.

"You sorry-ass bitch. Look at you now. Not the bully EZ Cash store manager anymore, huh? No more miss high-and-mighty manager who looks down on her employees and treats them like shit, huh? Funny how the tables can turn real quick, isn't it?" Trina spat cruelly. I could barely catch my breath.

"Did you really think you could steal from my man and get away with it? I know you thought I was just a dirty hood rat with a bunch of kids and fucked-up baby daddies, right? You treated me like shit all the time I worked for you too, but all along I was the one that was really the boss's girl, so really you worked for me," Trina said, kicking me again. More blood spilled from my lips. I was shaking now. My insides felt like they were going through a meat grinder.

"Why?" I rasped, my throat feeling like it had a three blaze fire lit in it.

"Why what? Why did I set you up?" Trina asked, laughing evilly after her questions. "Oh, Karlie. How stupid are you? You didn't expect me to be the inside woman, huh? You didn't think anybody with a little bit of money would want me, huh? You really believed Mr. Sherra was our boss? Even one of my kids could see that was a front."

I was too shocked to even respond. I couldn't believe that Trina was the devil in sheep's clothing. I had to hand it to her; she had played her hand very well. She had probably listened to my conversations when I thought no one was around while I was in the office and probably told her man who was involved with the robberies. She had played me close after the robberies, acting like she was concerned about me after the hit I took to the head. She had gained my trust. She had rushed to my aid because all along she'd known what she had planned.

"I knew right away that you had something to do with that robbery. Yeah, I played along as the victim, but I recognized your little boyfriend's voice when he was in the store with his cheap ski mask on. You didn't think I would recognize his hazel eyes. Ha! Shit, that's what it was about him that had all the bitches in Virginia Beach after him.

"I saw how you acted when they busted up in the store with guns waving in our face. You weren't scared at all. It took a few minutes for me to figure it out, but after you led them to the big safe instead of the small safe, I knew you were down. Only a dummy wouldn't be able to figure that out," she relayed. I couldn't believe what I was hearing. I would've never guessed it.

"Oh, and those tapes. You told them exactly where the machines were so they could get the surveillance tapes. There was no other way for them to know it would be hidden behind the wall of the woman's bathroom," she continued. I just closed my eyes. How could I have been so stupid in thinking she was just a stupid girl from the hood? I had definitely underestimated her.

"Now, where the fuck is the money?" Trina growled. "We want every dime of it back."

I kept my mouth shut. I had given up on life. Fuck it. If I was going to die anyway, I wasn't giving them shit; especially this traitorous bitch. If I couldn't have the money, this bitch and her man couldn't have it back either.

"She asked you a fucking question!" El Jefe spat. "Answer the question."

"Fu . . . fuck . . . you," I managed through my battered lips. This time, he kicked me in the head. Sparks of pain exploded through my skull like fireworks on the Fourth of July. I didn't scream as he kicked me again. I couldn't even feel any more pain. I began to pray silently that God would just take my life and Miley's too.

God, please forgive me. Don't let us suffer any longer. Just take us. Take us to wherever you took our mother. Take away the pain. Take away the struggle. Just take us.

"Pass me the gun," I heard Trina say. "If she's not going to tell us where the money is, she's not going to live either. I've been wanting to kill this bitch for a long time."

"Kill me. Please," I whispered. "Just kill me." I wasn't going to give her the satisfaction of seeing me beg and plead for my life. I wasn't going to scream anymore. I wasn't going to give them anything that they wanted. With the way I felt now, I was welcoming death anyway. No Sidney. No Miley. I was sure that my face had been obliterated, and I didn't want to live like that. I wanted to be put out of my misery once and for all.

"You ain't gotta tell me twice, bitch. I'm going to kill your grimy ass," Trina barked. I closed my eyes waiting for it all to end. I didn't want to look over at my sister because the pain was too much to endure. I tried to clear my mind, but all sorts of images from my childhood suddenly flooded to the forefront. I thought about my mother and all of the messed-up things she'd done to us as kids.

"I forgive you," I murmured.

"What? What's that?" Trina snarled.

I repeated myself, but I was not speaking to her. I was forgiving my mother . . . myself . . . Sidney . . . and anyone who'd ever done me and Miley wrong in our lives. I was letting go of all of my misery.

Finally, I felt the cold kiss of the gun's metal against my temple. I squeezed my eyes shut.

BANG! BOOM!

I heard an explosion of sound. I expected to be dead, but I quickly realized that the loud crashing noise I'd heard wasn't from the gun. Trina stumbled from the sound too.

"Police! Drop the weapon! Drop the fucking weapon now!"

I opened my eyes in time to see Trina drop her gun. It fell right in front of my face.

I heard more loud commands. "Police! Don't move! Put your fucking hands up! Clear the building!" The next thing I heard was the stampede of combat boots pounding around me. It sounded like the SWAT team and all of the police in Virginia Beach were flooding into the place.

Tears of joy drained from my eyes. I didn't think I would ever be happy to hear the police in the same room with me. I knew then that there was a god. I closed my eyes and finally let go.

"Ms. Houston! Ms. Houston!" I heard my name being called. The voice saying it was familiar to me. "Ms. Houston, can you hear me?" I knew that voice anywhere. I fought to open my eyes so that I could see his face again. A face I didn't think I'd ever be glad to see.

"You're going to be okay. We are going to get you some help. You're alive, and we are going to get you some help," Detective Castle said almost breathlessly. He reached down and squeezed my hand. That's when I realized I was no longer tied to the cold metal chair. "Looks like we got here in the nick of time. You're a little banged up, but I'm sure you're going to be fine," Detective Castle soothed in that smooth voice of his. My forehead creased and my lips pursed with a mixture of grief and joy. I was alive and grateful, but . . .

"Mi . . . Mil . . . Miley," I rasped. Detective Castle's eyes dropped to the floor. His facial expression seemed grave. My heart sank. Dread washed over me and melted my insides like someone had thrown hot lava at me. I felt an ache so far down in my soul that it threatened to send me into cardiac arrest. I started moving my head from left to right frantically.

"N . . . n . . . no." I flailed. I didn't care about my injuries. I was not ready to face the fact that my sister was dead.

"Shhh. Stop. You're going to hurt yourself. Shhh. She's alive, Karlie," Detective Castle assured me. "She's in pretty bad shape, but she's alive," he said, giving my hand a reassuring squeeze. His words were like music to my ears. Miley was alive! I knew she was probably in critical condition after what she'd endured, but at least she was alive! Finally, I closed my eyes and let my body relax against the stretcher. Nothing else mattered. Not even the fact that I'd probably get arrested for the robbery as soon as I was better. At this point, I felt like I deserved it.

"You two took it hard. You're pretty lucky to

still be alive," Detective Castle said, walking alongside the stretcher as the EMTs moved me to the ambulance.

"How . . . how did you . . . ?" I struggled to get my words out.

"Well, we had a little help," Detective Castle replied. We had finally made it to the open back doors of the ambulance.

"There was someone who cooperated and gave us just what we needed. Good thing too, or else you might be dead," Detective Castle continued. Then he stepped aside and Craig stepped from behind him. My heart jerked in my chest and my battered, swollen eyes went as wide as the swelling would allow.

"Damn, baby girl. Didn't think I'd see you like this." Craig smiled at me. "Glad you made it out of this shit on the right side of things." He shook his head.

"How?" I panted. It was all I could say.

"Man, these niggas picked me up after they couldn't find you and Sidney and Miley. I thought y'all had turned on me. But it's a good thing they got me when they did. If this pretty-boy detective didn't put the screws to me and make me talk about where the money was stashed, they would've never followed y'all to that gym and been able to follow the people who snatched Sidney and then in turn follow that bitch Trina to find you and Miley," Craig informed me. "I swear, that shit played out like something from a book or a movie. It was like one crazy event after another. I'm just glad a few of us could be saved from the same fate that fell on Troy, Mega, Ant, and Walt. That shit was fucked up what happened to all of them."

I just shook my head. Tears drained out of my eyes. It was all my fault.

"Yeah, that's how I felt talking to these pigs, but it turned out for the best," Craig said. "Never thought I would see the day that I would say talking to the cops turned out to be a good thing."

"Sid . . ." I started. Tears drained from the sides of my eyes just trying to say Sidney's name. Craig hung his head, but he didn't say anything. It looked like he was about to open his mouth to tell me something, but he didn't get a chance before he was pushed out of the way.

"Okay. Let's go. We need to get these girls to the hospital. They are pretty messed up," one of the EMTs announced. With that, I was whisked into the back of an ambulance.

"Knock, knock." I heard the soft voice of my regular nurse as she opened my hospital room door and tapped at the same time. I opened my eyes and noticed her bright smile. Although it was comforting, I was trying to get some sleep so I found it a little annoying. I looked in her direction quizzically.

"Ms. Houston . . . you have a visitor," the nurse announced. I groaned. If one more detective, news reporter, or city official came to ask me questions, I was going to scream. It had been three days, and I had repeated my story probably sixty times by now. Aside from all of those annoying people, I couldn't imagine who else would be visiting me. Miley was still in the Intensive Care Unit, so it couldn't be her. I crumpled my face, partly in confusion and partly in annoyance. My nurse noticed the struggle happening on my face.

"I'm sure you'll want to take this visitor," she assured me with a warm smile. I exhaled and moved my bandaged head slightly in acquiescence.

"Bring him in," the nurse turned around and called cheerfully to someone behind her. *Him? Who is him?* I said to myself. Now I was really curious. I stared at the door in rapt anticipation. My heart monitor was blipping off the meters as my heart raced with a mixture of fear and eagerness. Finally I saw the wheels moving through the door. My insides got warm as the wheelchair was pushed all the way through my door.

"Oh my God," I gasped, tears immediately began falling from my eyes in streams. I began crying so hard, my bandaged ribs ached. His face still had the remnants of his assault, but it was just as gorgeous as ever. Those beautiful eyes staring at me lit my insides up with warmth. I felt like my heart would explode with giddiness.

"Hey, beautiful," Sidney said in his usual smooth baritone. His infectious smile lit up his gorgeous face. I wished I didn't have casts on my legs and one of my arms, and bandages binding my ribs and head. I wanted so badly to jump out of the bed and into his lap.

"Oh my God," I gasped again. It was all I could manage through my sobs of joy.

"Not exactly how we thought this would all end, huh?" Sidney said as he was pushed right up to the side of my bed. I stretched my hand out toward him as far as the cast on my arm would allow. Sidney grabbed my hand and brought it up to his lips and kissed it. I closed my eyes and continued to sob with joy.

"All's well that ends well. I love you, Karlie," Sidney said.

"I love you more, Sidney," I whispered.

TWISTED DECEPTION

Saundra

CHAPTER 1

"Yazz, you down or what for Regina's party on Saturday night? I swear it's about to be ignorant off the hook. Hell, this is the first party since graduation." Mimi chopped my ear off as we made our way down McLaran Street, the block I lived on. We were heading back to my house from the store. As usual, my mom had me out walking in the burning-hot St. Louis heat wave to grab her some Salem cigarettes.

"I don't know yet. Really I'm just not feeling it—besides, I got other things I need to be worried about, but you know that already." I glanced in Mimi's direction without slowing my stride. "Ruthie still all over my ass about a damn job," I said, referring to my mother. "And you know how she is."

"Haven't I told you a thousand times before, I can get you a job at the Cheetah whenever you ready." That was the strip club that Mimi started dancing at the night of her eighteenth birthday. I mean, she made decent money, but . . . "I don't know why you scared—hell, Ax would hire you on the spot with that bangin'-ass body. You need to put it to use."

I don't know why she felt the need to remind me of what my body looked like, because I was well aware of it. I weighed a hundred thirty pounds easy, and had a thin waist, along with hips that curved around into a perfectly round butt. I also possessed a set of dark brown deep-dish eyes, with shoulder-length natural wavy hair that I wore in a ponytail. With a mahogany skin tone, I considered myself a natural beauty, but I was not impressed with that. And as much as I needed a job, I just could not see myself half naked, shaking my ass for a room full of thirsty niggas.

"I'm telling you, you could make some money to pay some bills, and that would shut Ruthie's mouth." That all sounded good, but . . .

"Nah, I'm good. Besides, the Cheetah ain't safe. Didn't somebody get shot down there a couple of nights ago? The last thing I feel like doing is dodging stray bullets."

"Girl, you know some niggas gon' act a fool no matter what. But Ax keeps that shit under control inside the club. That crazy shit you heard about happened outside. You would be safe. Trust me."

"Nah, I'm good." I was sticking with that.

Mimi sighed. It was apparent by the look on her face she was frustrated, only wanted to help. "At least come to the party then. Have some fun, Yazz. Ain't nothin' wrong with that."

"Even if I wanted to go, I don't have anything to wear. And I refuse to wear that old shit I wore to school. Ruthie has already cut me off financially. Shit, she complained about buying me clothes when I was in school." The plastic from the Salems was starting to make my hand feel sweaty.

"Is that what you worried about? Girl, I got you. I will hook you up with an outfit, you bony so it won't be hard. Aye, do you remember Keisha Watson?"

I shook my head in agreement. "Yeah, we took several classes together my senior year. And she used to be selling snacks and stuff."

"Well, now that chick boosts clothes. She's who I've been getting all my dancing outfits for the Cheetah from."

"For real. She boosts?" That surprised me. "You mean she went from selling chips and blow pops . . . to stealing clothes? Hmmm, what a career change." We both laughed. Keisha used to supply the whole school with snacks. She was a walking vending machine, only you didn't have to worry about your money getting jammed. Word on the streets was her mom used her food stamps to buy the snacks. Keisha then sold it for cash so they turned a good profit.

"That's what I said when I first heard about it, but she be having them good tags though. A couple weeks back, I got two pair of True Religion jeans from her for a hundred fifty dollars. I'm telling you she got the hook-up." I thought about what Mimi was saying. It sounded good. I knew she was trying hard to convince me to go, but I was still hesitant.

"I'll think about it" was all I was willing to

promise. I hoped this would shut her up. We walked in silence for the next couple of seconds and were only a few feet from my house when we both glanced at Kevon, a local dealer in our area. He was standing on the corner, chatting with a couple of knuckleheads from the block. They were a bunch of young peons hoping for a come-up. I noticed Kevon had his eyes set directly on me and hurriedly looked in the other direction.

Mimi's eyes were burning a hole in the side of my face. "I saw that. Don't even try to cover it up," she interjected. Every word of her statement told me she was about to start speculating. And I hated when she did that.

"What?" I played dumb.

"Don't you even try that innocent shit with me, I saw Kevon's fine ass checking you out. Don't play you peeped it too. That's why you tried to look away." She grinned. She had been watching me the whole time.

Trying to remain serious, I rolled my eyes at her. "No, you are seeing things because that ain't never happen."

"Yeah, whateva, you ain't slick. Kevon's sweet on you, and you know it's true." She folded her arms across her chest with a smirk on her face. There would be no changing her mind.

"See, that's why I ain't going to that wack-ass party with you. 'Cause you stay tryin' to hook some-body up. Ain't nobody got time for that."

"Heffa. I know you ain't tryin' to blame this on me? I ain't tried to hook you up. Yet." She laughed.

"I swear you get on my nerve." I playfully pushed

her. The one thing I could be really good at was pretending to be uninterested.

"Yazz." I heard my name soar through the air and paused. Turning to my left just a little bit, I almost smashed into Kevon—he was in my space within minutes. With a smile on his face he spoke again. His smile was sexy; he possessed one dime-size deep dimple on his left cheek. I acted casual.

"Hi," floated from my lips, in just above a whisper.

Mimi saw Katrina climbing out of a car in front of Ms. Peggy's house.

"Aye, I'ma about to go catch up with my girl Katrina. We have business to discuss. I'll call you later." Mimi winked at Kevon and then excused herself. I wanted to yell for her not to leave, but she was halfway down the block before I could say anything. Feeling awkward and trapped, I stood stock still staring at Kevon, praying he would walk away. After thirty seconds passed by, I attempted to walk away first. Turning around nervously and focusing on our run-down house, I made it my destination. I took only a few steps before I felt Kevon grab ahold of my left elbow, slowing me down. Spinning around to face him, I gave him an annoyed stare. But he smiled in spite of it.

"Why you always acting so mean? Do you hate me or something?"

I could not believe he had just asked me that. He had some nerve to question me. We were not cool like that.

I fired back, "Since we are asking questions, I have one. Where is your girlfriend?" Clearly he thought I was stupid. Everyone knew that Kevon dated Misti since forever. And I was not interested in being a man stealer. No fucking way. He was cute, but not that damn cute. A thot, I was not.

"Girlfriend? I don't have a girlfriend." His lips spread into a smile, but I didn't see any reason for him to be smiling. That was the problem with dope boys—they all thought they could have anyone they wanted, because of their reputation for having unlimited amounts of cash and power. But not this chick.

"Now you being a fraud," I read him. "Everyone around here knows that, so do not play with me." Again I turned to leave, but he stopped me, this time by brushing my elbow with his finger.

"Aye, all right, you're right. I had a girlfriend, but I don't anymore. That relationship is a wrap."

I wasn't really sure why I needed this information because I did not care. Kevon had been running this block for years. And as far as I could remember, he had never looked at me twice. So why he was sweating me so hard today was a mystery I did not care to solve. And I was about to tell him just that when my mother opened the front door and started yelling.

"Yazz, I don't have all day. Hurry up and bring me my cigarettes. Shit!" She slammed the door so hard the house looked like it shook. I blinked twice before turning my attention back to Kevon.

"Well, as you can see, I gotta go." I took off toward the grass that led into my yard. The sidewalk would only take longer. And I knew from experience that if Ruthie came back to the door, she would really embarrass me.

"Aye, can I take you out to eat or some? We could grab some wings," Kevon shouted.

Yes, almost flew out of my mouth, but I paused for a brief second. "I can't," was my reply instead. Without another word or glance in his direction, I twisted the brass knob on our front door and made my way inside the house. And just as I thought, Ruthie was waiting on me with an ashtray in her hand. Snatching the cigarettes out of my hand, she looked me up and down.

"Why do you have to snatch them?" I asked. I had just walked a full two miles, coming and going to Jack's Grocery to pick that up for her. The least she could have done was allow me to hand them to her, or say thank you. But typical Ruthie, she just strutted off in the opposite direction. Pulling one of the brown wooden chairs from the kitchen table, she sat down.

Walking over to the tan loveseat with burgundy and green stuffed pillows, I bounced down and grabbed the remote to watch some television. Because being raised by Ruthie had groomed me to understand that, in her house, you should pick your battles very carefully. And her being rude wasn't worth the hassle. I pressed the ON button, then selected the On-Demand menu. I needed to catch up on *Love and Hip Hop Atlanta.*

"So when you plan on gettin' a job?" Ruthie spat out aggressively at me. I should have known she would not let me sit in peace. "How long do you think I'm gon' let you live here rent free? You already wasted twelve years in school. Now it's time to get busy. There are bills that gotta be paid up here; this ain't no vacation spot with free cable, food, and utilities."

"I know that, Ruthie." I referred to her by her first name. Ever since I was in the fifth grade, she had forbid me from calling her Mom or Mother. She said she was too young to be called that. And if I ever made the mistake and called her that in public, she would whoop me to remind me to be more careful the next time. "I just graduated a month ago, Ruthie. Since that time, I been filling out applications everywhere. Somebody will call soon." I wanted to sound hopeful.

"Well, you must not be looking hard enough. Hell, by the time I was your age I was on my fifth job. Your ass just being lazy."

I almost responded, but I knew it would be a waste of my time. So I decided to try and ignore her. But that was damn near impossible to do when she wanted to be heard. I sighed as she mouthed off a few more complaints. Locating *Love and Hip Hop Atlanta* in the menu, I pushed PLAY on the remote. As I got comfortable on the loveseat, the living room door swung open. Rodney, Ruthie's deadbeat boyfriend, stepped inside. With a wide grin spread across his face, Rodney's ugly left front rotten tooth shone a grayish brown color. Ugh. I wanted to puke just looking at it and him. Sporting some dingy Lee jeans and a gray T-shirt with a pocket on it, Rodney walked over to Ruthie. He leaned in close to her left ear, so that I couldn't hear what he said to her. He did things like that to annoy me, but if he only knew that I didn't give a fuck. Soon after, he walked back over to where I was sitting and bounced down next to me on the loveseat. My stomach turned—he disgusted me.

Prepared to ignore him, I gave *Love and Hip Hop Atlanta* my undivided attention. But I could literally hear every rough, ragged breath Rodney took. Annoyed, I wished I could snatch out his nostrils. I almost said that out loud, but bit my tongue instead. Then he opened his mouth to speak. "This is the stupidest show I eva seen. Why do you watch this shit?" he asked me, as if I would answer him. It was no secret to the man that I could not stand his trifling, no-job-having, free-loading ass. Oh, did I mention his breath smelled like chitterlings that had not been cleaned? Ugh. Anyhow, all of a sudden he reached over next to me, snatched up the remote control, and turned the television off.

Talk about stunned. I wanted to curse him out, scream even. But instead I got up off the couch, stared him dead in his face, and rolled my eyes at him so hard they burned. Pissed off, I stomped away to my room, where I slammed the door so hard, a picture in the hallway loudly smashed to the floor.

"Yazz, you done lost your mind, girl, slamming doors in my damn house, breaking shit," Ruthie screamed. I reached for one of my library books that had never been returned to school, knowing it would help me focus on something other than my miserable home life. Oddly enough, before a page was turned, Kevon popped in my mind. I tried hard to shake the thoughts, but they seemed to be refusing to go away. Reaching for my government-issued phone, which gave me five hundred free calling minutes each month, I dialed Mimi. Maybe a conversation with her would help get Kevon off my brain. When Mimi answered, I told her I'd decided to go to Regina's party. I wasn't sure when I'd decided that, but maybe she was right. I needed to hang out. Because Ruthie and Rodney were getting on my last fucking nerve.

CHAPTER 2

Regina's party was off the hook, just as Mimi had predicted. It was at this club called Mystic. Regina's sister Rhashonda had set up the party and gotten us all inside because most of Regina's friends were not club age, except maybe a few from the block. But since Rhashonda was sleeping with the owner, Damon, there was no problem for us to get in. And as much as I had been against coming, I was glad to have changed my mind. True to her word, Mimi had come through for me with a hot outfit. I was rocking a midnight-blue wraparound fitted body dress, and some cute black stiletto pumps. With gold accessories to match, I was looking grown-up and cute, and feeling good. A margarita was secure in my underage hand. Nobody could tell me nothing—I was in turn-up mode. As for my girl Mimi . . . let's just say she was on one. She had taken two shots of Patrón and didn't seem the least bit tipsy. Party girl was her middle name.

"Oh shit, that's my song." Mimi threw her hands in the air as Young Jeezy's "Holy Ghost" blasted out of the speakers.

Bobbing my head to the beat with my drink raised in the air, I agreed. "Mine too." I had to talk loud because of the music.

"Let's dance." Mimi grabbed my elbow and we hit the dance floor, reciting most of the lyrics. We were having too much fun. Then, all of a sudden, I felt an arm wrap around my neck. Whirled around quick to see who had the nerve to be touching me because I was about to go ham. The arm released and I saw it was Regina.

"Girl, you almost got the shit slapped outta you." I grinned as I embraced Regina with a hug.

"I'm so glad you came, Yazz." Regina was happy. Whenever she was around, her energy was always good.

"I had to damn near drag her," Mimi boasted, still moving to the beat.

"Whateva." I laughed. "For a minute I thought you were not coming to your own party. Where were you?" We had been there going on two hours and this was my first sighting of Regina.

"There was a slight malfunction with my wardrobe, which caused me to be late," she explained.

"Well, I'm glad I decided to come. Rhashonda, really hooked this up."

"You know how it is anything for her baby sister. Besides, she owes me for moving out and leaving me at home with our crazy-ass mother."

"Trust me, I know your pain," I cosigned. While

I didn't find pleasure in calling Ruthie crazy, she could be a real bitch. And she never apologized for it.

"Anyway, stick around, have fun and some drinks. The turn-up just gettin' started!" She was hype. "I'ma make my rounds and speak to everybody. Oh, and let them get a peek at this bangin'-ass body and this outfit." She struck a pose and we all laughed.

"Okay, we see you. You better work, bitch!" Mimi shouted over the music, then snapped her fingers. Regina turned and made her way through the hefty crowd on the dance floor. The place was already packed, and people were still coming through the door.

"Let's grab another drink?" Mimi suggested. "Maybe this time you will get something stronger."

"Stronger? What's wrong with the margarita I had?"

"Yazz, that shit ain't nothin' but Kool-Aid," Mimi joked, as we made our way through the crowd and to the bar. This time, I ordered a shot of Patrón. Maybe this would shut Mimi up. As the bartender passed me my drink, I saw Kevon.

Turning my head away from him, I stared at Mimi. "Look behind me. There goes Kevon." I felt the pit of my stomach shifting.

"Ummmph," Mimi slowly dragged out. "And damn, does he look good." She smirked.

"Is he watching me?" I asked out of curiosity. Fuck that—on the real, I was looking good and wanted him to have a peek.

"Are you kidding me, that nigga ain't took his eyes off you yet. Hell, his eyes are feasting on you.

Dude is drooling all over himself." Mimi sipped her drink.

Thanks to her, I was now nervous knowing that I had his undivided attention. I had wanted him to look at me but not stare. I had to get out of his sight. The other side of the club would be a good start at putting some distance between us. Polishing off my shot really quick, I slid the glass across the bar to the bartender. Eyeing Mimi, I said, "Let's go back to our table."

"Why you want to go sit down? Don't you want to let Kevon eat his heart out?"

"Mimi, I'm not a thot. Besides, he done saw enough already."

Mimi shrugged her shoulders. "Cool. You better hope that table still empty." I nodded. Stirring her straw in her drink she led the way.

Walking away, I tried to keep it cute and play it cool, but my first step was a little wobbly. That shot of Patrón had taken its toll. But a few more strides and my balance came back. Making my way through the crowds of people, I started to feel more secure. Because now I knew Kevon and his watchful eyes were a few feet behind me.

Relief flooded over me as my butt settled into my seat. I let out a slight sigh. Mimi wasted no time. "Girl, you can't run from Kevon forever. For one, this lil-ass club just ain't big enough." She was enjoying watching me sweat.

"Who said I was running from him?" I looked around in a suspicious manner.

"What are you looking for, or should I say who?" She laughed and sipped from her almost-empty glass.

"You know what, Mimi . . ." I started to speak but stalled when Kevon leaned down in my ear.

"What's up, Yazz?" He scared the shit out of me. My heart felt like it would burst into a million pieces, it was beating so rapidly.

"Hi," fell softly but steadily from my lips. The smell of Palo cologne that floated off him, and up my nostrils almost made me melt in my seat. It also made it hard for me to resist him. I looked at Mimi, who was wearing a smile so big that she resembled the Kool-Aid man. I wanted to kick her for enjoying watching me squirm.

"Hey, Kevon," Mimi spoke.

"Aye, what's good? Can I get you two something to drink?" He stood up straight with his left hand in his left front pants pocket; his right hand cradled a small glass of something dark brown. I assumed it was Hennessey, or at least it resembled it. One thing I knew for certain: Hennessey was the hood anthem so I had probably guessed right.

"No thanks. I'm good," I answered right away. Truth be told, I was one drink away from being drunk.

Swallowing down the last of her drink, Mimi answered, "Yeah, I'll take a martini dry with two olives." I stared at her with astonishment; working at the Cheetah had turned Mimi into a full-blown drunk. We both had been stealing liquor out of Ruthie's stash since we were about fifteen. But I had never seen Mimi drink this much. Not only was she drinking like a fish, but she knew exactly what drink she wanted, and how. She could easily get a job bartending.

"A'ight, I'll be right back." Kevon started to

leave but then turned back around to face me. "Aye, Yazz. Are you sure you don't want anything?"

"Nah, I'm . . ." Mimi cut me off.

"Yeah, Kevon, just bring her back one of those martinis."

I started to protest but decided against it. He glanced at me for approval. His stare was making me weak.

"Yes, that's cool," I agreed, all while praying he would hurry up and just go. Smiling, he turned and continued to the bar.

"Now, why did you do that?" I turned to face Mimi. "You heard me say I didn't want nothin' to drink." I pouted.

"Yazz, come on, why you trippin'? What's up?" She had the nerve to call me out. "Have you really looked at Kevon? He fine as hell, and a baller. Dude is full-blown catch." The facial expression Mimi was making was comical. But I agreed with her so much, plus it was becoming hard to keep playing uninterested. And at this point, I had to be real.

"Mimi, yes, Kevon is all that you say he is, but I just can't fuck with him."

"Why not?"

"He has a girlfriend. Or did you forget all about that Misti chick? Everybody knows he been with that girl forever."

"Is that why you're trippin'? Man, you better forget about that girl. Do you see her anywhere around here? Shit, I would not be thinkin' about that bitch. Besides, I heard they split."

Sitting back in my seat, I sighed. "That's the

same thing he told me. But you know how these niggas will lie just to get what they want."

"Listen to me. Fuck Misti. You don't need to be worried about no other chick, because they wouldn't be worried about you. Besides, Kevon ain't like these other lames, plus he worth the trouble. Shit, if you don't want him I'll take him." Mimi grinned.

"Oh, really? Well, here's your chance," I said with a playful smirk on my face as Kevon approached with two martinis. One in each hand.

As he placed the drink in my hand, the KeKe Wyatt and Avant song "You and I" came blasting out of the speakers. I loved that song. I was sure the excitement that rushed to my cheeks gave me away.

"Would you like to dance?" he asked me without hesitation. If I didn't love that song so much I would have said no, but that was not the case. Without giving him an answer, I passed Mimi my drink and stood. Gently grabbing me by the hand Kevon led me to the dance floor, wrapping my arms around his neck, I lost myself in the song and his strong hold. Safe was the best way to describe the feeling. For the life of me, I could never remember feeling safe in my entire eighteen years of living.

When the weekend was over, it was time to get back to real life. Job hunting was the word of the day for me—it was a must that I find something. Not that I hadn't been everywhere already, or at least that's exactly what it felt like. Today was Wal-mart day so after waiting in line for two hours to use the one computer they had working to fill out applications, it was finally my turn. The ancient computer kept stalling and was running hella slow, but I was determined to finish. Besides they were in desperate need of a customer service person. And I mean bad; the girl they had working the return desk did all but curse the customers out. Every time someone stepped up with a return, she would breathe loud, smack her gum, and damn near argue with them. I was so annoyed with her, I almost turned around and fired her ass myself. Near the end of my application, my phone started to ring. The number was not familiar, but I answered anyway. Right away, I recognized the voice. But what I didn't know was how he had gotten my number.

"What's up, Yazz?"

"Ahh, who is this?" I played dumb.

"Kevon," he answered, then went silent. I wondered if he had hung up, but there was no click. And I thought I could hear him breathing.

"Oh, hi. Kevon, how did you get this number?" That was a question I had to ask. After the party the other night, he had asked for my number. But I had told him no without hesitation. So his call was definitely a surprise.

"Your girl Mimi." To be honest, I had known the answer to that before he said it. Mimi was one hundred percent a Kevon and Yazz fan. "So what's good witcha?"

"Nothin' really. I'm just out and about handling some business. Hold on just a minute." The last thing I wanted to do was tell him my business, but I needed to answer the last few questions on my application. After pressing the SEND button, I picked up the phone. Clearly he really wanted to talk to me because he had stayed on hold for every bit of five minutes.

"Hello." I stood up and started for the Walmart exit. I had to hurry up to catch the next bus. Missing it would mean waiting a half hour for the next one.

"Aye, look, I was calling to see if you would let me take you out tomorrow night. We could eat or something? Whatever you wanna do."

I briefly considered his offer. "Okay, that's cool. We can go eat. Where?"

"We can grab a steak or something. What you think about Outback Steakhouse?"

"That's cool." A juicy steak didn't sound bad. Not to mention some time away from Ruthie and her bitching. "What time?"

"About seven-thirty."

"Cool, I will meet you there." There was no way I was inviting him to my house. Rodney would not get the chance to embarrass me with his brown tooth, bad manners, and bad breath. That was not about to go down on my watch. Rodney was an asshole at all times. It was his special talent.

"You sure you don't want me to pick you up? I could swing through and scoop you. That's not a problem," Kevon assured me.

"No, I'm cool. I will meet you there at seven-thirty. I gotta go." I quickly ended the call before he could contest any further. Sliding my phone into my pants pocket, I climbed onto the musty city bus headed back to the crib.

It took Mimi two hours to convince her sister Sheila to allow her to use her broken-down mini-van so that she could drop me off at Outback to meet Kevon. Sheila hated parting with that piece-of-junk van. It looked decent on the outside, but it really was a piece of junk engine wise. It had this constant *knock-knock* sound that could not be explained. Or at least that was what Sheila had convinced us. But beggars could not be choosers and I did not want to ride the bus.

Mimi let me out in the front of the restaurant, and Kevon was already seated when I made it inside. The hostess delivered me to our table.

Kevon stood up and pulled my chair out for me. I had seen that on television but never in the hood. I almost laughed. But noted that gesture was sweet.

"Damn, you lookin' nice." Kevon complimented me as he slid back into his seat. I wanted to say the same to him, but I kept my cool. He didn't need to get any ideas. I was sure he knew that he was fine and his swag was on ten. He had a caramel complexion and a medium build. He was about five-ten, a little short for my taste, but it fit him well. And that dimple was to die for. Still, I wondered why he was no longer with Misti. As far as I could remember, they had been together for at least four years. Possibly longer. Everyone knew how close they were.

After we both ordered the same thing off the menu—salad, baked potato, and T-bone steak—we ate and chatted.

"So what's good with you? Got any plans since you graduated?"

I was almost reluctant to talk about myself, but decided it was okay to share a few things. My life was so pathetic, I was sure he would be bored.

"Ain't much to tell. I have been looking for a job in this seemingly jobless-ass town." I forked through my salad. Talking about my life was a good way for me to lose my appetite.

"Lookin' for a job? What you need a job for?"

I gave him a perplexed look because that was the dumbest damn question I had ever been asked. "Why else do people look for jobs, Kevon?" Eye contact at that moment was necessary. I put my fork down. My hostility was clear.

"Wait a minute. Hold up." He grinned and reached his hands across the table in attempt to hold mine, but I moved them. "Let me say that different, since I understand why you would look for a job. But what I meant to say was, you are too beautiful to work."

"Really?" I laughed. Because he sounded stupid as fuck and clearly did not live under Ruthie's roof of constant employment demands. Deciding to ignore that conversation, I blew off his comment and changed the conversation. We were just getting to know each other and did not need to go there. Surprisingly, when the conversation changed, things got better. After eating a wonderful meal, we topped it off with cinnamon apple pie soaked in vanilla ice cream. We talked, laughed, and almost bonded. So, when he asked me out again, I agreed. Who was it who said drug dealers couldn't converse?

CHAPTER 3

Kicking it with Kevon the last couple of weeks had been great. Every time we were together, he made it all about me. And I sucked up every minute of it. I could have never predicted we would click like we did. It felt good to have him in my life at this time. Because Ruthie was making my life a living hell on a daily basis. All she did was bitch, day and night. "Job, Job, Job, Yazz, you need to get a job," was constantly coming out of Ruthie's mouth. The shit was successfully driving me crazy. It had gotten to the point where I would stay in my room, with my door locked, when I was home. That was the only way to keep her from barging in. But even that could not save me from Ruthie and her mouth. She would just yell out loud with her insults.

The other day, it had me so depressed that I decided to share some of what was going on with Kevon. He offered to let me move in with him. But we had only been dating for a few weeks and I didn't feel comfortable with that. And, to be honest, as bad as things were, I was not ready to leave home yet. That was where I was supposed to feel wanted, safe, and just maybe it wasn't too late. What pissed me off even more was how Rodney sat around on his sorry ass, ate all the food, never contributed, and she never dared say a word. Here I was her daughter, and she treated me like a visitor who had worn out her welcome.

This morning was no different. She had woken up with that same shit, so I split early. Straight to Mimi's house is where I ran off to. There, I was able to unwind a little.

"I'm just so sick of Ruthie and her complaining. She sits around and reprimands me as if I'm not even looking for a job." I sat on the living room couch with Mimi. At night, that same burnt orange couch rolled out into Mimi's bed. Rolling a blunt, Mimi shook her head with sadness as I talked. This conversation was all too familiar to her. I had been coming over crying this same song for months now. And not much had changed besides the fact that, Ruthie had really lost her mind.

"Well, you know she ain't gon' stop. Shit, what else she got to do besides bitch and moan at you? The woman hates her job and her life." Mimi continued to fill the swisher blunt, which, in my opinion, was about to overflow with weed.

I sighed. "I know, but I got to do something though, because this morning she once again threatened to put me out."

"Don't pay that shit no mind. She always says that."

"I know, but this time was different. I guess it's the way she said it. I'm telling you she means it this time. Sometimes I feel like she really just wants me gone anyway. It's like she's trying to drive me mad so I'll leave." I shook my head as a tear tried to slide down my face. Instead of allowing it to fall, I took in a deep breath and exhaled. Ruthie had never shown me the love that I knew a mother should give to her child. Lately, I was really starting to wonder if she loved me at all. Because all I felt like was a burden to her, a piece of junk in the house that was blocking her way.

Mimi stopped rolling her blunt. Her forehead displayed lines that looked scrunched up, as if she was in deep thought. Sometimes it felt like she was the only family I had. At least she loved me. No matter what. We had been friends since grade school and had always been there for each other.

"Look, you know I would invite you to stay here if there was any room. But this motherfucker packed. Shit, with Sheila, the kids, and me. Now she done moved Ronald's ass up in here. It's a damn fire-code violation. I swear, if the landlord finds out anyone else here, they gon' throw her ass out. Soon as I can save some money, I'm outta here. But that's hard to do since I'm always helping Sheila." Sadly enough, everything she was saying was the truth. Mimi had been living with Sheila since ninth grade, when their mother got locked up for killing her abusive boyfriend. But back then it wasn't so bad because Sheila only had two children. That had changed drastically over the past few years. Not only did they live in a two-bedroom small apartment, Sheila had six kids, a part-time job, and only made a buck over minimum wage. The whole situation was not the best. But the one thing they did have in the overcrowded apartment was love. That was one of the reasons why Mimi didn't move when she started making money. She wanted to be sure Sheila and kids were good first.

"Don't sweat it. I know you would help if you could. But it's gon' be a'ight. A job bound to come through soon. I got applications in all over the city. Until then, I'm just gon' try my best to stay outta Ruthie's sight."

"That sounds easier said than done, but anything is possible. So what's up with Kevon's fine ass?" Now that was a conversation we could have. Hearing Kevon's name dragged a smile out of me. "Damn, I guess that's my answer." Mimi started licking the sides of her blunt—without a doubt, the finishing touch. With Sheila and the kids gone, she was about to have the apartment lit up with smoke.

"He straight. Actually, he's been keeping my mind off this craziness. . . ." A knock at the door caught us both off guard. "You expecting someone?"

"Nope. Look out the peephole and see who it is." Mimi started fidgeting with the plastic sack the weed was in.

Stepping over the folded blanket and two pillows that Mimi had not put away, I placed my left eye to the peephole. At first, I couldn't see because the person was pacing around, but finally he stood still. "Oh, that's Devin." Devin was Mimi's ex-boyfriend whom she could not seem to shake. Deep down, he still cared about her a lot, so he could not let Mimi go. Anytime someone tried to hook up with Mimi, he would show up and start blocking. But he was cool people though and could be funny as hell.

"Let him in." Mimi pulled the blunt from under her leg, where she was hiding it.

"Hey, Devin," I spoke, soon as I opened the door.

"What's up, Yazz? Damn, girl, it's been a minute since I last saw you."

"It has," I agreed. We three used to hang out all the time when he and Mimi were in love. He never tripped about me being the third wheel. And I appreciated him for that. "You know I don't do shit."

"Nigga, why you ain't call first?" Mimi broke our reunion.

"I told you yesterday I might come through and fuck wit ya." Devin was nonchalant as usual. But Mimi knew why he was popping up unannounced. Really he was coming by to see who was there. He was still slick jealous of other dudes. Even though he tried hard to deny it.

"That was yesterday, this is today, Devin. You can't just be popping up wheneva you want. You ain't my man, so have some respect." She sounded annoyed, but I knew it wouldn't take long for her to get over it.

"Damn, Mimi, why you trippin'? You see what she put me through, Yazz?"

I just smiled. There was nothing I could do to rescue him from Mimi's wrath. When she went there, only she could turn it off.

Shake my head at them was all I could do because they stayed arguing. Well, at least Mimi was always putting him in his place. They had love for each other; they just could not be in a relationship together.

"Whatever, Devin. Come on, let's smoke this blunt." Mimi pulled out a lighter, ready to blaze up. Just like that, they were cool again.

"Now, that is what I'm talkin' 'bout, less arguing and more smoke." Excited and anticipating the high he was about to experience, Devin rubbed his hands together.

"Mimi, I'm out, I'll call you later." I decided to bounce.

"See, you always running when it's smoke time. I'm tellin' you, this is exactly what you need to clear your head," Mimi informed me, then inhaled the blunt.

"I'm sure you're right." I smiled. "But I'm good. I'll hit you later. It was nice seeing you, Devin."

"A'ight, Yazz," Devin replied, then blew out smoke. The room was already clouded.

Closing the door behind me, I stepped out into the heat and headed back to the crib. My growling stomach confirmed how hungry I was. Ruthie was at work so there would be silence at home. And if I was really lucky, Rodney would be gone too. This time of day, he normally ran the streets nickel and diming. He swore he was getting money, but the real truth was he was a forty-year-old sack boy with no respect in the streets.

Sliding my key in the lock, I opened the door slowly and was greeted with cold air and the relaxing sound of quietness. I breathed a sigh of relief my prayers had been answered. The kitchen was my first stop. I opened up some oatmeal and popped it in the microwave for a minute, grabbed an unopened bag of Cheetos, and headed to my room. After I ate, my stomach calmed down and my blood sugar was back to normal. I reached on top of my dresser drawer and picked up two *Vogue* magazines. Lying across my bed, I started flipping the pages, checking out the designs. I loved clothes so much. Too bad they were out of my broke budget, but skimming through these magazines gave me hope. It also gave something to look forward to. And there was nothing wrong with that.

With a full stomach and some hope from the *Vogue* magazine, I was feeling good and energized. Then all of a sudden there was a *BOOM*. It sounded like someone had kicked my bedroom door off the hinges. Startled, I almost fall off my bed. Sitting up on the edge of the bed, I had been able to stop my fall. It was struggle at first, but eventually I gathered my composure. That was when I saw my door was not off the hinges but had indeed been kicked open.

Staring at me with a scowl on her face was Ruthie. "Where the hell you been all day?" she screamed. The look on her face expressed that she had gone mad.

"Why?" I asked. I was still in shock over her unnecessary behavior. My heart was pounding. I held on to my chest.

"What? Why?" She stared at me as if I were missing an eye or something. "Because," she screamed again. Spit flew out of her mouth across the room. "This is my house, and I asked your black ass a question. Now, where have you been all day?" Once again, she screamed. I was certain she had turned into a crazed woman. Hopefully it wasn't drugs.

"I was at Mimi's house." This was the first time I had actually seen her loose in this way. It was making me a little nervous.

"Mimi's house?" She acted as if that were unbelievable. "Is it a job at Mimi's house? Because, if not, I don't see why you would waste a full day over there. Have you ever seen me go down to the school parking lot and stand there all day? You know why? Because it don't pay money."

Now she was just saying stupid shit and being sarcastic to piss me off. "Ruthie, I have been looking for a job. Ain't nobody hiring." Sick of her craziness, I rolled my eyes at her.

"You can roll your eyes all you want. Your ass just being lazy and trifling," she accused. The worst part was that she believed every word she said.

"I'm lazy. How you gon' call me lazy? When all Rodney do is lay around on his ass, eat, sleep, and shit. And you don't say one word." Normally, I never cursed when talking to her, but I was fed up. Plain tired of being treated like an outsider in my own mother's home.

"Listen, lil girl, you don't worry about my man. He is my problem." She stabbed herself in the chest while making her point. "Besides, he is good to me and makes me happy. And you should be happy that he has accepted you like you were his own daughter. Most men wouldn't even put up with me because of you."

Now she wanted to blame me for the lack of men in her life. "Don't blame me if you could not keep a man. And Rodney's bum ass is not my father," I shot back in disgust. Every time she said that, I wanted to throw up.

For a moment, Ruthie stood still, staring at me as if she could not believe a word that had just come out of my mouth. Like she was the victim. That was a role that she loved to play. "Yazz, you're as ungrateful today as you were the day you were born." Without another word she left my room.

Her last words replayed in my mind like a tape recorder. I had no clue what they meant. But the look in her eyes said that they meant a lot. I was reaching down to grab the magazines that had fallen on the floor when all of a sudden Ruthie was in my doorway again.

"Do you ever wonder why you don't have a father? Huh? Do you ever wonder why he's not around?" The coldness on her face made me wonder if she really wanted me to answer that. In fact, I had wondered, even asked her once when I was four. And, with a blank look on her face, Ruthie hadn't answered. So I'd never asked again.

"When I was sixteen . . ." She paused for a minute. She wore a calm look on her face. It made me feel uneasy, but I sat still, hoping she would go on. "When I was sixteen, I dated this guy named Clyde. We were inseparable and in love. Or at least that's what I thought. No one could have told me different." She smiled. But something about the smile was forced. "One day, he comes to me and says that he had lost a bet to his friend. . . ." She paused. "You know what? To this day, I have no idea what the bet was. He never said, and I didn't ask. But Clyde needed my help, and all I wanted to do was help him. Anyway, he had lost a bet, and to pay the debt back he needed me to sleep with his friend. Now, at first I was like, hell no. I mean I was still a virgin. Clyde hadn't even got lucky yet. But after a couple of days of Clyde begging and crying, I agreed to do it. It hurt that he would even ask me to do this for him, but just the same, I agreed.

"Couple of months later, my cycle don't come, then the vomiting, and I knew I was pregnant. Scared, I went to Clyde's house in tears. I was lost and didn't know what to do. I told him I was pregnant, thinking he would help me in some way. Hmmph. Instead, he broke up with me and called me a thousand hos when he knew it was not true. I could not believe the words that came out of his mouth. How could he talk to me like that? When my mom found out, I begged her to let me have an abortion, but she said no. Said she didn't believe in that. As time went by, I started to show so people knew, and when that happened, people started to talk. Well, Momma was a proud woman. She always had been. One day, she came home from work and told me I had to go. Just like that, she was done with me I could no longer live with her. I was horrified. Here I was, sixteen, six months pregnant, and nowhere to go. The only place for me then was the shelter, which turned out to be where I gave birth to you. After that, I worked hard and got us a place. I tried very hard to be happy and accept the fate that had been given to me. But deep down, from the day my mother had kicked me out, I felt like I struggled to take care of a baby who had caused me to lose everything but by no means gave me anything in return. And to be honest, to this day that ain't changed much. I'm not sure if I will ever feel any different." She shrugged her shoulders and went silent. Like she was unhappy with what she'd had for dinner.

As I sat and listened to her story, I sympathized with her. But suddenly the point of her story sunk in and I understood. She did not love me, her own daughter, and that truth broke my heart. The thought broke me down where I sat. I had tried for years and fought very hard for my mother's love. But now I knew, and one thing was very clear to me. She had never, nor would she ever be able to love me. The pit of my stomach was so sick with hurt it twisted in knots. I felt as if I would throw up everything that was inside me until my gut was empty. With both of my eyes clouded from tears, I could no longer see anything but spots. Those spots were actually Ruthie. Wiping those tears away with the back of my hand, I found the strength to stand. Full of anger, I burst out of the room, past Ruthie. Reaching the front door, I dared myself to look back. This part of my life that included my so-called mother, Ruthie, was done. I had never had a father. Now the same thing was true when it came to my mother. I no longer had one.

CHAPTER 4

After I left home, the streets became my refuge for a couple hours as I tried to clear my head. I needed to be alone for a minute. It was still hard for me to soak up and wrap my head around my mother's story. The sun started to shift behind the clouds so the time came when I had to figure out where I really wanted to go. Mimi and Sheila would never turn me away if I didn't have any place to go. But I felt like overcrowding them more than they already were would be selfish of me. So in the end I landed on Kevon's doorstep. From the time he opened the door, he welcomed me with open arms. His hugs, kisses, and understanding were therapeutic. A couple of days blew by without me doing anything but lying around. The only thing that forced me out of the bed was the shower. I could barely eat; my appetite just didn't seem to exist. Inside, I felt as if someone had died. But I knew there was no way a person could survive like this forever. I would have to brush myself off and move on. Ruthie had lost out. She was dead to me, and I was over it.

With my mind made up to get my life back, I climbed out of bed, took a hot shower, and grabbed one of the few outfits Kevon had brought for me. When I left Ruthie's house, I'd left everything behind. At the time, getting out had been more important. And, at this moment, there was still no regret about that. This was my time to heal. Anything from that house would only trigger bad memories that were best forgotten. Kevon had gone out a few days before, since he could not convince me to get out of bed, and grabbed me a few things that I would need.

By the time I had decided to get dressed for the day, he had already left. In the kitchen, I threw a slice of toast in the Black and Decker toaster, drank a glass of Tropicana orange juice, and was out. The day went by fast as I hit several temp agencies, filling out more applications and talking to any human resources person who was available. When it got late, I decided to head back to Kevon's condo. Another shower was calling my name; today had been just as scorching hot as the days in the previous weeks. Kevon was still not home when I made it so I wasted no time jumping in the shower. He would be happy to see me up and moving around. Adjusting the shower knobs before climbing inside, I watched the water as it sprayed smoothly from the showerhead, the sound of it comforting. Ready to feel that sprinkle sensation all over my hot, tired body, I pulled at my clothes and allowed them to drop to the floor, then slipped into the shower. As the water sprayed all over my face, the feeling of it relaxed me, the sweat that had attacked me all day melting away. Turning in twist motions, my body soaked up the water. Kevon's voice soared in the background as he called my name, announcing that he was home. I reached for the Dove bodywash and lathered myself all over. It felt great.

Climbing out of the shower, I felt refreshed, and as I reached for my dry-off towel, I caught a glimpse of my body in the mirror. *Beautiful* was the only way I could label it. I smiled; my tight skin and perky breasts were perfect. Thinking of Kevon caused my middle to tingle. We had not slept together yet. Not once had he pressured me in any way, but I was more than ready. After applying lotion to my entire body, I took hold of my silk bathrobe and slid it on.

Making my way to the kitchen, I found Kevon pulling plates from the cabinet.

"Kevon?" His name sounded sweet as it rolled off my tongue.

"Oh, hey." He looked surprised to see me. "You finally got out of bed. Can I fix you something to eat? I brought all this food. I was going to fix you a plate and bring it up to you." He pointed to the bags on the stove that said PETE'S SOUL FOOD. I had only eaten there once in my life, and the food was bomb. But right now my mind was not on food.

Without saying one word, I allowed my robe to drop to the floor, exposing my entire naked body. Kevon's mouth dropped open as I walked slowly and seductively over to him. When I stood in front of him, a grin was the only thing I was wearing. Slowly, he reached out and pulled me close to him, and I instantly felt his hardness.

"You sure you ready for this?" He planted soft kisses to my neck.

"How about this? I want you, and I want you now," I announced, looking him square in the eyes. And to be sure he understood, I started un-buckling his pants. I was on fire. And the proof was leaking down my thighs. Kevon picked me up and sat me on his member, taking control, and the ride was long and steady. The word *good* could not describe how I felt. All of my problems were irrel-evant.

CHAPTER 5

The next couple of weeks, I was the happiest I had ever been in my life. Kevon was there for me in more ways than one. Not to mention, he showered me with everything a girl could want. I had transformed into a totally new person. I now owned a wardrobe full of name-brand this or that. For the first time in my life, I wore my hair in a style other than a ponytail. My new, improved hairstyle was ridiculously cute; my beautician had sewn in Brazilian hair that she styled into big lock curls that cascaded down my back, or sometimes I wore it straight. Cute honey was what I was, a new me, and it felt great.

Kevon treated me like a queen, and I welcomed it. And I didn't miss Ruthie the least little bit. Now I had someone who loved me, and he proved it every day.

Kevon opened the front door and called my name.

"What?" I was in the middle of applying MAC lip gloss. Smacking my lips together to be sure it smoothed out, I turned my face in the mirror to see if it looked good from all angles.

"Somebody's outside for you."

"Who is it?" I asked. Reaching atop the dresser I grabbed my cell phone before exiting the room. I had no idea who could be looking for me; I wasn't expecting anyone. And since Kevon had never answered my question, I would have to see for myself. I made it to the living room, and it was empty. The front door was ajar so I snatched it open to find Kevon standing next to a red BMW. Wearing a huge smile, he dangled keys at me. That could only mean one thing.

"Is this car for me?" I asked.

"Damn, right. All yours, babe."

"Aww, babe, I love it." I jumped in Kevon's waiting arms. This was the nicest thing that anyone had ever done for me. My very own BMW. As I opened the door, the smell of new leather filled my nostrils. My hands slowly roamed across the seats, and I gazed up at the sun roof. The car was perfect. A month ago, I would have never imagined owning one. Climbing back out of the car, I hugged Kevon.

"I have to go show Mimi," I informed him.

"I already know, so go ahead take your new baby for a spin. Trust me, it's good." He smiled.

"Babe, thanks so much." I kissed him on the lips. Climbing into my car, I sat down slowly, and the leather seats immediately sucked me in. "Wait, my purse," I yelled, just as Kevon reached to shut my door. Kevon stopped me as I attempted to scramble out of the car. He reached into his pants pocket.

"Don't worry about that, you good. Buy another bag while you're out." He handed me a stack of hundred-dollar bills. I counted about four thousand dollars slowly. Like I said, he treated me like a queen. The only thing for me to do was smile. What girl didn't like stacks of green dough?

When I started up the engine, it was silent. Adjusting my rearview mirror, I gently put my foot on the gas. I slowly backed out, careful not to hit anything, then placed the car in drive. Finally, in traffic, it felt as if I were riding on a cloud. It was official: this BMW was my new toy. Before I could drive a full block, the Chris Brown and Nicki Minaj ringtone I'd set for Kevon started singing on my phone.

"Hey, is it all that you thought it would be?"

"Yes, and more. I wouldn't mind having two just like it," I commented. I had never imagined that riding in a car could be this comfortable or fun. Luxury was not overrated.

"That's what's up." His tone revealed that he was pleased that he was able to make me happy. "Listen, pick up something nice to wear while you're out shopping. Caesar is throwing a set tonight, and I want my lady on my arm. Time to show everybody what a bad chick I got at home."

Caesar was Kevon's boss and a true boss in Missouri. Meeting him would be an honor.

"Aww, thanks, babe. Wait, can I bring Mimi? Gotta have my ride-or-die chick."

"Sure, bring your girl. She cool people. I gotta go though—we'll talk later."

After ending the call with Kevon, I pulled up to Mimi's crib. I dialed her number as I scoped a park. "Yo, come outside."

"You out there?" The tone of her voice told me she was surprised. Normally, when I was coming over, I told her first.

"Why else would I ask you to come out? Stop with the questions already."

"Damn, a'ight. Calm down."

Pulling into a secure parking space, I caught Mimi peeking out of the front door, trying to find me. Shutting off the car, I opened the door and stepped out. "Oh, hell no!" she shouted. The smile on her face was stretched from one ear to the next. "This your whip?"

I nodded.

Mimi started screaming with excitement as she walked around the car, checking it out.

"This shit is cold as a motherfucker! These bitches better fall back. Wait, you gotta take me for a spin. Hell yes, I want to turn some corners in this bad-ass whip."

She only had to say that once because I was ready. "Well, hop in, let's go." Opening the driver's-side door, I climbed back inside. "We need to go shopping anyway. Kevon's taking us to a party tonight."

"What party?" Mimi shut the passenger-side door once she was safely inside.

"You heard of Caesar, right?"

"Caesar the drug dealer? Hell yeah, I heard of that nigga. Who in Missouri ain't?"

I guessed that was a dumb question to ask. You would have to be living under a rock or stupid not to know who Caesar was.

"Good, because we gon' be guests at his party tonight."

"Aww, shit, that is what's up!" Mimi was excited. "Oh, but wait, I can't go." Her facial expression went from eager to disturbed.

"Why not?" Now the worry was mine. There was no way I was going around all those strangers without my best friend. I did not want to go without her.

"Why do you think? I don't have shit to wear, and I will not be caught dead at Caesar's party in no cheap knock-off-ass clothes. That dude is a boss—he don't want no scrubs hanging around. No. My shit would have to be on point for me to attend. This is just too short of notice."

Suddenly I could breathe again. I'd thought she had a real reason she couldn't go. "Girl, don't worry about clothes—I got you. Now let's go. We gon' hit up Saks Fifth. Our shit is gon' be on point."

And I meant just that.

CHAPTER 6

As we pulled up to Sikes, the club where Caesar's party was being held, it looked like the scene of the BET red carpet. People were out in droves, waiting, trying to get in. If I didn't know any better, I would have thought some type of celebrity was inside. Coming to a complete stop, Kevon threw his cream-colored 2014 Cadillac Escalade in park. One of the valet guys came over, and Kevon handed him the keys. Climbing out of the truck, I wasn't nervous at all because I looked good after spending three hours in Saks. My outfit was a banger, and did not disappoint: an open-back black halter jumpsuit by Theory, with some leather pointy-toe Manolo pumps. My outfit was indeed beat to capacity.

My girl Mimi was also on point—five-four, with her cream-colored skin tone and booty that had been said to come from eating pinto beans and cornbread. She was killing it in an Elizabeth and James sheer body-con dress. Eye candy was both our names tonight. Kevon had made it clear he would not be taking his eyes off me, because I belonged to him.

Coming around to my side of the truck, Kevon reached for my free hand while I held on to my clutch with the other. Mimi looked at us both and smiled. "Kevon, are you sure we gon' be able to get in? Niggas is out here thick." The same question had crossed my mind.

"No worries. I got you. You are rollin' with me tonight." Kevon walked past everyone standing in line, and the two bouncers at the door greeted him as they removed the rope. We walked straight in.

When we stepped inside the club, the atmosphere said top-notch. It was nothing like club Mystic. Not to get it twisted—Mystic was nice—but Sikes was definitely more updated. It resembled something like a scene out of the STARZ TV show *Power*. And, yes, the DJ was already on fire. The song "Rich," by Kirko Bangz, was blasting out of the speakers. I could tell by the look on Mimi's face she was ready to hit the dance floor, but she chilled. Kevon led us up some stairs to a VIP room, and sexy and important was the only way to describe how I felt. There were a bunch of unfamiliar faces that glanced in our direction as we entered.

"Yo, what up?" Kevon yelled. Everyone spoke as Kevon kept moving through the crowd until we made it to the back. It was obvious he was loved. People were stopping whatever they were doing to show him love. They greeted him as if he were Jay Z or something.

There was a tall, dark-skinned guy with a goatee and the deepest set of big eyes I had seen in a long time standing toward the back. I assumed he was just another person at the party until Kevon greeted him. "My main guy, Caesar, what's up, my nigga?"

"It ain't shit," Caesar replied as they did this handshake that I had never seen. "Who are these beautiful females?" He gazed at Mimi and myself, where we stood to the right of Kevon.

"This my girl, Yazz." Kevon eyed me proudly as he wrapped his arm around my waist and pulled me in close. "Yazz, baby, this is Caesar."

"Hi, it's nice to meet you." The words flowed out of my mouth just above a whisper. For me, Caesar's appearance had been a surprise. For some silly reason, I'd envisioned him to be this Rick Ross-type-looking dude because of his name. But that assumption couldn't be further from the truth. Caesar reminded me of Omar Epps from *Love and Basketball*, only he was taller.

"And this is my best friend, Mimi." I pointed to Mimi since Kevon seemed to have forgotten to introduce her.

"What's up?" Mimi spoke, then focused her attention back on the crowd. She was ready to turn up, and that meant a drink in her hand, then the dance floor.

"Well, I'm glad both you ladies decided to come out and party with us. The night is young, but you are my guests and can have anything you want."

Mimi spoke up without hesitation. "How about a drink? I'm ready to sip." She had never been one to hold back or beat around the bush. I, on the other hand, was a little more reserved.

"I see you." Caesar smiled at Mimi. "We got whateva you need over at the bar—it's fully stocked. Just hit the bartender up." If he only knew—he didn't have to tell Mimi twice.

"Come on, Yazz. Let's get a drink." She pulled me in the direction of the bar without warning.

"Babe, I'll be back," I managed to warn Kevon as she all but dragged me with her.

"Yeah, after we turn up," Mimi added.

At the bar, we both took our first shots to get the night started. The tingling sensation went to my head, then straight to my toes. I needed to chill for a minute on the drinking. But not Mimi—she was on shot number four in no time flat. We hit the dance floor and did our thing, but my girl was krunk off them shots. She took twerking to a new level—just watching her was exhausting.

"Mimi, let's have a seat for a minute, girl. Hell, I'm tired and need to catch my breath."

"Dang, Yazz, why you gotta ruin it? You know this my jam," she said, referring to Rich Homie Quan's "Type of Way."

"Mimi, bring your ass over here. Every song that comes on is your song." It was my turn to drag her. That would be the only way to get her to sit down.

"I know, right?" Mimi laughed.

The plan for me was to find a seat and ignore the uneasy feeling I'd had all night. I hoped it was just my imagination, but who was I kidding. Caesar had his eyes all over me. Glued. And it was starting to make me feel uncomfortable. I was feeling guilty, as if it was my fault, or was that what Kevon would think? Either way, I was ready to go. But Kevon was nowhere in sight. He had been pretty much handling business all night; I had hardly seen him since we'd arrived. Spending time with him was what I'd assumed would happen. I'd been wrong.

While Mimi and I were chilling, this dude who went by Soulja, who also happened to be a part of Cash, which was Caesar's crew, came over and introduced himself. He was cute—tall and light skinned, with dreads. Mimi gave him her number, but she didn't say much about him after that. That normally meant she wasn't interested, and since leaving was my only concern, I didn't ask.

Finally, the night came to an end. The turn-up was real, but it was time for me to enjoy my man. After dropping Mimi off at home, Kevon sped off toward his place and we arrived in no time.

"Did you enjoy yourself tonight?" he asked as he slid the key into the lock, twisted it, and pushed the door open.

"Yes, it was nice. And you know Mimi enjoyed it. I just wish I'd seen more of you." I pouted.

"I know, babe. I was feeling the same thing. But there was business that had to be handled. It never stops. No worries though—I'm all yours now. For whateva you might need." Wrapping his arms around me from the back, Kevon started kissing the back of my neck. Instantly, I was turned on. Turning around to face him, I took a step back. He watched as I undressed, then kicked off my heels. Standing upright in my birthday suit, I watched as Kevon's eyes roamed over every inch of me.

"Damn, babe. You must be tryin' to drive a nigga crazy. Look at them thighs. I swear, you a masterpiece." He licked his lips.

"You think so?" I smiled seductively. "Follow me." I led the way to the bedroom. Once inside, I lay down on the bed and spread my legs. Without instruction, Kevon dropped to his knees and feasted down south. Not able to hold on, he filled me up.

"Hmmm," I sighed from pure happiness, then flipped onto my stomach, and kissed Kevon on the cheek. "Tonight has been a good night."

"Fo sho, you was sexy as hell in that outfit. I couldn't keep my eyes off you." He winked at me.

"Oh, really?" I couldn't help but blush. But his statement was a surprise because he had been absent most of the night. "How is that? When you were missing in action." Resting my breast on his chest, I touched the tip of his nose with my finger.

"See, that's what you think. A nigga was handling business, true enough. But like I told you, I was gon' keep my eyes on you all night. Nothin' was gon' change that. Please believe me." He wrapped his arms around me, and I snuggled up in his embrace. "You were the baddest chick in there without question." His flattery was cute. "Even Caesar couldn't take his eyes off you."

I froze. He had seen it too.

"So you saw it too? For a moment, I thought I was imagining it or overreacting. I even moved out of his sight at one point. However, when I looked up again, his wandering eyes had found me." Admitting this to my man was really uncomfortable for me. But what I really wanted to know was, how did he feel about his boss eating me up with his eyes? By this time, I had turned my back to him and was resting against his chest.

Then the opposite of what I had been expecting came out of his mouth. "Caesar has a thing for beautiful women." He rubbed my breast and kissed the back of my neck. Squirming, I beamed at his touch. It was driving me crazy.

"So you think I'm that beautiful, huh?"

"Hell yeah, you are that beautiful, and you belong to me. I'm a proud man right here." Lifting my neck and adjusting it so that my face met his, he kissed my lips softly. Positioning myself comfortably back in his arms, I started to feel sleepy.

"Babe, I was thinkin' that . . ." He paused and became silent.

"What, babe?" I yawned. Sleep was taking complete control, and my body was starting to feel sluggish.

"What I was about to say was . . ." He paused again. That was becoming annoying. "Maybe it would not be such a bad idea for Caesar to be feeling you. Actually, it would work out great if you made yourself more available to him. Kinda gain his trust."

Either I was sleepy as hell or Kevon was fucking with me. Laughing, I said, "Babe, that is not a good joke." I yawned again, this time using my free hand to cover my mouth.

"Babe, I know this sounds crazy. Nevertheless, important things gotta be done, and if operations ain't ran right, they fail. Simple as that. But a good leader steps up to that challenge. I'm making major moves to right some wrongs. This could be a part of the perfect plan. Caesar's my man, but he's been disloyal to his street soldiers. Real niggas that respect him, would even take a bullet for him—that includes me. Loyalty is the key to success in these streets. He has violated that code one fucking time too many. So his time is over. Now it's time for me to do what's right and step up. I am next in line to run the empire that's known as Cash. I just gotta take the proof to the big man. And, with your help, I can do just that. You and me can rule the streets of Missouri as man and wifey. The world would be at our feet. You ain't seen the love we could get."

Soaking up everything that Kevon had just said to me, I still waited for him to say he was playing around. Because he could not be seriously telling me he wanted me to reel in his boss. Basically set up the most notorious drug dealer in St. Louis. Even I knew that was death territory. And I was not about that life.

"Okay, babe, your joke is funny, but you can stop playing now. Come on, let's get some sleep. I'm tired."

"Yazz, this ain't a joke, and I ain't playin'. This shit is real right here." The unusual tone of his voice got my attention.

For the first time since he'd started jabbering about it, I believed him. Sitting up in bed and turning to face him, I looked in his eyes. "Kevon, exactly what are you asking me to do?"

"I'm asking you to step up and be my lady. Have

my back on this. It'll be simple. All you got to do is be cute, earn his trust, and make him happy. It'll be like taking candy from a baby."

The look on Kevon's face was something I had not experienced yet. I tried to look deep within him to be sure I was not missing something. How could he be asking me to basically bed his boss so that he could be the next kingpin and fatten his pockets? What man would ask his lady to do such a thing? I was confused. He couldn't possibly want an answer right now. Suddenly, I was extremely tired—no, I was exhausted. Slowly I eased back down onto my soft pillow and settled down under the covers with my back to him.

"Yazz, it'll be okay," he tried to assure me. But as I drifted off to a sleep with a fast-beating heart and a gut full of uncertainty, the last thing I remembered was Ruthie's face.

CHAPTER 7

A week had gone by, and I was still in horrible shock over Kevon's request. Honestly, I was lying dormant, waiting on him to say I was being punked. Except that had not happened yet. I even weighed my options. That didn't last long, as I realized, without Kevon, I didn't have shit. That thought was as fucked up as it was lonely. Getting up that morning, I tried to be as upbeat as I could. Kevon knew my mind was heavy, so he kissed me and handed me a stack of cash as he ran out the door. Another day of hustling had started for him. Grabbing the keys to my car, I was out too. I was picking up Mimi for a little shopping. She had just got paid so she had blown me up the day before, making me promise to pick her up.

She stood next to me at the mirror in Macy's, checking out some pants I was trying on. "Those

GUESS jeans are cute on you. Kevon must be sexing you crazy because them hips is spreading."

"You and your one-track mind." I turned from side to side and started sizing up my hips. She wasn't lying—they were spreading. It would be safe to say I was coming into my womanly curves. And, to be truthful, it looked good on me. At least, I thought so.

"Bitch, don't downplay me. You know that everybody thinks like me. They just don't admit it," Mimi boasted. She now held a burnt-orange one-shoulder crop top in front of herself in the mirror to see if it would look good on her.

"Are you getting both pairs of those jeans? They are like two hundred and forty-nine apiece."

For me, the price was not an issue. Like I said, Kevon kept my pocket laced.

"Yeah, I'm gettin' both pairs. Why not?" I sighed.

"Damn, I guess you do have it like that since your man spoiling your ass rotten."

"Yeah, that he does on a daily," I agreed, then strolled over to the blouses on the rack closest to me.

"Cool, but what's up with you?" Mimi followed close behind me. The girl could read me like a book. She knew something was bothering me.

"What do you mean?" I browsed the shirts nonchalantly.

"You tell me. Since you the one with the grave look on your face. Is something bothering you?"

I had to tell her something because she would not leave it alone otherwise. "No, everything is cool. But sometimes this new life with Kevon seems too good to be true," I lied. There was no way I could tell her about Kevon's request. She would be threatening to get him fucked up and some more. No, telling her would be a mistake. This was one secret I had no choice but to keep to myself. Whatever decision I made would be on me. "The clothes, the car, the money, and happiness—just can't believe it's all mine."

"Well, get used to it because it is, girl. Shit, ain't nothin' wrong with enjoying the good life. Hell, I'm just waiting on my turn. We are going to have matching ballers, watch. And trust I ain't gon' have shit but a smile on my face. All these thirsty, broke-down hos gon' have to fall back."

"Aye, what about that dude Soulja? He a baller, plus he cute. What's up?"

"No doubt he is fine, but I don't know about him. He left me a couple of messages; I never had time to call him back though." She shrugged her shoulders. "Then, you know, I had to get my number changed because of Devin's ass. I still remembered Soulja's number, but I was like, 'fuck it,' after that."

"It's like that?"

"I don't know. . . ." She shrugged her shoulders again. "Maybe he too cute though. He just looks like the type that got a bunch of bitches. And I ain't tryin' to be fighting these crazy hos. Because you and I both know I will beat a bitch ass if they get me in the wrong."

Looking at Mimi's facial expression, I couldn't do anything but laugh. She was telling the truth, so maybe she was right.

"Your ass is so crazy. But I feel you. Besides, it shouldn't be that hard for you to find another baller in Missouri. Now, let's pay for this stuff and get the hell outta here."

Both of us were weighed down with bags as we made our way toward the Macy's exit so that we could get to the car. I did a double take as I caught a glimpse of Ruthie in the shoe section. The devil must have been busy, because there was no way possible we could end up in the same store at the same damn time. St. Louis could not be that small. It had been a while since I'd run out of her house, never to return. And, still, it was too soon. She was the last person on earth I was ready to see.

Seeing her made me feel lonely all over again. I felt unworthy of anything good. She would not approve of me being the least bit happy; to her, I didn't deserve it. But Kevon popped in my head instantly, and there was the feeling of me being loved. I could go home and he would throw his arms around me. Things would be okay. At that moment, I missed him awful bad. Ruthie was a non-factor. Without a second thought, I gripped my bags tighter. My getaway would be my destination.

"Yazz." Ruthie had the nerve to call my name. She could not possibly think we were on speaking terms. But, even if she did, I knew better, so I sped up.

"Dang, Yazz, wait up for me, girl," Mimi hollered. Hearing her voice made me pause for a brief second. Mimi was out of breath trying to catch up with me. Ruthie had caused me to forget all about her. That woman had the craziest effect on me.

Literally throwing our bags in the back of my

BMW, we jumped inside and bailed out. The ride was quiet. Mimi knew how I was feeling so she didn't pressure me to talk about it. After dropping her off, home was my destination. Seeing Ruthie had put things in perspective for me. She always made me feel like a stranger. But Kevon had gone out of his way to make me feel wanted. Walking in the house and seeing his face smoothed out the rugged edges that seeing Ruthie had bestowed on me. Everything was going to be okay.

"What's up, babe? Did you enjoy shopping?"

"Yep, like always—that is, until I saw Ruthie." I dropped my bags in the middle of the living room floor.

"Damn, you saw your moms?" His eyes grew big. I nodded. "Did y'all talk?"

"Heck no, I don't have anything to say to that evil woman. Why should I? What mother blames her own kid for being born? She never cared about me, so why should I care about her? I'm sure she just wanted to remind me of how miserable I made her life," I yelled. I had so much built-up anger inside. Exploding was probably my only chance at relief.

"Babe, babe, calm down." Kevon came over and wrapped his arms around me as tears flooded my face. Seeing Ruthie just brought back all the hurt and pain. Feeling Kevon's love all around me helped me fight it. Lowering my hands to my face, I dried my tears.

"Being with you the past few months has been great. I trust you and I want you to know that I do have your back. . . . So I'm ready." I looked him in the eyes.

"Are you sure you're up to this? I don't want you to feel pressured."

"There is no pressure. I'm just going to be here for my man when he needs me. After all, isn't that what being in a relationship is all about?"

And just like that everything was a go. I would show Kevon that I could be his down, ride-or-die chick. The same love he had shown me would be returned. I would be his loyalty, his wifey.

CHAPTER 8

It had taken two of the longest weeks of my life, but Kevon had finally set up the first trap that would cause me to run into Caesar. The plan was for me to go to the dealership, where he was closing the deal on a Ferrari whose interior he was having custom made. On the way over to the dealership I became nervous as hell. My stomach turned so much until it spilled over. I couldn't help it. And since throwing up was not a part of the plan, it threw me off schedule, I stopped off at a Walgreens to buy a toothbrush and toothpaste. The last thing I wanted to do was turn the dude off with sour-smelling puke breath.

Finally I arrived. After finding a place to park my car, I worked up the nerve to get out. *It's game time*, I tried to coach myself. I knew I looked good—I just needed to play the part. As soon as I stepped out of my car, I noticed several salesmen from the dealership observing me. But only one had the nerve to approach me.

"Hi, I'm Steve. How can I help you, ma'am?" He extended his right hand to me.

I almost laughed in this dude's face. He'd called me ma'am—he had to be fucking kidding me. There was no way I looked that old, shit. Instead of blasting his short, shiny baldhead ass, I played it cool. Luckily, for him I was on a different mission.

"Hi, Steve. I wanted to take a look at a couple of your toys today." I referred to the cars on the lot. And boy, were they bad. I'm talking about Audis, Range Rovers, Mercedes Maybach, you name it I was in car heaven. Clicking my heels is what I felt like doing.

"Sure, that would be my pleasure. Did you have any one in particular in mind?"

That was the wrong question to ask me. My eyes were roaming the lot like I was in a candy shop. All of them were what I had in mind, really, but I named one. "How about a Mercedes?"

"Follow me. I have the perfect one on the showroom floor."

Inside, the showroom floor's new-car smell sucked me up, overwhelmed me even. The building itself was so luxurious I could have driven it around. And the car, as we approached it, sang love songs to me. Suddenly, I craved a Mercedes. The car was to die for—it was a silver two-door E550-Class Coupe. Its leather interior greeted me with open arms. The reason for me being there was easily forgotten, but as I climbed out of the car, I came face-to-face with Caesar himself.

"Yazz, right?" he asked me, as if he were not sure. First off, I knew his ass was playing a game because the look on his face told me he knew exactly who I was. But I played along.

"Yes," I managed, then looked at Steve, the car salesman, who seemed to be staring at us both. Steve's presence played well in my court. I used it to make it seem as if I was not interested in talking to Caesar. "So, Steve, what's the asking price for this one?"

"About sixty-five thousand. And as you can see, it's worth every dime." He gently rubbed his hand across the hood.

"Indeed, it's cool. I'm sure a beautiful lady could enjoy it," Caesar spoke up, and his slick flirting didn't go unnoticed. "Are you gon' cop this today?" he asked me.

"Maybe." My response was short on purpose.

Someone came over the pager system and called Steve, catching us all off guard. He excused himself with the promise of returning.

"Do you think this car might be too fast for you?"

"No, this I could handle." I softly rubbed the roof of the car like it was precious to me. The connection to the car was not a part of my plan. I sincerely loved it.

"Well, you should have Kevon pick this up for you. I think it fits you."

"Maybe I will."

"All right, I think we have everything ready to go." The salesman Caesar had been working with approached him.

"Okay, I'll be right over." Caesar turned his attention back to me. "It was nice running into you here, Yazz. Maybe I'll see you again sometime."

"St. Louis is small," was my reply. I felt stupid for saying that. I sounded like a stalker. Kevon was going to be disappointed in me. Making replies like that, I had probably blown it. It seemed every word that came out of my mouth was wrong.

Before he walked away, Caesar turned to me. "By the way, you look nice today." He smiled. And boom, there it was. I had him after all. Next, I had to get out of there before Steve came back to hassle me about buying that damn car. As much as it would please me to have it, I knew that was not the reason for this trip. So I was out.

As soon as the door to my BMW was closed, I dialed Kevon's number. "What's up, babe?" Kevon answered on the second ring. "How'd it go?" It was obvious from his voice that he was anxious.

"I think it went good. The only change was he noticed me first. I was looking at this Mercedes, then out of nowhere he appeared. He approached me with small talk about the car, but then he had to go because he had to finish up his paperwork. He did, however, comment on how good I looked before he walked away. All in all, I think it was a win." At least I was pretty sure it was.

"A'ight, that sounds good." He seemed satisfied. "Check this out though—I need you to get ready for a party at Caesar's crib tonight. You gotta be on your bad-chick shit because we about to kick this into overdrive. Shit about to get real and quick. But you got this, so don't worry. Plus, I got your back one hundred grand, a'ight. So let's get it."

"I'm ready, babe. I'm going home to take a good hot bubble bath, and I'll see you tonight."

"Cool, I'll be to the crib after I make a few more pickups." With that, he hung up. I was all in now— the nervousness was a distant memory. There was no turning back. Increasing the volume on my car radio, I drove to the house in relaxation mode, no distractions. Just me and Keyshia Cole's "Love."

CHAPTER 9

Arriving at Caesar's house was a breathtaking moment. It was nothing short of a mansion. He lived in Region Estates, a nice gated community. The three-story, six-car garage looked like something off the show *Cribs*. Any celebrity could live right next door. Stepping inside, onto his flawless marble floors, left me feeling anxious. I fought hard not to *ooh* and *ahh* at all the beautiful things that I had never seen up close and personal in all my life. I calmly walked beside Kevon as if I were used to this style of the drug-dealing wealthy.

Stepping out by the pool where the party was being held, I was floored by the beauty. The massive yard didn't have only one pool; it had two. It resembled an island. Off to the side was a huge hot tub that was bubbling, waiting to be taken advantage of. Never once had I experienced a hot tub, but it looked so comfortable. At this point, stripping and stepping inside didn't seem like such a bad idea. I shook the thought away and held on to Kevon's elbow as a waiter approached us with some drinks. Reaching a little too quickly, I grabbed one.

"Nervous?" Kevon eyed me and grinned.

Gulping down the whole glass, I lied, "No." As I handed him my glass, my eyes searched for the next waiter. "I am thirsty though."

Signaling a waitress who was walking close by, Kevon set the empty glass I had given him on the tray before retrieving a new one. "Yazz, there is no need for you to be nervous. I'm here for you." Passing me the wineglass, he seemed so confident.

"I know, and I got this." I smiled with confidence. I wanted him to believe in me.

"Well, I gotta go inside for a minute to handle a few things. Just be cool. Remember you the baddest chick here. And lookin' hella sexy."

Winking at Kevon, I grinned at his compliment. That, he was not lying about; my face was beat, courtesy of Macy's. Not to mention, my outfit was on point. The Bailey 44 cutout stretch dress I had copped fit me like a glove, and my pink Jimmy Choo suede pumps were killing the shoe game. Nothing about me said lacking, and with all the eye action I was receiving, it was a fact.

Deciding to mingle with the crowd, I sipped and walked slowly. A slight touch on my shoulder caught my attention.

"What's up with your girl?" Soulja boldly asked.

"Hmmm, I guess saying hi or hello would be a stretch?" I was sarcastic on purpose.

"Oh my bad." He smiled. "Hi, how are you?"

"I'm just messing with you." I laughed. "But Mimi, she's cool."

"Really, well, I think she got her number changed to avoid me."

"Avoid you?" I smirked. He couldn't possibly be for real. "No, I doubt that," was my reply. If he only knew how Devin, Mimi's ex-boyfriend, had busted up her phone because of him. Devin had gotten pissed when he'd seen Soulja's name light up on her phone back to back. Even though he played the part of being over Mimi, jealousy had taken over. However, none of this was my business to tell Soulja.

"Yo, my man, are you tryin' to step to my girl?" Kevon joked as he approached us.

"Nah. But her girl would be good though." Soulja laughed as they locked hands in a gangster handshake.

"That's what's up. They be playin' hard to get." Kevon smiled in my direction.

"Whateva," I replied, playfully rolling my eyes.

"I'ma catch her though. Then she'll be mine." Soulja kept his confidence. "I'ma get up with y'all later though," he excused himself before disappearing in the crowd.

"Look, it's game time. Get ready to bait your hook. Go inside through the kitchen, then out into the hallway facing north. Walk past the first two sets of doors, then walk through the den. That will take you over to another hallway. Take your first right, which will be Caesar's office. Play it cool, as if you were going to the bathroom."

Taking in all the information, I stored it into my brain.

"I got it." I smiled with reassurance. Rubbing my hand over my front torso as if to smooth out my already fitted dress, I was ready.

Once inside, I followed Kevon's instructions to a T. As soon as Caesar's office was in view, I froze. The game was on. Slowly, and seductively, I walked past Caesar's office, pretending to be lost, yet on a mission. I was almost out of his doorway and in the clear when he called out my name.

"Yazz." His voice was low, just above a whisper.

My footsteps came to a halt. Facing him, I spoke. "Hey."

"So you came to my party. Are you enjoying yourself?"

"Yeah, it's nice."

"Would you like to see my office?"

"Actually, I was on my way . . ."

He cut me off as I pretended to hesitate. "It'll only take a minute," he encouraged me.

Putting one foot in front of the other I almost kicked myself at how easy this was.

"So did you get your new whip today?"

"No, not yet." I walked around his office as if I was interested in his things. But honestly they were nice. There was an Armani clock hanging on the wall. Now that was some rich-nigga shit.

"Well, you should, because you deserve it." Even though my back was to him, there was this feeling his eyes were all over me.

"Now that I don't deny, but money don't ex-actly grow on trees." Why I said that, I had no idea. The last thing I wanted to do was make it seem like Kevon could not afford it. Because he could.

But Caesar didn't seem to judge my words.

"You got a point," he responded. There was silence for a minute as I continued to browse. "So what's up with you and my man Kevon?"

That question caught me off guard. Was he blind? The answer to that should have been clear, or at least I'd thought so.

It was obvious this needed to be played differently. "What do you mean? Or better yet, why?" I gave him a slight attitude as if I was offended.

"A'ight, ma." His tone was apologetic. "I like that."

"What is it you like?"

"Your spunk. You don't take no shit."

"That would be true." I played along. "As for Kevon, you look smart, so you know the deal."

"No doubt." Things got quiet again. I started to move closer to the door, as if I were leaving.

"If you don't mind, I want to be cool wit you too." *Bingo*. He had finally said it. I subtly took in a deep breath.

Without facing him, I asked, "What is it you want from me?" Just like that, I had flipped it. Caesar was no longer the pawn in our game. I was the pawn in his.

"Conversation." He was blunt, very matter of fact.

"And Kevon?" I asked.

"What about him? Besides, you need more. I knew that the first time we met." Damn, he was bold. That was a fuck-Kevon statement if I had ever heard one. "But don't stress. It'll be our secret." He'd only said that so that I would feel comfortable.

Playing it cool, I walked over to the wall closest

to the exit to admire a painting. "What is this paint-ing?" I played interested.

"This?" He pointed to the painting. "Well, I would tell you, but I have no idea. My sister loves art. She bought that painting as a housewarming gift on one of her trips to Europe."

"Well, it's interesting." I turned to face him. "Yep, just like life." Without another word, and bearing only a smile, I exited his office. Shit had just gotten real. I was officially Caesar's new side chick.

"Girl, I'm telling you he thinks you changed your number to avoid him. Dude was trippin' me out."

Mimi laughed listening to my story about Soulja and his ridiculous assumption of why she had a dif-ferent number. We were at her crib, chilling and chatting about the party. "That shit is crazy. We had a few conversations, but . . . I think he's like a player or something though. Like I told you be-fore, he probably got a bunch of bitches, and you know I ain't got time for the drama. That shit is for the birds."

"You might be right, maybe you don't need to hook up with him. 'Cause you can get crazy, and the last thing I want to see is you in jail for slicing some female."

"Right," Mimi cosigned. "Because you know for me to check a bitch is not a problem." Mimi was not to be played with. She could be as sweet as pie one minute, and pulling your tracks out the next. "He is fine though."

"He is, and he was lookin' good last night. You should have been there."

"You know I woulda been there, but there was money to be made. The Cheetah was on fire. Those niggas were spendin' mad money. And you know I wasn't about to miss that."

"So we are shopping tomorrow right?" My cell phone started to ring before she could answer. The number on the caller ID was not recognizable, but I decided not to ignore it.

"Hello." I sounded annoyed on purpose. Unknown and private numbers bugged me.

"Hi, I need to speak with Yazz?" The voice was not familiar, and he only used my first name.

"This is Yazz."

"Hi, Yazz, this is Steve."

Whoever this Steve was, he said his name as if I knew him. "Who?"

"Steve," he repeated his name. "We met yesterday down at the dealership."

I could not believe it. How and where in the world had he gotten my number? The surprise must have been apparent on my face because Mimi was gawking at me. Since she knew nothing about the dealership, I played it cool.

"Oh, hi." But now I was confused. Why was he calling me?

"Yazz, would you be able to come by the dealership today? Yesterday you left without saying goodbye." This was why I'd had to sneak away, because clearly he was a bugaboo. My leaving should have summed it up. I wasn't buying. Mimi had started to put on makeup while I was on the phone.

Silence took over me for a minute. There were

several things running through my mind. Like, most importantly, why was he asking me to come down to the dealership? And I would have asked him that, but Mimi was only inches away from me so she couldn't help but hear.

"Okay, cool. I'll be there." That was the best way to end the call.

"Who was that?" Mimi was concerned.

"Girl, nobody important. Just a reminder that I need to pick up a prescription from the pharmacy. You know my memory sucks."

"Oh." Mimi folded up the clothes that laid across the couch.

"But look, I'ma need to get outta here. I'll call you later." Not wasting any time, I grabbed my Coach bag and was outta there.

The redheaded girl sitting at the front desk that was labeled CUSTOMER SERVICE alerted Steve to my arrival. Grinning from ear to ear, he appeared. If he thought he could convince me to buy that car, he was in for a rude awakening. There was no way I could afford it on my own. And Kevon had just purchased the BMW for me. So there was no way I was asking him. And since I didn't have all day, I decided to cut straight to the chase. "Look, Steve, I skipped out on you the other day because I couldn't afford that car. And the same is true today." I wanted to be clear.

"Well, you don't need to worry about that be-cause the car has been paid for." He continued to showcase that silly grin. I wondered if I was going deaf because there was no way the car belonged to me. Unless Kevon was trying to surprise me again. But why would he do that? There had to be some type of mix-up.

"There must be some mistake. You need to recheck your paperwork, Steve."

"Yazz, this car belongs to you, and you need to take it because I can't store it here. This is a dealership, not a garage." This time, he was serious. "Now all you need to do is sign all the paperwork that makes it official." At the present moment, I was completely confused.

"Who paid for this?"

"I can't disclose that." Steve tried to sound professional. Containing my laugh was hard. I felt as if I would choke. "Are you ready to get your new keys and drive it right off the showroom floor?" I was not crazy. He was trying to change the subject, but it would not be that easy.

Reverse psychology was my next move. "Listen, I totally understand you not being able to tell me. But if you don't tell me, those papers will not get signed. Which means the sale is not official." I pretended to walk away. That car was Steve's commission. There was no way he would let me walk away. If only he knew my threat was idle and full of shit, because I wanted that car just as much as he wanted that commission.

"All right, all right. Caesar bought it for you this morning. He showed up and took care of the financial part. All you have to do is sign your name and it belongs to you."

"Caesar." I said his name, a surprised look on my face. That sealed it. I signed the papers, then jumped in my new Mercedes and skidded out of the dealership. Steve followed behind me in my BMW. The dealership shuttle would be picking him up. I could not believe that Caesar had bought me the car without me even asking.

"You will not believe what just happened." I was so excited I could barely talk when Kevon said hello.

"Try me."

"I got this call from the salesman, Steve, who showed me a car yesterday. He asked me to come back down to the dealership. I almost didn't go because I thought he was just going to try and convince me to buy the car. But it turns out Caesar had already bought and paid for it. All I had to do was sign the paperwork, and as we speak I'm in my new Mercedes."

"Damn, baby, what you say to that nigga last night?" Kevon joked on the other end of the phone.

"Shut up." I smiled. "I only did what you instructed."

"Real talk though. Now we know we got him. The nigga buying Mercedes n' shit after one conversation. *Shiiit*, this might be easier than I thought. From now on, you come with nothin' but that game," he schooled me.

"I gotcha. Should I call him and thank him for the car?"

"Nah, don't worry. He just dropped a bunch of stacks for the whip. Trust me, he will be callin' you any minute. Just be ready."

"Trust I will. What are you doing later? Maybe we should have dinner."

"That's cool—just text me where you want to go. I'm about to make a move. I'll see you later."

As soon as Kevon and I ended our call, my cell rang. It was another unknown number. Since I was in a good mood, I did not hesitate to answer.

"Are you enjoying your new toy?" Caesar's voice was familiar right away. I wondered if Kevon had a Caesar tracker on him because Caesar had called just like he'd predicted.

"Yes, I am. Thank you."

"No need to thank me. That was nothin'. You just enjoy it."

"Trust me, I already am." And I meant that. If I had somewhere to go, I would have jumped straight on the highway.

"So you got some free time." There it was, the job I was expected to do. Caesar was fine and all, but Kevon was my man. This would feel odd no matter what.

"Sure. What's up?"

"Meet me tonight at my condo downtown about eight. I'll text you the address."

"I'll see you then." I ended the call right away I could not believe he had a condo downtown. Wasn't that mansion big enough? But I guess when you're the kingpin of the city, you live like a boss. But none of that was my business. I dialed Kevon's number again to tell him that our dinner plans were canceled. Boyfriend number two had me tied up.

CHAPTER 10

The GPS on the new Mercedes that Caesar had copped for me confirmed that my destination had been reached. Checking my makeup one last time and telling myself over and over that I was not nervous, I made my way up to the door and rang the doorbell. Caesar opened the door and did not try to hide his delight to see me. His eyes ate me up from head to toe. I'm sure the sleeveless bandage dress that was hugging my body was to blame. "Wow," glided off his tongue. "You . . . you made it," he stuttered. Did I look that damn good? I had to drop my head to keep from smiling. "Thought you had stood me up."

I would have been on time, but Kevon was so anal about me being on point with everything that his coaching had made me late. Too bad this bit of information was confidential. Right?

"I'm just running behind—traffic on the freeway into downtown was a mess," I lied. It was past five o'clock so rush-hour traffic was long over, but it was the best excuse I had. He could take it or leave it. "Are you going to invite me in?"

Again, I got that Omar Epps feeling when I looked at him. Whether I wanted to admit it or not, the brother was as attractive as they come. There had to be bitches knocking down his door. Either way, I enjoyed watching him drool all over me.

"My bad. Come on in." He stepped to the side, allowing me full access.

Full of confidence, I stepped inside. I didn't know what to expect, but I told myself I was pretty much ready for anything. No, I believed it. I had to.

"You have a nice place here," was my empty comment. "Do you have an interior decorator or something?"

"Nah, just threw some shit together myself. I don't like strange ass people snooping through my things. You know how it is. But I'm glad you like it. Would you like to take a look around?"

"Sure, you can give me the grand tour."

Thirty minutes later, he had shown me every inch of his condo, and just like his mansion, it was nice. Caesar's personal chef, Leon, brought us both a glass of Moscato to sip on. I finished my first glass in two swallows. I wasn't really nervous, but the more confidence I had, the better.

"You okay?" Caesar asked. He watched me polish off the wine like I had not drunk anything in days.

"I'm fine." I smirked. "Just thirsty."

"Dinner is ready to be served," Leon announced.

"You bring your appetite with you? 'Cause my man makes a juicy steak."

"I could eat." Preparing for the date, there had been no time for eating or snacking so I was hungry for real.

The dinner table was set when we entered the dining room. Leon had prepared T-bone steaks, salad, asparagus, and baked potato. My mouth watered as I took it all in. With no shame, I dug in. Cute was going to have to take a backseat to my silently growling stomach.

"So where you from?" Caesar asked as he watched me devour my meal. I actually wished he would eat instead of watching me, but I was too hungry to let that distract me.

Wiping my mouth with my napkin, I replied, "I'm from here, born and raised right over on McLaran Street."

"Okay, I grew up a couple of blocks from there. . . ." Pausing, he took a bite of his steak while I went in on my baked potato. "You got any kids?"

The fuck he say? Shocked, I almost gagged on my food. This nigga was tripping.

"Do I look like I got any kids?" I snapped my neck in his direction, and my attitude was for real.

"Wait. I'm sorry. I didn't mean it like that."

The look on his face was sincere, but not even that could keep me from rolling my eyes. "No, I don't have any kids. But just so you know, it's rude to ask that shit on the first date." What could I say, my life situation had made me defensive and I would not apologize for that.

"Aye, I'm sorry."

His apology was not accepted yet. "You got any kids?" I shot back since he wanted to be so personal on the first date.

"Actually, no, I don't. But I love kids."

"Hmmm," was my stiff reply. This was not getting off to a good start. The last thing he needed to witness was how much of a bitch I could be when pushed. Ruthie could be thanked for that side of me. "Look, it's cool."

Chewing, he nodded in agreement. "No worries. So what do you like to do for fun?"

"That's easy. Shopping, it's my absolute favorite thing to do. It's safe to say I'm hooked on clothes. My dream would be to own a clothing store one day." I rarely shared this kind of information. It had to be the alcohol.

"That's what's up. You want to be like a stylist or something?"

"Not really a stylist. Selling them is what I had in mind, but being able to design them would be a bonus." Usually, when clothes crossed my mind, it was me dressed up in them. Not other people. But I did enjoy putting certain things together or wishing they were designed a certain way. But other than that, I didn't give it much thought. Besides, Ruthie only wanted me to get a quick job to help with bills. Dreams, she didn't have time for.

"Enough about me. What about you?"

"Me? I don't know." He seemed in deep thought. "Having a strong empire and loyalty. To me, that's survival, always has been."

His answer made me curious, especially knowing he was supposed to be anything but loyal. This conversation was starting to be a bit much. I needed more to drink. After dinner, we retired into this room that he called "the man's den." It had like a seventy-inch television on the wall, with a huge, real-leather sectional. *Comfortable* would not be a good enough word to describe it. Caesar turned on the television, and we both decided on the movie *The Long Kiss Goodnight*. I loved that movie. Time flew by because, before long, the movie had gone off and we were still talking. Realizing it was getting late, I decided it was time for me to leave. Caesar walked me outside to my car. Without notice, he leaned in and very gently kissed me on the forehead, then both of my cheeks. Next, I thought he would kiss me on the lips, but instead he said goodnight.

On the ride home, I felt a bit confused. Caesar just didn't seem like the guy I'd imagined he would be. His reputation in the streets was monstrous at best, and he didn't take no shit. But not only was he fine as hell, he was gentle. Kevon had told me the real from the start so I expected the real, but had received anything but.

My ringing cell phone interrupted my thoughts.

"Hello."

"Where the hell you at? I called you four times. Tell Kevon to let you ass up for some air, at least for a few minutes," Mimi babbled, a mile a minute.

"Shut up." I giggled at her assumptions. "I was watching a movie and dozed off earlier," I lied. "What's so urgent that you been blowing me up? Ain't you at the Cheetah?"

"Hell no, I'm just gettin' off. Sheila just picked me up. We on our way to the crib. Girl, the club was on point tonight. Money was in the air thick, got them racks on racks." Her excitement was obvious.

"That's what's up."

"I just broke Sheila off eight bills, and I'm still stacked up. So I'm straight. Now I'm ready to shop, and you know I got that date with Soulja. So what's up?"

I had been so busy with the whole Caesar situation, I had forgotten that Mimi had accepted a date with Soulja. "Cool, we gon' hit up the stores. You know I'm always down with shopping. And we gotta get you laced for your date. So I'll hit you tomorrow."

"A'ight, bet." She hung up, ending the call.

The bright sun shining through the window woke me up. My eyes and body felt heavy. Turning over on my back, I realized Kevon was still in bed beside me, asleep. Lifting myself up on my left elbow, I grabbed my cell phone off the nightstand. One o'clock—I could not believe I had slept for so long. Scrolling through my contacts, I texted Mimi that I would pick her up in about two hours. Throwing the covers back and grabbing my robe, the bathroom became my destination. After a long, hot shower, I got dressed.

As I was reaching in the top of the closet for my brown leather Coach bag, Kevon wrapped his arms around my waist.

"So you decided to wake up?"

"Yeah, my body said it was time to get up. Besides, once you get out of the bed, I can't sleep. The warmth of your body gives me comfort."

"Really?" I beamed. "Well, kissing you on the

lips gives me comfort." Slowly turning to face him, I kissed him softly on the lips.

"So how'd it go last night?"

"I'm not telling you. If you had come home before I went to sleep, you would know," I teased him.

"Sorry, babe. I was busy as hell. Niggas was actin' crazy last night. Lil Pete got hit—shit was just ridiculous," he explained.

"It's cool. I was tired anyway. But everything went fine. We had dinner, watched a movie, and talked."

"What y'all talk about?"

"Just random things. All in all, I think it went really well." I hope this was enough for him. The last thing I wanted to do was go into full details.

"A'ight." He was content. "Sounds like everything's on track."

"Yes, I would say so. He wants to see me tonight. He called last night when I made it home," I informed him.

"Damn, already? I can't believe he's calling this quick. But a'ight, cool, I want you to be ready. Pick up some lingerie while you're out."

"Hmmm, you ready to see me in something different." I grinned while rubbing each of his cheeks with my hands.

The smile he was wearing on his face faded. "Not for me. Take it with you when you go to Caesar's tonight."

"What?" I shook my head. "Why?" was my follow-up question while searching his eyes for answers. But instead all I found was a dumb look and a closed mouth. I backed up from him. "I can't do that, Kevon. I don't want to fuck him," I yelled. "Is that what you think of me?" Again, I searched his eyes for answers but found none. Hot tears escaped my eyes, instantly covering my face. My vision became blurred so I couldn't see him approaching me.

I felt soft kisses on my lips. "Yazz, this is business. You have to follow through. I already know it won't mean nothing to you." He was crazy if he thought that would make me feel better.

"So are you saying that you will turn me into a ho so that you can conquer the world?" My throat felt tight and dry, as if my airways were closing. Had I not been standing up, I would have thought an elephant was standing on my chest.

"Absolutely not, but I will sacrifice to give you the world on a platter. You deserve that. And one day I'm going to make it official. I love you, Yazz." Brushing his hands across my cheeks, he wiped the tears away.

Taking a step back from his grasp, I reached for my Michael Kors bag instead of the Coach and left. The drive to Mimi's house and Macy's was a blur. I couldn't even feel my heartbeat. I tried hard not to tip Mimi off that I was upset. The smile on my face was painted on.

"Tonight, it is going to go down. I must look good. When Soulja sees me, I'm going to be the only thing on his mind."

"I know, right? 'Cause she bad," I joked, referring to her in the third person. I really was happy for her. "So what you gon' do about Devin?"

"Girl, he better go somewhere. We been broke up and that's it. I told him the next time he tries to break something that belongs to me, I'm gon' fuck him up, then call the police."

"At least that's all cleared up." I laughed.

"Shit, it better be. But tonight all I'm tryna see is Soulja wit his fine ass. He better not disappoint me neither. Or his ass will be ex'd." And she was not playing. The one thing Mimi did not give in relationships were second chances. When she was done, she was done. "I think everything is going to be all good though. At least I'm keeping my fingers crossed anyway. Because, like I said before, I need me a man like Kevon."

"And what kind of man is that?" I was curious to know.

"You know, a man that's down for his chick. Girl, you are lucky." She looked at me as if she wanted me to agree. "Yo, what's up? There you go with that look again."

"Look? What look?" I played dumb. "There is nothin' the matter with me." I forced a smile.

"No, try something different. Because that's exactly what you said the last time."

I sighed because I knew I had to tell her something to stop her from prying. "It's Ruthie." I hunched my shoulders. Shit was what I felt like for continuing to lie to my best friend. It was the one thing I hated to do, but what other choice was there?

"Ruthie? She still got you stressin'?" Mimi questioned.

"Yeah, she's been on my mind a lot lately. I'm not sure why, but I can't seem to shake her."

"Yazz, you have to let this go. Everything between you and her is not on you. She is the one that has lost out on a great daughter. Hopefully, one day she comes around and realizes that. And if she doesn't, just know that you have people who love you."

"That lady," I jawed, referring to Ruthie. "No, she won't be coming around. At least I won't count on it or hold my fucking breath." The memory of Ruthie as she'd shared her vow, that she could not see herself ever changing her feelings for me, filled my head. At that moment, I realized again that Kevon was my only home. The only real home that had doors and windows, and real love inside, that I had ever had in my life.

CHAPTER 11

Seven months had passed so fast that I had lost track, but things were going great. Happy was the new me. I had nothing to complain about. In my eyes, the sun shined every day, even when it rained. I couldn't remember the last time I'd seen a grey sky. Hanging out with Caesar had turned out to be easy, fun, and prosperous. The guy gave me everything a girl could want. He made sure I didn't want or wish for much of anything. And even though it was wrong, I loved it.

Kevon, on the other hand, lately seemed to be getting a little jealous of Caesar and all the things he did for me. But, unfortunately, it was nothing that could be done about that. There was no way I could stop accepting Caesar's gifts. The last thing we wanted to do was make him suspicious about anything. So Kevon had to get over it. Besides, I reminded him, this whole thing had been his idea.

However, it was dragging on longer than I'd initially thought, but according to Kevon, these things took time. And either way I was happy.

But lately Kevon had been saying it would be over soon and that I should prepare to be first lady of the city. Honestly, I didn't understand what all that meant, but I guessed it would be a cool role. As for Caesar, we spent so much time together that I was used to him. I was becoming very familiar with his habits. He had actually turned out to be a good dude.

"Some shit came up so I'ma be outta town for a few days on business," Kevon informed me. We were at Red Lobster having lunch and drinks. "Plus I gotta put a few things in place so we can wrap all this shit up with Caesar. It's been long enough."

"That's cool." I was more interested in the hot garlic biscuits the waitress had put on the table. This was the third basket the waitress had brought to the table, but between Kevon and me, they were going fast.

"Be ready to start looking for a bigger house."

That got my attention, "Really, babe?" I was excited.

"Yep."

"My very own house? Where? I mean, how big and what's the price range?" I wanted to know. I didn't know much about buying a house, but I knew I would need a Realtor.

"It's whatever you want so just think about it."

"Thank you, thank you, thank you, baby," I chanted. Between Caesar and his shopping sprees and Kevon, I was being treated like a queen, and I had outgrown the closet space Kevon had given me in his bedroom and spare room months ago. A huge walk-in closet that I could turn flips in was definitely on my house-shopping wish list. I could not wait.

Mimi's name lit up on my cell phone. "One second, I need to get this." I held up a finger like we were in church so Kevon could excuse me. "What's up, Mimi?"

"Are you coming?"

"Yeah, I'm on my way. I'm having lunch with Kevon. I'll be there in about twenty minutes."

"Hurry up." She hung up before I could say another word.

"Sounds like your girl ain't happy." He had heard her through the phone.

"Nope, she's not." I grinned. "We were supposed to be meeting up to look at baby beds. And I swear, ever since she got pregnant, she's been impatient, so I better hurry up."

"A'ight, well, I'll see you later before I hit the highway."

"Okay. I'll be done in a couple hours." Leaning across the table, meeting each other halfway, we kissed.

Walking inside the Babies "R" Us that was located on the top level of the mall, I found Mimi with her huge belly sitting down in a rocking chair in the section close to the baby cribs. "You need to get your big ass up," I joked.

"Whatever, bitch. My feet are swollen, and you got me waiting on your diva ass."

Looking at my friend, the only thing I could do was smile. I could not believe she was almost due to have her first baby. Being a godmother was going to be great. I had already purchased bags and bags of shit.

"Come on, big momma." I reached out to help Mimi stand up with her round basketball belly sticking out.

"Look at this one over here. This is kind of what I'm looking for." She led the way.

"Yes, this is nice. You should get it." The all-white Larkin fixed crib was beautiful. "Now you just need to pick the bedding."

"That's what I was thinking. Yazz, I can't believe Soulja and I are about to have a baby together." She blushed.

"Me neither, and she's going to be beautiful." Mimi's ultrasound had revealed a huge baby girl weeks ago. "How is Sheila lately? Is she finally coming around?"

"She's okay with it, I guess, but she is still disappointed and I understand why. She wanted things to be different for me—not always having to struggle to get by the way she has to. But I assured her that she doesn't need to worry about that though. Soulja loves me and this baby. He's got my back."

"He does." I agreed with her on that. "If he tries anything different, I'll kick his ass." I felt bad for Sheila. She was such a good mother to her kids, but with no real education, it was difficult for her to find a good-paying job. So, to make ends meet, she had to work two jobs, which meant she was hardly ever home. I hoped that seeing Soulja take care of Mimi and the baby might help to ease her mind. "Let's go cash out on the bed, and I'm paying. It's my treat."

"Nope, Soulja is paying for this bed. He gave me two thousand dollars just to do it."

"Well, you keep that in your stash because I'm paying for this bed. Like I said, it's my treat. And don't argue with me."

"Why you so damn stubborn?" Mimi smiled.

"You got the nerve to be callin' me stubborn? You gotta be kiddin' me." I grabbed the tag off the bed and headed toward the checkout counter.

After leaving the store, we walked right past the food court. "I swear all that food smells so good." Mimi rubbed her round belly. "If Soulja wasn't waitin' on me, I would sit down on my fat ass and stuff my face."

"Girl, you better feed that baby if you're hungry. You could grab you some pretzel sticks, or something that you can take with you."

"Damn, Yazz, that's a good idea, because pregnant people need to keep food on deck," she agreed. I followed Mimi as she headed toward the Auntie Anne's pretzel booth. A glimpse of Kevon's ex caused me to do a double take.

Mimi must have seen her at the same time because she glanced at me. "Ain't that Misti?"

"Either that or she has an identical twin," was my reply.

"Damn, where that bitch been at? I ain't seen her in . . . well, I guess since you been talkin' to Kevon."

"Me either. It's like she dropped off the face of the earth."

"They asses used to be everywhere together, remember?" Mimi seemed to have forgotten all about the food for the moment.

"Yep," I agreed.

"Shit, I thought the bitch had jumped off a building or something." Mimi laughed.

After Mimi ordered her pretzel sticks, we left the mall in our separate cars. Yeah, Mimi had her own car now. No more begging Sheila to drive her beat-up van. Soulja had wasted no time picking her up an Audi, and she loved it. On my drive home, Misti crossed my mind. Kevon and I had been dating for about nine months, and not once had I laid eyes on her. Strange.

CHAPTER 12

Two more months passed by, and our plan for Caesar was still building. But Kevon kept reassuring me that it would be soon. He also kept reassuring me that I would have my new home soon. Either way, I was good. I had more important things to be happy about. Mimi had given birth to a healthy seven-pound, two-ounce beautiful baby girl that she and Soulja named Alijah. And she was so precious; I spent almost all of my free time at Mimi and Soulja's house, holding and spoiling her. Today was no different.

"Look, give her back to me." I reached for Alijah as Mimi sat rocking her to sleep. "You need to just sit back and relax. Trust, all new moms need help adjusting," I fussed over Mimi. She was determined to be the perfect mom.

"Adjust, my ass. You just want to keep holding

Alijah and spoiling her. Tonight, when she wakes up, I'm gon' jump in the car and drop her off at your house." Mimi stood up and gently positioned Alijah in the crease of my waiting arms.

"Aww, you go right ahead. I'll snap right out of my sleep. She's my love." I snuggled Alijah up to me tighter. I couldn't have been more in love with her if she had been my own. "Look, at this cute button nose. I just want to bite it off." She was just the cutest. I couldn't stop doting over her.

"You bite my baby, I'ma bite you," Mimi joked as she went through Alijah's closet, moving things around. She just refused to sit still.

"Mimi, get out of that closet. You need to sit down and rest. You have only been out of the hospital for a week. The doctor told you with a C-section that you need to take it easy," I continued to fuss. Alijah had been a stubborn baby who refused to come out on her own so Mimi had had to have a Caesarean.

"Damn, Yazz, I can't sit down all day. Calm down." She picked up a shoe box. "Would you look at all these Jordans Soulja done bought? In a minute, we gon' need another closet for her."

"She deserves it. And while you in that closet you may as well make room for all those bags." I pointed toward the four Macy's bags sitting on the floor. Before coming over, I had gone on yet another baby Alijah shopping spree.

"Yazz, come on, you have got to stop. There is no way she gonna be able to wear all this shit you guys are buying. She has too much already."

"Yes, she will. She's a princess. That means she

wears everything only once. Ain't that right, Alijah?" I softly tickled her nose, careful not to wake her. She was sleeping like an angel.

"I swear you never listen," Mimi accused me.

"I'm a godmother. I can't have limits. And you know I'm leaving tonight on this trip with Kevon so I'ma come back with more. So be prepared," I warned.

"You better not. What time does your flight leave?"

"In two hours, so I gotta get outta here."

"You better call me when you get there."

"I will, and I'll only be gone for a couple of days. But you call me if you need anything?"

"Don't say that. I will bug your ass until you get back on the plane headed home." Mimi laughed. As much as I hated letting go of baby Alijah, I had to get going. So, after kissing Alijah on the cheek and hugging Mimi, I was out.

On my way to the airport, I called Kevon several times but got no answer. We hadn't talked since earlier in the day. He had told me to call him before I got with Caesar to board the plane. Telling Mimi I was going with Kevon was a lie. Things had not changed; I still could not share my secret with her. Circling the packed airport parking lot, I finally found an empty space. As I turned off my engine, Kevon's name lit up on my phone.

"What's up?" I said, annoyed. "Why can't you answer your phone?"

"My bad, babe, I was busy."

"Yeah, but I called you twice, Kevon. You said you wanted to talk before I leave for Vegas. Now, I'm here at the airport and there ain't enough time to talk. I gotta get inside or I might miss my flight."

"I'm sorry about that, babe. Shit just crazy and I'm tryin' to maintain. But I want you to go and don't worry about anything. Just enjoy yourself. I love you."

"I love you too."

"A'ight, call me if you can. Bye." Just like that, he hung up the phone. Looking at my phone, I was feeling some type of way. Here I was, flying off to Vegas with another man, and I got the feeling Kevon could not be the least bit concerned. Deciding not to dwell on it, I got out of the car, grabbed my bags, and headed inside. I was really looking forward to the trip with Caesar—somehow I knew he would show me a good time. Caesar always seemed to care about our time together; lately I felt more as if I were in a relationship with Caesar than with Kevon. Maybe I was tripping though. Kevon was working hard to make things happen—he just needed my support. Shaking it off, I headed inside the airport, where I found Caesar, wearing a grin.

Vegas turned out to be a dream come true. I could have never imagined. Never before had I stepped foot out of St. Louis, so I hadn't had any idea what other parts of the world could be like. Caesar had acquired a fake ID for me so Vegas was wide open. And he spared no expense—we shopped, gambled, and partied. Caesar took only two bodyguards with us so we were not overcrowded with an entourage. Plus, they were the only two in the crew who knew about us.

When our last day in the city arrived, we started to pack our things.

"Don't forget to pack this." Caesar held a bag in his hand.

"What's that? I packed everything already." I continued to zip up my suitcase.

"Well, you must have forgot this." He handed me the bag and I realized it was from Saks. Opening it up I recognized a Saint Laurent tote that I had looked at while we were out shopping the day before. "When did you buy this? You do know it costs ten thousand dollars? *For a purse.*" That was the exact reason why I'd decided not to get it, because I'd thought ten thousand was too much to pay for a purse. Period.

"It's only money, Yazz." He grinned.

"Aww, thank you, Caesar." I hugged him tight. "You are so good to me." I almost cried because it was the truth. "How did you know I wanted this purse?"

"I'm pretty good at observing, and you eyed that particular one at least three times. That was enough for me. Yazz, you can have whateva you like if you don't know that by now. So get used to this." I wasn't sure what he meant, but that bag had me blushing and I could not stop.

CHAPTER 13

Arriving home from Vegas I was tired and craved a hot shower and the bed. It was around seven o'clock in the evening so I knew Kevon should have been out collecting on plays. But, to my surprise, he was home sitting on the living room couch.

"Hey, babe. I wasn't expecting you to be home."

"Why not? You've been gone four days and three long nights. Shit, I miss you." He stood up and made his way over to me.

"Aww, really? I'm glad to hear that." I dropped my suitcase and wrapped my arms around his neck. But, to be honest, I had been too busy to miss him while I was gone. Nevertheless, it was good seeing him.

"Why don't you come over and sit down? I'll put your things away for you."

"That sounds really good, babe. But I am so tired. All I really want is a shower and some sleep."

"Okay, well, let me take your things to the room."

"You got it. Go ahead and be my guest." I grinned while heading to my bedroom.

"So how was the trip?" Kevon asked as he put my suitcase on top of the bed.

"It was so much fun," I admitted while unzipping my suitcase. There were some new silk pajamas inside that I wanted to sleep in.

"So what did Caesar do while you were there? Did he have any meetings?"

"Actually, no, we spent every minute together."

"You mean he never left you alone?"

"Nope. Everywhere I went, he went. All we did was shop, gamble, and party. Babe, Vegas was so much fun. We gotta go together. Oh, and look at this purse Caesar bought me. This damn purse costs ten thousand dollars." I beamed as I admired my purse again. I was in complete love with it.

"Is that all you care about, that damn purse and designer shit? What the fuck, Yazz? Have you lost focus on what the goal is? This is not some fucking vacation, shopping-spree game. You must want to be with this nigga or some!" He snatched the purse from me and threw it. Dumbfounded could not have described how I felt. But this was not my fault. And watching my Saint Laurent bag fly across the room was the final straw.

"Fuck you, Kevon," I yelled. "You can kiss my natural black ass. I know this ain't a fucking game.

But all this shit was your idea. It was you who asked me to get close to him, then fuck him, all this to take his mind off the fact that I'm your fuckin' girl. Now you want to accuse me of wanting him and losing focus. Your ass must be crazy. This right here is some shit I don't need. I'm outta here."

Grabbing the keys to my Mercedes, I dashed out the house, then out of the driveway, so fast I almost hit a car that was passing by. Kevon snatched the front door open, yelling my name as I burned rubber, not sure if I would ever return.

As I drove around the city, my mind drifted back to Ruthie. I was trying so hard to remember some of the good times we had shared when I was little. Sadly, there were none, except maybe on a Christmas morning when she bought me toys. And I had to admit, she had always bought me good toys. Was that some form of love? God, how I wished I knew. Before I knew it, I was parked across the street from Ruthie's house. She must have been home because all the lights were on. Thinking about the last words she had said to me made me realize I had become her. The man who was supposed to love me had convinced me to sleep with another man for his own personal gain. The only difference was me being smart enough not to get pregnant and have an unwanted baby to blame.

Racking my brain trying to figure out how anybody could be so stupid, I drove to the Hilton and rented a room for two nights. Still craving that hot shower, I undressed and jumped right into the warm water. After a good scrub, I felt refreshed. I grabbed one of the robes provided by the hotel. As I crawled under the covers, the tears fell and soaked my pillow until sleep claimed me.

The first thing on my mind the next morning was clothes. I could not walk around naked or in the same clothes for two days. And going to Kevon's house to get clothes was not an option. Both Caesar's cribs had clothes that belonged to me, but I didn't want to run into anybody. Now was just not the time. So instead I threw on my old clothes and headed out to retrieve a few outfits. After I got dressed, Mimi's house was my first destination. On my way there, I finally turned my cell phone back on. There were twenty missed calls from Kevon with messages. Mimi had called as well.

As soon as she opened the door, she reached out and hugged me tight. "Where have you been? Are you okay?"

"I'm fine. I booked a room at the Hilton last night."

"Why didn't you come here?"

"I needed to be alone for a minute."

"What happened?"

"Kevon and I had an argument," I admitted.

"So that's what happened. He came by last night and has been calling this morning, looking for you. Was it that bad that you had to run off though, Yazz? It's not like you not to call me. Wait a minute—did that motherfucker hit you or something?" Mimi got fired up.

"No, he didn't hit me. He was just actin' crazy and being jealous of some guys that were on the trip. He tried to accuse me of giving one of them my number. I got tired of hearing it so I split," I lied, but some truth did follow. "I'm just going through a hard time right now. This may sound crazy, but I miss Ruthie." Tears fell freely down my face. "I know she has always been horrible to me, but something deep down in me still loves her." I cried like a baby. Was it wrong to crave your mother's love when she had been nothing but a bitch to you?

"It's okay, Yazz. All these feelings are normal." Mimi hugged me. "Maybe you should go visit her I know it sounds insane, but seeing her might help."

"No, I'm not ready for that yet." I sniffed. Mimi handed me a Kleenex and I blew my nose.

"Okay, well, when you are ready, I'll go with you if you like."

Everyone needed a friend like Mimi. She always had my back, no matter what. Without her, I may not even know what love is. Kevon's name lit up my phone. Pressing the IGNORE button was my response to him. But he called right back.

"Yazz, go ahead and answer," Mimi tried to encourage me.

"Fuck him." I rolled my eyes at the phone. He deserved to be ignored. If she only knew what was really going down. She would hate him.

"At least let him know that you are okay."

"Why should I?" I groaned. His name lit up again on my phone. He had some nerve to keep calling me. Punk ass.

"Go ahead and answer," Mimi pled. At that moment, I wanted to roll my eyes at her, but she looked so pitiful.

"Hello," I answered reluctantly, my attitude in tow. If he thought I would be nice or reasonable, he was wrong.

"Babe." Kevon's voice sounded shaky, like he had been crying.

I sighed loudly. "Yes, it's me, Kevon. Who else would answer my phone?"

"Yazz, babe, I know you are mad at me, but I am so sorry about every foul and fucked-up word that came outta my reckless-ass mouth. Please come home. I'll never, ever disrespect you again."

As much as I wanted to remain mad, he sounded so sincere. But I wasn't no fool. He would suffer some more.

"Right now I'm kinda busy, but if you're home later I may swing by. But I'm busy right now so I have to go." With that said, I ended the call before he could reply. That would leave him worrying about what I was doing while I decided what I wanted to do and when.

"What happened?" Mimi inquired.

"He apologized and begged for me to come home. What else?" I remarked snidely. That was what all guys did to get their way. I wasn't stupid.

"Awww, that's so sweet."

"Yeah, yeah, whateva. You know how it goes, but I'ma make his ass sweat a minute." I grinned. "You don't piss me off and expect for me to give in with one call and a tear."

"I feel you, and that, you learned from me." She laughed.

I hung out with Mimi for the rest of the day. We dropped Alijah off at Sheila's and went out for dinner and drinks. And since I was paid up at the Hilton for one more night, I stayed. Shit, I was no fool.

CHAPTER 14

The next morning, when I unlocked the door to the condo and walked in, I found Kevon sitting on the living room couch wide awake. It was clear he had waited up for me. One look at his red, swollen eyes, and I knew he hadn't slept a wink since I'd been gone. Maybe he really was sorry. Easing off the couch and making his way over to me, he apologized over and over. My original plan had been to play hard to get, but as he started to kiss me all over, I melted. His tender touches were more than I could resist. Right in the middle of the living room floor, he laid me down, then tasted me until I exploded all over him. Afterward, I was too exhausted to move so I lay there and drifted off to sleep.

Kevon didn't let me sleep for long though. He started to stroke my back softly. While I had not enjoyed the fight we'd had, the makeup was more than worth it. Turning over to face him, I climbed on top and rode him like he was a stallion.

The constant repeat of the Rick Ross song that was coming from Kevon's cell phone was annoying the hell out of me. Slowly opening my eyes, I realized we were still in the living room on the floor, where we had fallen asleep. This time of day, he was normally out handling business. So it was probably someone from Cash checking up on him. Either way, the ringing was disturbing my sleep.

"Babe." I shook him lightly. Sleeping well, he didn't budge. "Kevon!" I yelled his name this time.

He started to stir. "Hmmm?" He opened his eyes.

"Your phone keeps ringing."

He sat up slowly and crawled over to the couch. Picking up his iPhone, he gazed at the screen before answering. And, just like that, the streets were calling. Not long after hanging up, he informed me he had to leave because it was re-up time. After a quick shower, he was out. I was tired and hungry so, after also taking a hot shower, I ordered up some Chinese takeout and grabbed the remote to watch a movie and relax for the rest of the evening. After watching two good movies, I fell asleep. The next morning, I woke up feeling refreshed.

St. Louis was looking good outside when I pulled back the curtains. Rifling through my closet for something to wear, I found an outfit and got dressed. Starbucks was my first stop of the day. Coffee would give me life so that I could be on top of my game.

"Hello," I answered the phone after taking my fist sip of chocolate goodness. It was Caesar. He had been worried about me since he had not heard from me for a couple days. After I assured him that everything was cool, he invited me out to his crib in the country. And I was happy to go because, honestly, I enjoyed his company and the sex. Needless to say, I missed him. I tried hard to fight that truth, but it was becoming harder and harder. But this was something else that I had to keep to myself. It wasn't like I could share it with Mimi.

"Hey, sexy lady," Caesar greeted me when he opened the door. Towering over me, he reached down and gave me a big hug.

Grabbing his face, I tongued-kissed him long and hard. Like I said, it was part of the role that Kevon had me playing. But, shamefully, I enjoyed it.

"Damn, I guess you missed me too." He smiled after coming up for air.

"You guessed right." I looked him up and down, trying hard to fight the attraction, but he was lookin' fine as hell. I thought more and more of Kevon's accusations, and that he was right. But it was his fault for putting me in this situation.

Caesar softly grabbed both my hands. "Vegas wore you out, huh? My intentions were for you to enjoy yourself, not run off," he joked.

"I didn't run off." I laughed. "But I enjoyed myself so much a little rest was needed."

Leon interrupted so that he could serve us drinks. He handed me a margarita that he had prepared special for me. He was so used to me coming over that he had learned my drink of choice by heart.

"We should travel more. I would never get tired of that," I suggested, then sipped my drink.

"If that's what you want, then you got it." Caesar winked at me. "Let's go sit out by the pool." I followed as he led the way. Suddenly, he stopped walking and spun around, wearing a sexy smile. "Why don't you go to my room and change?"

Glancing down at myself, I confirmed that my look was indeed on fleek. So this was a surprise question. "Change?" I asked. "Is something wrong with what I have on?"

He smiled. "I'll be out by the pool when you're done."

That was not the answer I was looking for.

Sipping on my margarita again, I gave him the benefit of the doubt before heading off to his room. Minutes later, I opened the big doors to his room to find the cutest two-piece Louis Vuitton bathing suit I had ever laid eyes on. He was definitely learning my taste. It was probably the same bathing suit I would have picked myself. A few more sips of my margarita, and I was sliding into my bathing suit, feeling good.

Out by the pool, Caesar sat patiently, holding his glass of Hennessey, as I modeled the Louis Vuitton bathing suit around the pool.

"You like?" I strutted, spinning around so he could see every inch of me.

"You don't have any idea how much. Yazz, you are a dime, baby." His eyes glistened.

Giving him a huge grin, I dove into the pool.

He sat back and watched me dip and dive in the water like a fish. The water felt so good against my skin. Climbing out of the pool, I felt born again. Grubbing on steamed shrimp, chicken breast strips sautéed in teriyaki sauce, broccoli, and grilled fish, I was having a good time. Afterwards, I was full and ready to put on some pj's and relax.

Sitting on the couch, cuddled in Caesar's arms, I could feel sleep claiming me, but it was already like one o'clock in the morning. "I got a long drive so I'ma get going." I yawned as I tried to sit up, but Caesar held on tight.

I knew the words before he uttered them. "Why you gotta leave? I want you to spend the night." His soft lips brushed my neck, and it felt so good. *Shit. Fight it.* I almost screamed.

"You know I can't."

"Yes, you can. Just do it." Those lips brushed my neck again, and that was it. I had to have him.

"Okay, let me call Kevon. I'll tell him I'ma stay over at Mimi's house tonight to help with the baby. He'll understand. It should be cool." Cell phone in hand, I went outside for privacy. Inside my car, I dialed Kevon.

He answered on the fourth ring. "What's up, babe?"

"Nothin', just filling my obligations. Look, Caesar's asking me to stay over. And he really wants this to happen."

The line was quiet for a minute. Kevon sighed. "A'ight, just do it. We want to keep him happy, right? It's a part of the plan."

"Are you sure, babe? I just want you to be cool. It's whatever you need me to do."

"It's all good. We gon' take this shit for the team. I'll see you in the morning."

Ending the call, I headed back inside, ready for whateva. And true to it, Caesar gave me that and more. By morning, I was super sleepy and exhausted, but I knew Kevon would be waiting on me. Jumping in a hot bubble bath, I soaked all of my strained muscles, got dressed, kissed Caesar, and was out.

CHAPTER 15

"You drink coffee now?"

Gripping my Starbucks cup tightly to my chest, I stopped in mid step. Had she been any closer, I would have stepped directly on her feet. I tried to think fast, desperately seeking a clear exit, but there was no way to run. I was trapped.

"Can you step back, Ruthie?" I grunted.

"Do you have to be so rude? I am your mother, Yazz." That was a shocking statement. Never in my life had she referred to herself as that.

"So is that what you call yourself these days?" I sneered. "Move out of my way, Ruthie." I ordered her again, but she didn't budge. This time, I took a step around her.

"Yazz," she called.

I maneuvered my way around two people swiftly as they attempted to get to the counter in the Starbucks line. I wouldn't have stopped, but her voice sounded like a cry. Something else I was not used to hearing from Ruthie.

She was in my face in no time. "Can we chat for just a minute?"

Gazing around the room, I decided there were too many people inside and their eyes were watching us. I felt as if I were guilty of something. "Outside," I replied. In the parking lot, I faced her, waiting to hear what she had to say.

"How have you been?" She seemed nervous.

"Fine." I was annoyed by her presence. "What is it you want, Ruthie? I don't have all day."

"Oh, you in a hurry. . . ." She stalled. She stared at me as if I were an odd ornament on a Christmas tree. "It's been a while since you been home. I just wanted to know how you been." At first, I could not look at her, but the crazy shit that was coming out of her mouth was strange. If my memory served me right, she didn't want me in her home because, as she put it, I was "lame and trifling." Or had she forgotten?

"Ruthie, you need to make some sense. You didn't want me so I left. So what now? What is it you want?" My heart was heavy once again. She had me confused.

"Look, I know things ain't been the best, but that day at the house you just left without allowing me to finish."

"Allow you to finish? What else could you possibly have said?" Was she fucking kidding me?

"Trust me, there was more to be said. First off, you could have tried to understand instead of being a brat. Shit was not easy for me, raising you. I struggled to get by with no help from anyone."

There she was again, blaming me. "Well, Ruthie, it wasn't my fault. Even though, every day of my life, you made me feel like the mistake I was. So thanks to you, I understand. But my leaving gave you exactly what you had been praying for. Shouldn't you be somewhere happy? Not here bothering me. I gave you the freedom you wanted."

This scene was over for me. Nothing she said made any sense to me anymore. And I simply didn't need the already dramatic scene to get any worse. I walked away.

"That's right, Yazz. Just walk away. That's how you're supposed to handle problems. What? You think you too good to talk to me now?"

I stopped at my car, but could not get inside.

"Yeah, I see you dressed all fancy, in your name-brand clothes, driving nice new cars, and all. Now, you a big shot. Humph." She was sarcastic on purpose. I hated every word that she spat out.

Throwing my coffee to the ground, I jumped in her face, my fist balled, and it took everything in me not to strike her. The hurt and pain was real. All she wanted to do was mess with my head. Keep me unhappy, as she had already managed to do all my life.

"I have something now that you never gave me, Ruthie," I screamed. "It's called happiness, the shit that people get every day for free. I have people who love me, care about me, and want me around. Something that you never did at all. Now, all I need from you is for you to back off. Go back to your house, your man, and your life." Tears cascaded down my face nonstop. "Just forget about me. After all, that should be easy for you to do." A few people had piled out of Starbucks and stopped to enjoy the show. Wiping my tears, I walked back toward my car.

"That's right, blame me, Yazz. Blame your poor mom. But you'll be back home to me. 'Cause I see you just like these other chicks out here. Running after a drug dealer—yeah, you think I don't know. But I know all about that Kevon."

I stopped walking at the mention of Kevon's name. How did she know about him?

"Don't be surprised when I say this, but he don't love you. And when he is done with you, I'll be on McLaran Street and you are welcome to come home."

I could not believe her, still hurtful and evil. Nothing I would say to her could make a difference. Jumping in my car, I sped out of the Starbucks parking lot. This would be the last time I patronized this particular one. It was too close to Ruthie's house. And if I never saw her again, it would be too soon.

"Kevon," I voice-dialed. All I got were rings and a voice mail. I tried one more time before giving up. He was home so I would just tell him when I got there. Since I was still craving coffee, the Dunkin' Donuts drive through became a pit stop on my route to the house. The caffeine was needed now more than ever to calm my nerves. The first taste slid down my throat, then shot straight to my brain.

Going in for one more taste, I damn near dropped the whole hot cup into my lap as I pulled up to Kevon's house. Climbing into an all-white four-door Lexus truck was none other than Misti.

Kevon watched her pull off, then walked back into his place. I was shocked and pissed because what I was seeing was unbelievable. This could not be what it seemed because it looked as if my boyfriend's ex-girlfriend was leaving his place, where I had left him home alone. My hands were shaking as I shut off my car engine. Storming into the house, I slammed the door shut.

"Kevon," I screamed his name.

"What, babe?" He stuck his head out of the kitchen like it was a normal day.

"What the hell was Misti just doing here?" I was not calm. "Was she in this damn house?" That was a stupid question. I had seen him walking her out with my own two eyes.

"Babe, calm down."

"Don't tell me to calm down," I yelled. "Here I am, stressed over Ruthie and her bullshit. Then I come here, where I hope to find comfort, only to find your ex here." My words were accusing and justified, in my opinion.

"Babe, chill. I promise you, it ain't what it seems."

Was that his explanation? I could slap the shit out of him. He would have to do better than that. "What do you mean, it ain't what it seems? Fuck that. I know what I saw, and that shit ain't okay."

"Look, Misti came by here to see me. We hadn't seen each other since we split. And she had no idea I was in another relationship. But now she knows, and that's it. Nothing happened when she was here, I promise." He seemed sincere. "Yazz, I love you, and ain't nothin' or nobody changing that. Misti is old news. And you know I would never disrespect you. Soon as we get all this shit straightened out with Caesar, we gon' get our shit together and concentrate on us." He wrapped his arms around me.

This may sound stupid, but I believed him and there was no reason for me not to. And his arms around me made me feel safe again. That argument with Ruthie had shaken me up. His embrace was therapeutic. But Ruthie's words about Kevon not wanting me haunted my mind. It was a must that I shake them.

CHAPTER 16

Days later, I was still trying to shake the Misti situation. It wasn't that I didn't trust Kevon, but seeing Misti walk away from his house still bothered me a little. The bitch was just starting to pop up everywhere all of a sudden. And even though it had been months, I still remembered seeing her at the mall when Mimi was pregnant like it was yesterday. I guess just knowing their history of being together for so long made me feel insecure. Hopefully, the feeling would pass. But, for now, I just wanted to visit with my girl Mimi and tell her all about it.

After calling her several times without her picking up, I decided just to head over to her house. Lately, she had been keeping her cell ringer off, to keep unexpected calls from waking Alijah. At her house, my knocks went unanswered, so I tried calling her phone again, but still, no answer. Her car was parked outside, but it was possible they were out with Soulja.

Back at the house, I poured myself a much-needed drink. Going hard was a must. Hennessey and coke would be perfect. This would take my mind off Misti and Ruthie. They were the last two people I wanted to invade my mind. The thought of them gave off negative energy and, at this point in my life, positive energy was the key to my happiness. Lately, I had been contemplating really opening up my own clothing store. Location was my main concern. Where would I open it in St. Louis? And what would I call it? One thing was for sure, I would not name it nothing ghetto-affiliated. Walking over to Kevon's printer, I took two sheets of paper out of the feed tray. I reached for a pen and sat down at the dining room table to brainstorm names. Considering the clothes I would sell really got me to thinking. With twenty names on the paper, nothing, not one, appeared good enough.

Caesar came to mind. I had shared my desire to open up a clothing store with him. That had been a dream of mine for a long time. Kevon had no knowledge of this dream because we never had conversations anymore. Nothing that dealt with me or my interests was ever discussed. He was always preoccupied with Cash; that was his only concern. But Caesar was different, or at least he made me feel that way. Either way, this store was something I wanted for me, and I would be my motivation for that. A lie was what I would make out of Ruthie. I was not like other chicks. I had goals.

Pulling out my cell phone, I start a game of

Candy Crush to clear my mind. I would brainstorm store names another night.

"Yazz," Kevon called my name. I looked at the time on my phone to confirm it was still early. And Kevon didn't come home early that often. More than likely, he wouldn't be staying long.

Laying my phone down, I stood up with a smile, glad to have him for company even if only for a few minutes. "Hey, babe." I reached out to hug him. But instantly I knew something was wrong. The look Kevon was wearing on his face was that of devastation.

"I just got a call that Mimi was found dead."

My arms, which had been in midair, dropped like heavy logs to my sides. My vision blurred; my ears felt clogged. I needed him to repeat himself.

"Kevon, what'd you say about Mimi?" I asked for clarification.

"She was . . ." He paused. "She is dead."

"Wait, are you sure? Let me get my phone and call her. No, I'll call Sheila first to clear this up." I rushed toward the table for my cell phone. Picking up the phone, my hand was shaking so bad I could barely hold it steady.

"Babe, come here. She's gone." Kevon walked up behind me as I dialed Sheila's number on the phone, ignoring him.

Sheila's phone rang five times before her boyfriend picked up. But there was no need to ask because the screams that were coming from Sheila in the background confirmed it. Devastated, I let the cell phone in my hand plunge to the floor. My body went after it, but Kevon caught me before I hit the floor. Bile rose to the top of my stomach and spilled all over him. I was sick with grief. This had to be some type of terrible dream, a nightmare from which I would give anything to wake up. How and why was this happening? The scream from deep within my soul asked that question. But there was no answer.

CHAPTER 17

A month later, and still there were no answers as to why Mimi had been murdered. There was no motive beside some possible bullshit robbery. The monster who had pulled the trigger had gone into her home and shot her in broad daylight while Alijah napped. Soulja had come home to find her on the floor in the living room, shot to death. No rhyme or reason. The detectives said it looked like a robbery gone bad. Soulja, who was struggling with it, blamed himself. He figured they were out for him. He had put out a hit on whoever was responsible, but he was so grief-stricken, he'd decided to leave town. His mother lived in California so he went out there to get help with Alijah. Sheila had not wanted him to take Alijah, but she could not afford to care for her so she had no choice. Soulja promised to bring her back to visit occasionally, but said he needed to get his head together.

I just felt lost. I didn't have a clue as to what to do next, or where to turn. And when Soulja took off with Alijah, it only got worse. I felt helpless. But I understood that he had to do what was best for himself and Alijah.

"Here, this should help you relax a little." Caesar passed me a cup of hot tea. Lying back on the couch, I was trying to watch *The White Queen*, this new show on STARZ. Keeping my mind occupied sometimes helped. But talking to Caesar helped a lot as well. He had been here for me the whole time I had been grieving. When I cried, he held me; when I wanted to talk, regardless of what he was out doing, I could call him and he made time for me. The support he was giving me while I went through this was unbelievable. I appreciated it so much. Had it not been for him, I would have been alone.

Kevon, my so-called man, was too busy for what I was going through. When I cried at night, he slept; when I woke up in the morning sad, he had to get going. He behaved as though his whole life depended on bringing down Caesar. My problems with losing my best friend were just that—my problems. I would've been upset with him, but Mimi's death was the only thing on my mind.

"Thanks." I reached for the cup. The warmth of the cup soothed me. Taking a swallow, I cherished its goodness. "So no word yet, huh?"

"Nah, still waiting. Even with the bounty out, motherfuckers ain't talkin'."

"How much is the bounty for?"

"Eighty thousand."

"And still nothing?" I was shocked—all that money and nobody reporting shit. I shook my head.

"This shit got me puzzled too. It's strange as fuck. But I promise you, when Cash finds out who that motherfucker is, it's a wrap. You don't have to worry about that."

"I just can't believe that nobody don't know nothing. These streets can't hold water, but my best friend get murdered and everybody decides to mind their own fucking business." Caesar came over to comfort me.

"Look, I don't want you to worry about this. The time will come. We just gotta chill. They didn't know who they were fucking wit. But they will, and I don't want you stressing over this. I got you if nobody else does." Softly stroking my face, Caesar took me in his arms. Feeling safe, I sat back and fell asleep, comforted. Tonight, there would be no going home to Kevon or calling him. I wondered if he would even realize I wasn't there. With his mind being so preoccupied and all.

Two days later, lying in the bed at Kevon's house, I contemplated getting up and going shopping. I hadn't been shopping since Mimi died. That was one of the things we had done to pass time. We'd both loved it. For some reason, though, I just couldn't will myself outta the bed. Mimi was too heavy on my mind. I imagined Mimi talking shit about me procrastinating. She would call me all the time and force me out the bed, but instead she was gone. Forever.

Kevon had gotten up early and had been out already. He had a mild cold, and like any other man, when he was sick, he turned into a big baby. So he had come home for a midday nap. I hadn't been out of bed all day, but was craving a hot shower. As usual, Kevon's cell phone started to ring. I had already made up my mind not to wake him up. He was sneezing all over everything, and his body needed rest. With my back turned to him, I pretended I was still asleep and listened as he answered the phone.

"Damn, nigga, can't you handle that shit?" Kevon was aggressive with whomever he was having a conversation with. "I don't give a fuck. You already know what needs to be done." Silence . . . "Sometimes I wonder about you, nigga. Just hold the fuck on I'll be there in a minute. What?" he yelled. "I said, I'll be there in a minute. Don't do shit until I get there."

Sitting up in the bed, I faced him. "Kevon. you are sick. You need to get some rest."

"Babe, I know, but I gotta go handle this though. I'll be back in a minute. This won't take long."

I left it at that. If he wanted to kill himself for a stupid-ass crew, then he had my blessing. I had my own fucking problems.

"Whateva." I sighed and laid back down.

"Are you cool?" he asked. "You have been in this bed all day."

"Yeah, just missing Mimi, but I'm thinking about

going shopping. You know, do a little retail therapy."

"That's what you should do. Get up out this house, get some fresh air. Besides, lying in this bed with me will only make you sick." He threw the covers back and climbed out of bed and started to lace up his gym shoes. Once he was done, he stood up, reached in his pocket, and pulled out a stack of hundreds and handed them to me. "Try to enjoy yourself and get whatever you want, babe." Walking around on my side of the bed, he bent down and kissed me on the cheek. "Time heals all." With that, he told me he had to get going and would try to make it back soon.

Sitting in the bed, holding a handful of cash, I realized that Kevon could only give me money because he had no time. His money was his quality time and comfort; that was the only support he could provide for me. Once again, I was frustrated. I threw the money on the bed next to me and reached for my cell phone. I no longer wanted to be home alone, let alone go shopping. What I needed was emotional comfort. I dialed Caesar's number, and he picked up on the second ring.

"Hey, you," his voice soothed me.

"Are you busy?" I asked.

"Never too busy for you. I'm at the condo. Why don't you come over?" He only had to say it once. In no time, I had showered and dressed, and was out.

CHAPTER 18

"So they finally hired you in permanently?" I was excited for Sheila. We were sitting outside her apartment, having a drink for a small celebration. She had finally gotten a full-time job with General Mills. She had been working for them through a temp agency for over a year. But finally the company had hired her. And she was happy to know that soon she would be able to move out of her small apartment.

"Hell yes, girl, I can't believe it. This is the break I needed; soon, the kids and I will be gettin' up out of this small-ass, run-down apartment."

"That's what up." I smiled.

"Damn, I just wish Mimi was here for this. She watched me struggle for so long. And I always felt bad because I was the oldest. It's all my fault that she never had a role model. Then I had the nerve to bash her for making a family of her own." A tear slid down Sheila's cheek.

"Sheila, Mimi loved you, and she knew you worked hard to try and get ahead. So don't feel bad." I tried to reassure her. "Even though you all didn't have much, you had love and each other. And that's more than I ever had growing up. Being around you and Mimi taught me what love is. So don't beat yourself up."

Sheila looked at me with tears in her eyes. "I'm sorry about you and your mom situation. I know you always wanted to work that out."

"That's nothing. I'm over it." I blew it off. Ruthie was a conversation that I avoided at all costs. "Have you heard anything from Soulja about Alijah?"

"Well, he called about a week ago and said that she was okay. He promised to bring her home in about a month to visit."

"Really?" I was glad to hear that.

"Yeah, the kids and I can't wait to see her. I hate that I was not able to raise her. But I just couldn't afford it, plus this place is too small. The last thing I wanted to do was lose her in this crowd. She deserves so much better. I just hope, when she grows up, she doesn't think I didn't love her enough to take her."

"She won't think that. Besides, she's with Soulja. That's her father. He's a good dad. It's good she has one of her parents left. It was hard for me too. It's still hard, but I do believe her being with him may be for the best."

"I'm sure it is also." Sheila's voice was shaking. I

looked over at her, and she was crying. "I just miss Mimi so much."

Getting up, I walked over and hugged her, trying to be strong. "Me too. We just gotta be there for each other." The struggle for all of us trying to get over Mimi being gone was real. But we had to lean on each other and try to be strong. That was our only chance at getting back to somewhat of a normal life.

It was close to dark when I left Sheila's house. On my drive home, Kevon crossed my mind, and I realized this was the night. My mind had been so occupied with other things going on that I had almost forgotten. Kevon had told me a couple of days prior that he would meet with his leader on this night to tie up the loose ends on Caesar. This would be it—I no longer had to play the game of vixen to Caesar.

The thought of it ending sped up my heart rate. The last year had been hard at times, but fun at others. Things only soured when Mimi was murdered. But after all that time, I had spent with Caesar, not once had I seen anything that even suggested that he had been disloyal to his crew. In fact, everything he did was full of loyalty. And here I was, supposedly distracting him so that Kevon could expose him. But in this moment I realized there was nothing to expose. Caesar was probably the best thing that could happen to Cash. Not only that, he was human and one of the best men I had ever met.

There was just no way I could go through with this. I could not sit back and watch him lose everything over lies. Over a month ago, I had questioned Kevon about Caesar's disloyalty just to get to some clarification. Because, in my mind, things were not adding up. Kevon had instantly shut me down, telling me not to concern myself, that he had it under control. I then tried to press the issue by telling him that I saw no signs of Caesar doing anything out of the ordinary. He became very angry and made it clear to me that I should drop the issue. After that, I concluded this was for his own personal gain, and that anything he said about Caesar was probably a lie or exaggerated. Either way, things were about to get crazy, and I had to get away. Now.

I pointed my car in the direction of Caesar's house; there were a few things I needed to pick up. After that, I would catch the first plane out of town I could board. As I pulled up to the house, the coast seemed to be clear. Leon let me inside. Without exchanging any dialogue about why I was there, I went into Caesar's room and started to grab my things. Just as I was almost done, Caesar entered the room. His presence surprised me because I had assumed he was not home.

"I didn't know you were coming by."

"I didn't call because I figured you were busy so I didn't want to bother you. But it's cool. I just needed to grab some things." Without giving him much eye contact, I continued my mission.

"Are you sure you can't stay a minute?"

"No, not tonight. I have other plans." Not wanting to tell him any more lies, I left it at that. My movements made it clear I was in a hurry.

"Yazz, I love you." Those three little words got my

attention. I stopped moving, but couldn't bring my eyes to meet his. "I love you," he repeated. Maybe he thought I didn't hear him the first time. "I'm sure you think this seems all of a sudden, but it's not. I have loved you since the first time I laid eyes on you. I understand that you are with Kevon, but it changes nothin' about how I feel. I thought about setting you up in an apartment in New York. We can start a life together." I could not believe he had it all planned out. Every word that had left his lips clouded my brain.

"New York," I repeated. *Shocked* is the only way to describe how I felt about the words that were coming out of his mouth. New York was a long way from St. Louis in more ways than one. "What about the crew? How are you going to live in New York and run a crew here?" I was puzzled. For a second, I forgot about Kevon's scheme.

"Baby, relax. All that will be taken care of. Besides, I'm thinkin' about givin' it up. I have been in this game since I was fifteen. Some things just get old, and I done made a lot of money. Shit, I'm rich, got more money than I know what to do wit. There is nothin' else in it for me. All I want now is to share my life with you."

His words left me feeling dumbfounded. I couldn't believe he was willing to give up all he had ever known just to be with me. That meant a lot.

"I can't let you do this."

"Yazz, it's what I want. Furthermore, I have other business ventures I've been working on, and you can shop around for a spot to sell your clothes. I'm going to give you the money to start your business.

It's time you lived out your dream. I want you to be happy."

Every word that slid off his tongue sounded so convincing. He was offering me a new life, in a new city, and a chance to live out my dream. How could I turn that down? No one had ever cared about what I wanted to do. No one had ever put me first. Not until I met Caesar. He had consistently shown me how much he cared for me. I wanted to run and jump in his arms and stay there happy and secure forever.

But Kevon popped into my mind. What had I allowed him to convince me to do? Because of him, I had committed the ultimate betrayal. Caesar had trusted me with his most private moments; never once had he suspected me of anything. And when Mimi was killed, he had been there for me, had shown me nothing but compassion when I was at my lowest. When, the entire time, I was just a slut put in his sight to distract him, by someone who claimed to care for me. For that, I would surely pay, if and when Caesar found out about it. So there was no way I could run away with him, as much as I was tempted. Because one day Caesar may very well have to kill me, my life was at stake.

"Caesar, I care about you too. Really I do. But I just can't. I have to go. I'll call you later," I lied. Grabbing the things I had off the bed, I bounced. As tough as it was, it was for the best. This was the last time I would see him. The reality of it left me feeling empty inside.

CHAPTER 19

Tears clouded my face as I drove like a mad woman from Caesar's crib. He was probably the only real chance I would have at love in my life. But I tried hard to shake it. It just could not be; there was nothing I could do about that. And there were only a few hours left before Kevon would meet up with the supplier to expose Caesar. My mind was made up—there was something I must do. I could not sit back and watch Caesar lose everything, over things that were clearly not true.

I headed to the spot where the meeting was being held. Kevon was not expected to be there for at least another three hours, but the supplier would be there early. So I would have plenty of time to talk to him first, and then make my getaway before Kevon arrived. Because after I blew up his spot, he would probably want to kill me too. I was in too deep, but this had to be done.

As I pulled up to the spot, my mouth flew open as I spotted Kevon's car already outside.

"Think, think," I said aloud. He was not supposed to be here. Something in his plan must have changed. Kevon's tactic to pick up the cash from each trap changed daily, but the time that he finished was always the same. He must have juggled a few things to get here early. I was shocked, because the supplier would expect him to arrive after him. At least that's what I thought. Either way, I had to come up with something fast. This had definitely altered my plan.

Turning off my car lights, I parked in a dark area. Finding an unlocked window on the run-down building, I climbed inside and looked for a place to hide. It seemed as though Kevon had all the lights turned off, so the room was dark as hell. I tripped over something, but there was no way to make out what it was.

"Ouch," I said, as low as possible. It hurt bad. Screaming would have made me feel a whole lot better, but since I couldn't do that, I held on to my right ankle and doubled over in pain. As the pain subsided, I tried to stand up to get used to the weight of my ankle so I could stand securely on my foot again. Thankfully, it was okay. Maybe I had just pinched a nerve.

Now I had to figure out how I was going to burst in on Kevon and the supplier to say what needed to be said. Kevon would probably try to shut me up and not allow me to say a word. Or maybe he would have his crew tie me up and kill me, who knows. Because it was clear he wasn't willing to let nothing get in the way of the so-called empire that he planned to inherit.

In the process of trying to find a comfortable place to hide, I heard Kevon talking. Every word he said was tough for me to make out because of a slight echo in the room. At first, I thought someone was in the room with him, but soon it became clear he was on the phone. I listened hard as his word became clear.

"They should arrive in any minute now. You need to hurry up and get here." He paused, possibly listening to the caller. "Yeah, the guys finally agreed to get Caesar out of the house. . . ." Pause again. "Right, so you need to get yo ass here. I ain't wasting no time. We gon' dead that nigga on the spot. We gotta make sure that shit happens quickly, the faster the better. Once he's dead, that shit's a wrap. The game is changing tonight."

The words *dead him* made me double over with disgust. I could not believe my fucking ears. Kevon was planning to kill Caesar. Had that been his plan all along? Everything he had told me had been a lie. There was never any supplier coming. He had played me, and I had fallen for it. Suddenly, I went from feeling sick to feeling outraged. He owed me answers. I deserved that much from him, and since I was no longer afraid, I would get them.

"So you lied to me?" I approached Kevon, scaring the shit out of him. Jumping back, he reached for his waist to grab his gun until he recognized me.

"Yazz, baby, what are you doing here? How'd you find this place?"

He could not honestly believe he was in the position to question me. "Fuck all that. Kevon, how about you answer my question?" I demanded. "Are you planning to kill Caesar?"

"Look Yazz, you should not be here."

"Is that all you can say to me, Kevon? You used me all this time. How could you lie to me?" I cried.

"No, babe, you got it all wrong. I would never lie to you. Something happened and we had to change the plan, that's all, but now we have no choice. I got to kill 'im."

"Kevon, no . . . please don't," I begged him. But the look on his face told me that my cries were falling on deaf ears. His mind was made up.

"Yo, stop all that fuckin' cryin' over that fuckin' nigga. He don't give a fuck about you. All you been is his whore." He suddenly got angry. "Whose fucking side you on anyway? You want to be wit that fucking nigga? Huh? You choose him over me?" Kevon threw questions at me as he grabbed me by both wrists and started to shake me. Scared and crying, I begged him to let me go as I tried to wriggle free. His grip was so strong, it felt as if my blood circulation was being cut off.

"Let her go!" Caesar yelled. I recognized the voice without seeing the face. Slowly turning around to face Caesar, Kevon dropped both my hands. They landed beside me like two bricks. Frozen from fear, I could not move. Now I knew I was going to die for certain. All Kevon's lies and scheming would cost me more than I was willing to give up—my life. Silently I prayed.

"Yo, man, what you doing?" Kevon's voice sounded nervous, as both of our attention fell to the gun Caesar was holding.

"Don't test me, motherfucker. Did you really think you could kill me and get away with it?" The look on Caesar's face reflected what he had a reputation for being: notorious. The pupils in his eyes held nothing there; behind them was dark, cold as ice. This was it. I wanted to say something, but I was mute.

"Man, it ain't even what you think." Kevon's eyes were roaming around in his head. The guilt of a liar when he realizes it's over.

"Because of you, I just had to kill three of my bodyguards. Niggas I fucked wit before I even knew your disloyal ass. Damn, I can't believe I trusted you and treated your ass like a brother."

"Come on, Caesar, dog, let me explain," Kevon tried to beg.

"Nah, ain't nothin' for you to explain. Yazz, baby, come over here and stand next to me. I'm about to lullaby this disloyal-ass nigga." My brain told my legs to move, but I couldn't. He was calling me baby? But what was he going to do to me? Was I next? "Come on, baby. Don't be afraid. I know all about what he made you do." Caesar pointed the gun at Kevon's head, right between the eyes. "Yeah, motherfucker, you forced her to sleep with me for your own financial gain. I swear you a nigga of the worst kind."

"Is that what you think? You think I forced her? I ain't force that bitch to do shit. This bitch begged me to get down wit this shit." I could not believe my ears. The lies this dude was telling was awful, but still my voice would not come to defend myself.

"Shut the fuck up," Caesar yelled, then cocked the trigger on his gun. "Stop lying like a bitch nigga. Take ownership because this ain't a good look. Take this shit like a man. See your bitch Misti done called me up and told me everything all about your weak-ass plot. How do you think I know? I still can't believe them fuckin' niggas fell for that shit you fed them about me."

That answered the question that was burning a hole in my brain. Who had ratted Kevon out? Misti. But how did she even know about any of this? That was another question I would have liked to ask Kevon had I been able to speak. Kevon's entire jaw dropped. "Misti called you?" He looked at Caesar for confirmation.

Before Caesar could say a word, two gunshots rang out and I watched as he dropped to his knees. Stunned from the blow of the hot bullets, Caesar's eyes left Kevon and landed directly on me. Then his entire body rested on the floor. A loud scream followed before I recognized the scream had come from my own mouth. I immediately placed my hand over it. Taking my eyes from Caesar, I came face-to-face with Misti. The gunshots had come from the gun that she was now pointing at Kevon and me.

"Kevon, babe, are you okay?" Misti lowered the

gun and looked at him, concerned. "I'm so sorry I didn't get here sooner. Thank God I was able to get here in time to hear those lies Caesar told. None of it's true. Don't believe none of it. It had to be that backstabbing bitch that's standing behind you." She lifted the gun again and pointed it in my direction. Knowing she could not be speaking of me, I looked behind me. Somebody had to be standing there. Realizing that there was no one behind me, I turned back to face Misti.

Kevon, on the other hand, hadn't heard a word she said because what I saw next was strange as hell. Walking over to Misti, he started hugging her, and then kissing her all over her face.

"Don't worry about that. I know that nigga lying. I'm just glad you showed up when you did." Kevon held Misti tight. "That disloyal-ass snake was about to shoot me." Kevon continued to shit on Caesar with lies about his character.

"No worries babe. You know I will always be here for you," Misti cooed while massaging Kevon's right cheek.

Talk about shocked, I was it. They were at each other like lovebirds; they had even forgotten I was in the room. I was trying to wrap my head around what all this meant. Because here my man was with his ex-girlfriend whom he'd claimed he didn't fuck wit anymore. Yet they were about to rip each other's clothes off with me right in the room.

"What the fuck is going on?" I yelled, finally finding my voice. They both turned around in my direction, giving me an annoyed look.

Misti twisted her thin lips into a vicious grin as

she looked at Kevon, kissed him on the cheek, nodded her head in my direction, and said, "Go ahead."

He gazed in her eyes like a puppy ready for his Puppy Chow, then spun in my direction. "You see, Yazz, it's like this, sweetheart. Misti and I have never been separated. That was a lie." He paused for a minute like he was expecting me to say something, but I didn't. I needed to hear every word he wanted to share. "Misti here came up with a plan that involved us"—he pointed between the two of them—"recruiting you. We needed the most beautiful vulnerable girl from around the way. Naturally, my Misti thought of you because you fit that. The plan was to use you to seduce Caesar so that we"—again, he pointed at Misti, then back at himself. He must have thought I was slow too—"could take over Cash. So to make this work, Misti left town for a while. Meanwhile, I could flatter you into a relationship, gain your trust, and all plans would fall into place. And as you see, it worked." He grinned at me. "Actually it was easier than I thought it would be."

My whole face was on fire like a thousand bees had just finished feasting on it. I could not believe what had just came out of his mouth. He, along with his slut girlfriend, had not only used me, but played me like a fine tune. But the worst part was I had been naïve enough to fall for it. How could I not have known something was up? Kevon had been with this girl forever. Everyone, including me, knew that. This explained why I'd never seen her but then all of a sudden she was everywhere. I felt sick to my stomach.

"Damn, I can't wait to start this new life with me the head of Cash and you as my wifey." He kissed her on the nose and she beamed. Neither one of them felt any shame. Only victory. I could kill them both.

"You low-down, dirty-ass nigga. And you, you baldheaded bitch." I spat at Misti, but it landed before reaching her. "Both of you will pay for what you have done to me." My heart ached. Never had I felt so low. Not even Ruthie hated me this much.

"Don't threaten me, bitch." Kevon snarled at me. "You were useless. You couldn't even go through with the plan. Takin' that nigga's side over mine. What woman holds her man down like that?"

"Babe, don't even waste your breath. Let's just finish the plan. Shoot the bitch." Misti laughed.

"Yeah, I think I'll do just that." He reached in his waistband and wrapped his hand around his gun, pulled it out, then slid the trigger back. My heart skipped a beat as I closed my eyes tight and waited for the end, but nothing came but silence.

Opening up my eyes one at a time, I found Soulja standing in front of Kevon and Misti, with a gun pointed at them. I blinked to be sure I wasn't seeing things.

Soulja, I mouthed. He looked at me briefly before positioning his attention back to Misti and Kevon. Again, I was confused. Why Soulja would be here unless he was getting revenge for Caesar?

Misti took a quick glance at Kevon, then slowly but steadily made a few strides across the room, leaving Kevon alone. As I watched Misti wrap her arms around Soulja, my tongue went dry and the room swirled. "What the fuck?" I said out loud.

This shit was just getting out of control, not to mention bizarre. Nothing made any sense at all.

"Bitch, what the fuck is you doing?" Kevon yelled at Misti. I guess this was not a part of his two-timing scheme. The look on his face was shitty. That much I liked, but I could not celebrate until I understood what was going on. "You set me up? How could you do this to me? After all I done for your thirsty ass. Ain't this a motherfucking bitch? Damn, these hos ain't loyal." Kevon went on and on, shaking his head. He was hurt.

"Soulja, what's going on here?" I was calm. Maybe he could give me some answers. I mean, how could he be involved in this? Mimi had just died, and he was here rescuing Misti. "How could you do this to Mimi and your daughter?" I was emotional.

"Well, if you must know—" Misti started.

"Shut the fuck up because I ain't talkin' to you bitch!" I screech.

"Well, maybe you should be. 'Cause you know what? If you really want to know, it was Soulja here who killed your little friend." The room whirled, and my chest tightened. I looked down to see if I saw any blood, because surely I was shot. But there wasn't any. "See, your friend had a big mouth. She found out about us, then our plan, and threatened to tell. And for that, the bitch had to die. Because what you don't do is cross me."

That was it; I would shut Misti's mouth up for good. Running toward her, I prepared to kill her with my bare hands. Soulja pointed his gun at me and threatened to shoot. But losing his focus on Kevon was his first mistake. Kevon pulled his trigger, shooting Misti directly between the eyes. Her body hit the floor so hard you could hear her skull crack. But the battle didn't end there. Soulja fired off two or three rounds. One hit Kevon in the throat, but not before he fired again, shooting Soulja in the head.

I stood still, frozen in what had turned out to be a bloodbath. I could not believe my eyes as they darted from body to body. Even Caesar's body lay on the floor. Blood was everywhere. And there was no movement in sight. I looked down at my body to confirm that not one bullet had hit me.

Stepping over Misti and Soulja, I made my way outside. I took in a deep breath. The air was so refreshing. Putting one foot in front of the other I start walking toward where I had hid my car. I approached Soulja's Dodge Challenger and realized it was still running. As I walked past it, I couldn't help but notice a car seat in the front. Walking over to the car, I gazed inside. And there, sleeping peacefully, was Alijah. I cried out with joy before kissing her on the forehead. This precious bundle of joy had been robbed of a mother by her own father. This was something I never wanted her to know. At that moment, my life had been decided. Alijah would be raised as my own. Mimi would want that.

Taking the car seat out of Soulja's car, I carried it to my own car, where I carefully strapped her inside. St. Louis, Missouri, was going to be a memory for me. We were out of here, but there was still one more stop to make, Kevon's house. He kept his stash there, in a safe that he thought only he knew about. But I had always known; and that safe held over five hundred thousand dollars. That money would give Alijah and me a good start.

What do you think?

DON'T MISS

Triple Threat by Camryn King

A tenacious reporter. A millionaire philanthropist. And all-access secrets that won't leave anyone safe fuel Camryn King's relentless new thriller . . .

The Vows We Break by Briana Cole

Kimera Davis had a plan to jump start her life and land on easy street. But someone's playing a desperate, dangerous game with her life . . . and she'll have to win if she wants to survive.

ON SALE NOW!

Turn the page for an excerpt from these thrilling novels . . .

From *Triple Threat*

CHAPTER 1

Alexandria, Virginia
Six minutes earlier

Heads down, shoulders heaving, Jericho Quinn and Jacques Thibodaux faced each other, circling for the fifth time in as many minutes. Quinn's dark eyes narrowed above a week's growth of dark beard. Thibodaux's high and tight haircut glistened with perspiration in the orange light that filtered through the spring foliage on the sycamore and oaks. Gravel crunched under their boots on the concrete driveway in front of Emiko Miyagi's colonial brick, a short jog from George Washington's Mount Vernon estate.

Copper skin and a dark beard left him with what his ex-wife called an ambiguous ethnicity. At an extremely fit thirty-seven, he could, and often did, pass for someone of Middle Eastern descent, a Native American like his maternal grandmother, or the deeply tanned son of an Irish fisherman

that he was. His shaggy hair was just long enough
to curl over the top of his ears.

At five feet-ten, Jericho had held the Alaska
state Golden Gloves title in his weight classes
through five of the eight years from sixth grade
until he graduated high school, and had gone on
to box for the United States Air Force Academy,
winning the Wing Open his junior year. He'd
trained in several martial arts, but leaned toward
an ancient form of Japanese jujitsu—with plenty
of striking mixed in with joint manipulation and
throws. More than a series of techniques, it was a
way of strategy. Beyond his years of training, he
was an instinctive fighter, born with not only the
physique and intelligence for close quarters battle, but the willingness to inflict maximum sudden
violence on his fellow man when the need arose.

Officially a special agent with Air Force Office
of Special Investigations, he'd been seconded,
along with his partner, Marine Gunnery Sergeant
Jacques Thibodaux to the office of the national security advisor to the president. When they weren't
working, they were training—and according to
their instructor, Emiko Miyagi, there was always
something to learn.

Thibodaux had Quinn by six inches and sixty
pounds. The man was massive—but his were no
mere mirror muscles. He had plenty of experience in the octagon, where he fought amateur
MMA bouts under the name Dauxboy. The Marine's black eyepatch and an impossibly square jaw
added a severity to his already imposing look. Still,
his broad face generally held a smile, even in the
middle of a fight.

Both men were strategic thinkers, and both knew there were rarely any winners in an actual fight—only those who lived, and those who lost. Real fights were car-wreck quick, emergency-room gory, and brick-to-the-head final.

The problem with fighting someone who sparred with you weekly lay in the fact that you started to learn each other's rhythms, discovering each other's tricks. The benefit, as Miyagi explained, came from the need to constantly adapt in order to conceal one's strategy. If an opponent knew you favored a series of exploratory left jabs prior to bridging the gap of distance, he or she would be ready for the attack long before it came. As such, both Jericho and Jacques varied their movements in an attempt to throw the other off his game.

Neither man was a tentative fighter, though Quinn was a skosh more thoughtful. Thibodaux tended to use his tremendous size to crash in and overwhelm, but when sparring with Quinn the big Cajun often switched things up—as he was doing now—circling, waiting for just the right moment to make his move.

Jacques stutter-stepped, almost tripping on a patch of gravel and glancing for an instant down at his feet. Quinn seized the opportunity and moved in, catching a strike to the nose for his trouble, feeling the cartilage grind under Jacques Thibodaux's forearm.

Neither man was the sort to take it easy in a sparring match; training had to reflect life in order to be beneficial. So, the two men battled like bulls at eighty percent, taking care not to cause serious incapacitating injury. Unfortunately, reality came with a good deal of pain. Each man knew his abilities—and his limits. If a blow would have defined the fight at a hundred percent—the receiver would have no problem conceding that fact. Eighty percent from the mountainous Cajun would be enough to flatten anyone, but Quinn knew how to move, and a broken nose was nothing new to him.

Quinn let his head flow with the Cajun's forearm, following up with machine-gun strikes to Thibodaux's liver and neck as he turned sideways from the momentum of his arm-strike. The big Marine's neck was protected by thick muscles, but Quinn knew it was folly to hit the man in his iron jaw. The liver strikes were sickening, even at eighty percent.

The six-foot-four Cajun winced, both hands raised in surrender. "Fairly certain that one chopped me down to your size, Chair Force." Even in defeat, the Marine couldn't help the little jab at the Air Force. Blood trickled from a small cut Quinn had given him under his left eye.

"Sorry about that," Quinn said, dabbing at his bloody nose while he nodded to the gunny's swelling wound.

Thibodaux waved him off, chuckling. "I ain't no Cinderella, *mi ami*. Lucky enough I had a pretty face when I needed it to catch Camille."

A compact Asian woman with her hair pulled back in a ponytail stepped onto the concrete driveway from the lawn. Emiko Miyagi wore a white t-shirt and khaki 5.11 cargo pants. The scooping neckline and thin material of the shirt did little to hide the intricate and colorful Japanese tattoos that covered her torso. As the men's instructor, she insisted much of their training occur in street clothes—and most often on an actual street rather than the padded floor of a dojo. In this case, the concrete driveway in front of her brick home provided for the realistic backdrop—as well as plenty of bruises and raspberries for all three of the combatants.

Miyagi was forty-seven years old—but could have easily passed for a woman in her mid-thirties. Where the two men under her tutelage had years of experience in fighting, Miyagi had trained as a killer from her early teens. There was something other-worldly about the way she fought, as if she could anticipate her opponent's moves even before they knew they were about to make them.

Her training sessions always ended with a short bout between the instructor and each man. The fights were not short because she planned them that way, but because it did not take her long to win them. Jacques was good, and Jericho was very good, but Emiko Miyagi was better—a lot better.

"I truly hate this fighting friends shit," the monstrous Cajun said, four minutes later as he limped across the circular driveway toward a stainless steel water bottle in the shade of Miyagi's porch. He kept his arm tucked in tight against his side, wincing from Quinn's liver strike and the machine gun beating Miyagi had given him to his floating ribs.

Quinn stood at the edge of the driveway beside his gunmetal gray BMW GS Adventure motorcycle and pressed a wad of tissue to his bloody nose. "I'm with you there," he said, sounding like he had a bad cold. Jacques Thibodaux knew how to throw a forearm. That was an undeniable fact.

Miyagi took a long drink from her own water bottle, then shook her head. "Are you such an excellent judge of character, Jacques-kun?" she asked, using the more familiar form of the Japanese honorific *san*. "Sometimes, those we believe to be our friends turn out to be something else entirely."

"Yeah." Thibodaux rubbed his ribs again and nodded. "I'm gettin' that."

Miyagi canted her head to one side and shrugged at her disbelieving student. "On more than one occasion I have found myself engaged in battle with those who should have cared for me. Each year we read of men and women who believe themselves happily married—until their spouse tries to murder them." She gave a little nod to drive home the seriousness of her point. "Just last week an Alexandria police officer's wife was arrested for attempting to poison him by putting rat poison in his spaghetti."

Quinn sighed, but kept his thoughts to himself. He was sure there were times his ex-wife had been mad enough to feed him d-Con.

The big Cajun gave an adamant shake of his head.

"I trust my Camille completely."

"I'm sure many of those involved believed that same thing about their own companion," Miyagi said.

Thibodaux set his jaw, glaring with his good

eye. "I'm tellin' you, Camille wouldn't do such a thing."

"But suppose she did," Miyagi said. "What would you do then?"

"She wouldn't."

"But if she did?"

Thibodaux shrugged, as if it were all so clear.

"Then I'd eat the spaghetti. No point in goin' on if the last fourteen years have been a sham."

Miyagi smiled softly, displaying uncharacteristic emotion. "We should all be so fortunate to have—"

The chime of a cellphone cut her off, and caused all three to look at the black leather jacket lying across Quinn's BMW.

Thibodaux shot his friend a quizzical look. "What the hell, Chair Force? Since when did you start using a ringtone?"

A chill ran up Quinn's back. He kept his phone set to vibrate at incoming calls from everyone but the company dispatching his brother's emergency locator beacon.

He dug the cellphone out of his jacket pocket and answered it by the second ring. A male voice that sounded like a college student advised him that an SOS signal had been triggered at 7:46 a.m. local time on a device registered to Boaz Quinn. So far, the company had been unable to make contact with the registered number. Authorities in Buenos Aires had been notified but were not yet on scene.

Quinn looked at the TAG Heuer Aquaracer on his wrist and noted the time. It was 6:54 a.m. Eastern, an hour earlier than Argentina, eight minutes gone from the time of Bo's SOS. He asked the dispatcher to call him back as soon as he had more information, then hung up and started the protocol he and his brother had already worked out. When an SOS went up, it was too late to start planning.

First, he called Bo's cell, getting nothing but voice mail.

He scrolled through the list of contacts Bo had given him while he explained the situation to Jacques and Emiko. Both knew Quinn's brother was on a protection job in South America and they listened intently, stone faced. Neither had to say anything for Quinn to know he had their complete support. At length, Quinn found the number he was looking for and called the personal cell number for the man who had employed Bo's services.

"Riley Grey," the voice said.

"My name is Jericho Quinn. I just received an SOS message from my brother. Has anyone been in contact with you?"

The line was silent for a long moment. Quinn could imagine the stricken look on the face of the father at the other end. He'd been there himself.

"Steven?" Riley Grey whispered. "What about my son?"

"I don't have any more information yet," Quinn said. "I'd hoped you might have heard something."

"I . . . I haven't."

"Very well," Quinn said. "Bo's GPS puts them in Buenos Aires. Local authorities are en route to the coordinates where the SOS went up. I'll let you know when I get anything else."

"Any chance that this is a false alarm?"

Quinn took a deep breath. "It's possible," he said. "But unlikely. It takes two distinct movements to activate the SOS on his device—sliding a button sideways and then depressing it. Considering their location and your net worth, I'm afraid your son is a possible target . . ."

"I appreciate your honesty," Grey said.

Quinn looked at his watch again, though only seconds had passed since he'd done it last. "I'll call you back."

"Ten minutes," Grey said. "Even if you don't hear anything."

"I'll try," Quinn said. "Until then, I need to get started on some things. It's best to move quickly in this kind of event."

"You have experience with kidnappings?"

"I have experience with bad men," Quinn said. "Now if you'll excuse me, I need to make some calls."

"Wait!" Grey said, clinging to the call like a lifeline. "What are you going to do?"

Quinn groaned. He couldn't help but feel for the father's helplessness, but every moment he spent on the phone was time he could be moving toward Bo.

"I'm going to get a ticket on the next available flight to Buenos Aires out of Dulles. If this turns out to be a false alarm, I'll cancel. In the meantime, I need to be moving forward."

"I can help with that," Grey said, giving an audible sigh at being able to do something tangible. "I'm in Baltimore for meetings. My Citation is sitting at BWI airport right now. Are you closer to Dulles or Reagan?"

"I'm ten minutes from Reagan," Quinn said.

"Good," Grey said. "My plane will be waiting for you when you get there."

"And you?" Quinn asked, fearing the strings that always seemed to be attached to the goodwill of the rich and powerful.

"I broke my leg waterskiing in Tahoe three weeks ago," Grey said. "It kills me not to go down there myself, but I'll be more use to you working from here, providing resources."

"Okay then," Quinn said, relieved but anxious to end the call.

"Bo and I have been friends for a long time," Grey offered. "I don't know much about you, but I trust him completely, and I know he trusts you. He told me that you'd pulled his fat out of the fire on more than one occasion."

"And vice versa."

A tense chuckle came across the line. "Bo told me you'd say that."

From *The Vows We Break*

PROLOGUE

"We should just kill her."

Those words broke through my subconscious and sent a startling chill up my spine.

The pain, at first excruciating, had long since subsided into a dull ache and whether it was the handcuffs binding my wrists or the minimal rations of stale food and lukewarm water I'd been having to live on for the past few days, my body was now numb. Like a shell. But despite my snatches of blurred vision as I toggled in and out of consciousness, this man's face was crystal clear. What I didn't understand was why was he here? Why wasn't he helping me?

I struggled to lift my lids and through tears that blurred my vision, I stared into the eyes of a dead man.

"My love." His accent was deepened by the emotion clogging his voice. Pity. Apologetic. But he didn't move any closer, even though I'm sure I looked like the death I was slowly succumbing to.

I tried to replay everything that had happened in the past few months. Clues I had missed. Then, footsteps brought the other person into view and I remembered. My mind suddenly settled on the missing pieces that had been hidden in plain sight. How could I not have known? More importantly, what were they going to do with me now that I did?

CHAPTER 1

I knew I was wrong, even as I hiked up the bustle of chiffon and tulle that adorned my dress and quickened my pace toward the bathroom, my retreat causing the muffled noises of the wedding reception to fade against my back. At this point, I would just have to apologize later. For now, I needed peace. If only for a moment.

I swung into the restroom and quickly stooped to peer underneath the three stall doors. Empty. Grateful, I locked the door and walked to the porcelain countertop.

I almost didn't recognize myself. Sure, I was still Kimmy; same dramatic pixie cut, sharp cheekbones, and almond-shaped eyes. Physically, for sure, not much had changed. But what had changed, those mental and emotional scars sure as hell couldn't be hidden under makeup or a distracting smile. Those still waters ran deep.

I shut my eyes against my reflection, inhaling sharply through my nose before letting a heavy sigh escape my parted lips. For the first time all day, hell, weeks if I wanted to be honest with myself, I felt like I could breathe.

Of course I should have been happy. It was a wedding that I had long since given up hope would ever happen. But from the time I woke up that morning, it felt like both my brain and body were stuck on a déjà vu repeat. Everything was perfect, just like we had planned it. From the coral décor to the arrival of the vendors, right down to the gorgeous weather that hung appreciatively at seventy-four degrees despite the forecast of rain. Decorations had adorned the sanctuary, a collection of neosoul ballads had wafted through the speakers, and guests had arrived and arranged themselves in the pews with bottles of bubbles (because Daddy wasn't having rice thrown in his church) and tissues ready for the tears that were sure to come. Pictures were snapped, both from smart phones as well as by the professional photographer who crouched and maneuvered around to capture moments from every angle possible.

And I knew, even as I clutched my bouquet with sweaty palms and started my own descent down the sheer aisle runner, I knew exactly why it was taking all of my strength to feign the same excitement that was clearly evident among everyone else. And for that, I felt terrible.

Tears stung the corners of my eyes, and now that the ceremony was over, I finally let them spill over, trailing makeup streaks down my cheeks. I hadn't meant to spend the entire time comparing everything. They were two entirely different circumstances.

Last year, I had signed a contract to be a "love partner" or wife to the rich Leo Owusu. I would be just another along with the two women he already had. It had been nothing more than a business arrangement in my eyes, and I had treated it as such. But for Leo, I was his wife number three in every sense of the word. I couldn't help but shake my head at the memory of the lavish wedding from months ago, a wedding I neither wanted nor cared for. Nothing but an elaborate showcase of the extent of his money. So I stood at the altar with his other wives right up there by my side, like they too weren't wearing wedding rings vowing their lives and hearts to the same man. The entire event was fit for a queen, with all its bells and whistles and fake glory.

I grimaced at the thought, then turned my memories to the ceremony that had just taken place only moments before. I could not have foreseen I would be here again so soon. But sure enough, I was, listening to my dad's proud voice as he officiated. Genuine. That was the main word that came to mind as I reflected on the emotions that hung thick in the air. Vows and rings were exchanged, tears were shed, and every moment that ticked past I wanted to hold longer in my heart because it was so damn strong and authentic. This was how it was supposed to be. A constant reminder that was enough to heighten my own regret for selling myself so short before.

The door pushed against its lock as someone apparently tried to come in. I sniffed and wiped my hand against my face, smearing my makeup even more. Pathetic, I scolded myself as I snatched paper towels from the dispenser and blotted my cheeks. Turning, I flipped the lock and pulled open the door.

"Girl, I was looking for you." Adria breezed in with a laugh. She glanced at my face and immediately engulfed me in a hug. "Aw, I love you so much, sis. I can finally say that now."

I returned the hug with a small smile, swallowing my own pangs of jealousy. I was sure I was officially kicked out of the best friends club for being so damn selfish. While I was wallowing in my own self-pity and regret, I couldn't even be happy for my own best friend at her wedding.

Adria released me and turned to eye herself in the mirror. She had lost a few pounds, just enough to really accentuate her curves in the bead-embellished corset of her halter gown. A jewel-encrusted tiara fit neatly around her high bun and clasped an ivory veil to the back of her head, allowing it to cascade down to her mid-back. Despite the tears she had shed and the sweat that now peppered her forehead, my girl's makeup was still flawless from when I had spent two hours that morning brushing, contouring, blending, and getting it perfect. But more than anything, the pure joy that was emitted from her gaze and wide smile really made her glow with another level of beauty I hadn't seen before. Not in her, nor myself.

"I am hot as hell," Adria breathed, pulling paper towels from the dispenser and stuffing wads underneath her armpits. "Would I be too ghetto if I go back out there like this? They'll understand, right?"

I grinned, welcoming the humor. "Please don't," I said. "I don't think my brother could handle that."

Adria's lips turned up into a devious smirk as she winked. "Trust me," she said. "He can handle all of this and very, very well." She rolled her hips to exaggerate her statement, and I pursed my lips to keep from laughing out loud.

"Yeah, keep all that shit for the honeymoon."

"Honey, this honeymoon started four months ago when he proposed." Her eyes dropped to the three-carat diamond engagement ring and wedding band that glittered from her finger. I turned back to the mirror.

Her innocent gesture had tugged on another heartstring. Through the entire ceremony, I had wondered if Jahmad had been thinking about me. The man was still the love of my life, so I wondered if his imagination had taken over like mine, picturing me, instead of Adria, walking toward him in our own wedding ceremony of happily ever after. But, frankly, after everything that had happened between us, maybe that was too much wishful thinking.

"I actually came in here to talk to you about the store," Adria stated, pulling my attention back to her.

I frowned at her mention of our cosmetic store, Melanin Mystique. Thanks to the little seed money I had received from my husband's will, Adria and I had been able to rent a building and get the products for our dream business. "Girl, we are not about to talk business right now."

"I know, but I'm about to be off for a bit for the honeymoon—"

"And I can handle everything until you get back," I assured her, tossing a comforting smile in her direction. "Between me and the new guy. What's his name?"

"Tyree."

"Yeah. He started last week, and so far, he seems to be catching on quick."

"So you'll be able to make sure everything is ready for the grand opening?"

I nodded. Come hell or high water, we were opening that store. I had made too many sacrifices not to. "I'm not saying you can't," Adria went on, circling her arm through mine. She rested her head on my shoulder. "It's just that I would feel comfortable doing this last little bit of stuff with you. I don't want you to think I'm not doing my part. And with my nephew coming home next week too, you're going to have your hands full."

The mention of my son brought an unconscious smile to my lips. I couldn't wait to bring Jamaal home from the hospital. The overwhelming joy I had for that child made me wonder why I had even considered an abortion in the first place. No way could I have lived without him. But initially, the uncertainty about my child's father, whether it was my husband, Leo, or my boyfriend, Jahmad, was enough to scare me into making an appointment and even going as far as taking the first of two medicines that would cause the abortion. But by the grace of God, I had forgotten all about my pregnancy when I got a call about Leo's car accident. Now, my son's paternity didn't even matter. As far as I and Jahmad were concerned, he was the biological father. End of story. At least I hoped.

"It's all going to work out," I said, meeting her eyes in the mirror. "I don't want you worrying about the store, the baby, nothing. Just worry about enjoying my brother and being a newlywed. Can you do that?"

Adria's expression relaxed into an appreciative smile, and I didn't feel quite as bad anymore about my little selfish jealousy. At the end of the day, this girl was my best friend, now sister-in-law, and I loved her to pieces. Anything I was feeling was personal, and I would just have to deal with it myself. No way could I let it affect our relationship. Adria certainly didn't deserve that.

I let myself be steered back into the hallway and toward the reception hall. A collection of old-school mixes had everyone on the dance floor, moving in sync with the electric slide. I groaned, knowing no one but my dad had initiated the line dance that was a staple at every black wedding reception, family/class reunion, or cookout from coast to coast.

The venue was minimally decorated, to appeal more to comfort, with its beautiful assortment of coral flowers and floating candle centerpieces adorning each round table. Chiffon sashes draped from a stage where the wedding party sat, the remnants of the catered soul food dinner and white chocolate cake now being cleared by the waitstaff.

We hadn't even stepped all the way in the room before I was blinded by yet another flash from the photographer, and obediently I plastered another smile on my face. Adria would surely kill me if I messed up her wedding pictures.

Talking about cost efficient, Adria had certainly managed to save her coins when it came to planning this thing. Of course, my dad offered the couple his church and services free of charge, and the reception was now being held in the refurbished church basement, the sole location for numerous church events and family functions. Her aunt Pam was good friends with a caterer, and her small wedding party consisted of me and another young lady who worked at the bank with Adria. It had all worked out like it was supposed to, because Adria was set on putting as much money as possible toward their honeymoon and a house they were looking to close on in a few weeks. My sigh was wistful as her boisterous laugh rang throughout the room. Of course Adria had done everything right. Me, on the other hand, well, I was still picking up the pieces.

Speaking of pieces, my eyes scanned the crowd for Jahmad. Between this morning's argument and the chaos of the wedding operations as soon as we arrived to the church, we hadn't said much of anything to each other. Even as I had taken hold of his arm and allowed him to escort me down the aisle at the ceremony, the tension had been so thick I could taste it, and I prayed the discomfort hadn't been obvious to Adria nor to

Keon. Or the photographer. Wanting to break the ice, I had given his forearm a gentle squeeze. I even tossed a smile his way, but both gestures had gone ignored.

I sighed again as I noticed him on the dance floor, his arms around one of the guests, Acria's cousin Chantel. Her face was split with a flirtatious grin and Jahmad, well, he looked more relaxed than he had in months. And that shit pissed me off.

I was weighing how to get in between them and put hands on this chick in the most discreet way when an arm draped over my shoulder. Glancing up, I met my dad's eyes and allowed my anger to subside. For now.

"Beautiful ceremony, huh," he said, and I nodded.

"It really was, Daddy."

"I'm so happy your brother finally grew up," he went on with a chuckle. "I thought I was going to have to take him to the mountain for sacrifice like Abraham and Isaac."

I laughed. "You would've sacrificed my brother?"

"I was telling God to just say the word." He winked. The humor instantly faded from his smirk as he turned somber eyes on me. "What about you, baby girl?"

"What about me?"

"You know I wanted to officiate for both of my kids. And, well . . ." He trailed off, and I shrugged, trying to keep from looking back over at Jahmad and failing miserably. I knew what he meant. Of course he hadn't been able to do that with me when I decided to up and tie the knot with Leo. I hadn't given him that honor. And I knew he was still hurt by that.

A slow song now had Jahmad and Chantel swaying closer, his hand on the small of her back. If I wanted to be logical, the two didn't look all that intimate. Quite platonic, actually. But I didn't give a damn about logic at that point.

My dad could obviously sense the heightened fury in my demeanor, because he took my hand and gently guided me to the dance floor, in the opposite direction.

"When are you going back to the hospital to see Jamaal?" he asked as we started to dance.

I sighed. Obviously everyone had some secret mission to keep me from wallowing in my own self-pity. Dammit.

"I went up there yesterday," I said. "He's doing really good."

"You sure you don't want him to stay with us for a few weeks? Just until you get situated in your place with the move?"

I tightened my lips. If I played my cards right, I wasn't planning on going anywhere but to Jahmad's house. In fact that's what we had been arguing about this morning when I had come over so we could ride to the church together.

The thing was, my heart still completely belonged to that man. But somewhere in these past few months, he was becoming distant. One minute it was as if we were on the same page, trying to focus on us, or so I thought. But then I would feel like I was struggling to breathe under this suffocating tension that hung between us. And I really wasn't sure how to get us back on track.

So when I suggested we move in together now that our son was coming home, I certainly hadn't expected the frown nor the subsequent questions about my motive for asking like I was up to some shit.

"What is the big deal, Jahmad?" I had asked as I paced his bedroom. "I mean I thought we agreed we would try to work on this? Us?" I pointed a wild finger first at him, then myself.

"What does that have to do with us moving in together?"

The tone of his question had a twinge of hurt piercing my heart. Here I was thinking we were taking steps forward only to realize we were actually moving backward. Why else would the idea of living together come as such a shock to him? I mean after the whole ordeal with Leo, I had moved back in with my folks because I wanted to focus on the business, which was already stressful enough. And I honestly knew, however false the hope, that it would be temporary, because Jahmad's stubborn ass would finally realize exactly where I belonged. With him. Apparently I was still in Neverland.

"Kimmy, that's doing too much." Jahmad sighed in frustration as he shrugged into his suit jacket. "The way I see it, we don't even know if there is an 'us.' And we damn sure don't need any more complications."

I sucked in a sharp breath. "Complications? Since when is being with me a complication?"

"Since when? Since I found out you were married."

And there he went again. Throwing the shit up

in my face. As if I hadn't berated myself enough. As if I hadn't been laying on apology after apology so much that I was sick of hearing the words my damn self. I masked the embarrassment with anger.

"You know what my situation was about," I snapped, jabbing a finger in his direction. "And you know it wasn't real."

"That doesn't make it any better," he yelled back. "Hell, if anything that shines a negative light on you, because all the conniving and sneaky shit was for money. My love didn't mean anything to you."

"How can you stand here and say that? You know that's not true."

"Do I?" He narrowed his eyes. "How can I even trust you or anything you say?"

"Jahmad, we've had this same conversation every week for months." I threw up my arms to express my frustration. "I can't change the past. What else can I do? Or say to move past this?"

This time he was quiet so I used the opportunity to keep pushing. "There is no more marriage. No more Leo. No more lies and secrets, Jahmad. I promised you that before. Now it's just us. And our son. That is what's important to me."

I had to mentally repent even as the words left my lips. There were still a few lies between us. Among other things, whether he knew there was a question of paternity with my son. I sure as hell had to take that to my grave. And the money: Leo had given me plenty of it and since technically he had staged his death, that money was still tucked safely in my accounts. Like hell I would give that up. That would mean the whole arrangement would have been in vain.

Silence had ridden with us to the church, and we soon became so engrossed in the pre-wedding preparations we hadn't bothered, nor had time, to resume the conversation.

I tried to bring my attention back to my father as he swayed with me on the dance floor, but thoughts continued to consume me.

I glanced around, my eyes eager to catch Jahmad once more, but he had long since disappeared. I stopped my scan when I noticed a certain face appear in the crowd. I squinted through the dimness and distance, struggling to blink clarity into my vision. The face I couldn't make out but the dress, I knew that dress. And the hair was the same, too much to be a coincidence.

My dad spun me around, and I quickly angled my neck to catch another glimpse of the woman I thought I recognized. But by then, the Tina look-alike was gone.

Connect with U s

Visit us online at
KensingtonBooks.com
to read more from your favorite authors, see books
by series, view reading group guides, and more.

Join us on social media

for sneak peeks, chances to win books and prize packs,
and to share your thoughts with other readers.

facebook.com/kensingtonpublishing
twitter.com/kensingtonbooks

Tell us what you think!

To share your thoughts, submit a review,
or sign up for our eNewsletters, please visit:
KensingtonBooks.com/TellUs.